THEN AGAIN

Jenny Diski was born in 1947 in London where she
still lives. *Then Again* is her fourth novel, following
the much-acclaimed *Nothing Natural*, *Rainforest* and
Like Mother.

'Normally, my heart would sink when I heard an author describe her latest novel as being about the nature of time. All the more so when she admits that her knowledge of physics comes entirely from reading popular books on the subject. But then the author in question is Jenny Diski, whose previous three novels have speedily established her literary and intellectual credentials, and the book in question is *Then Again*, which, more than any of its predecessors, radiates confidence in its own ability to turn difficult ideas into pacy, accessible fiction'

Sunday Correspondent

'Is it possible to have a faith that rises out of questions? This is the question Jenny Diski sets herself in her weird but compelling new novel. To answer it she develops two stories concurrently. One is about a contemporary artist named Esther whose daughter, thought by some to have found God and by others to have lost her mind, has gone missing. While Esther sits at home and waits for news, she makes mysterious dream contact with the heroine of the second story, a fourteenth century Pole, also named Esther, but renamed Elizabeth by a Christian family after her own people are massacred in a pogrom... What is interesting and courageous is the way in which Diski plays her characters' ideas and stories off against one another – and the inspired madness with which she pulls them together in the end'

Independent on Sunday

Jenny Diski

THEN AGAIN

VINTAGE

VINTAGE

20 Vauxhall Bridge Road, London SW1V 2SA

London Melbourne Sydney Auckland Johannesburg
and agencies throughout the world

First published by Bloomsbury Publishing Ltd, 1990
Vintage edition 1991

Printed and bound in Great Britain by
Cox & Wyman Ltd, Reading, Berkshire

ISBN 0 09 978440 8

FOR JENNY STEIN WITH LOVE

Esther paints patterns on plates and sleeps while she waits to hear news of her fourteen-year-old daughter, Katya, who has disappeared in what some diagnose as a psychotic condition. Katya is certain that she danced with God in the particles of the universe. Esther is certain of nothing at all. She listens to the twentieth-century priests of mental health, each telling her different things: Katya's condition is Esther's fault, or just an accident of chemistry. But Esther knows that if and when Katya is found, she will have to decide what to do about her. In the mean time Katya wanders the streets, allowing whatever must happen to happen. She is trying to be good enough for God, but the world refuses to help. It knows that belief is not useful, and the only questions that should be asked are the ones that can be answered.

Somewhere at the limits of Esther's consciousness, in that borderland between the oblivion of sleep and the reclamation of her own soul at daylight, she becomes aware of a girl in danger. Not Katya, nor precisely Esther, but a separate life; another child, from another time. This girl, too, asks questions that make no sense to the world she lives in, and that world, different in ideology, but similar in its responses, must silence her heresy. Inexorably, a disturbing pattern is formed by the experiences of the two girls, far apart in time, but brought close through Esther and their common need to ask their unacceptable questions.

Jenny Diski takes her characters through several journeys in her transfixing new novel – into the wildernesses between sanity and madness, biology and nurturing, faith and rational discourse, to a place where reality and its difficulties are acknowledged, and questions that must always be asked are allowed to flourish.

ONE

As for the children, some were killed, others taken away to be baptised and brought up as Christians.

– Norman Cohn

1

WHEN ESTHER FIRST heard it, she thought the angels had
come. She looked up at the sky. She could see nothing out of
the ordinary, but the sound was so faint and seemed to come
from so far away that she supposed they were still beyond the
clouds; the thick mysterious substance muffling what would
be a glorious cacophony when the angels broke through, at
any moment, into her world.

'Is it Elijah?' she whispered to her sister, keeping her eyes
glued to the heavens. 'Is he coming with all the angels? Will
he speak to me?'

Rebekah stood still and felt the power of her little sister's
excitement and wonder at the magic that was about to descend
vibrate through the small hand that squeezed her own. She
heard the sound, too, but she didn't have the certainty of
four-year-old Esther. At ten, Rebekah was not immune to the
possibility of the sky opening and the world turning magic,
but some part of her pulled against her sister's vision. With
her longer experience of life, she was more habituated to the
world. She *wanted* to stare at the sky and watch Elijah descend,
fiery and magnificent, a host of angels smiling light behind him,
but she strained her eyes instead in the direction of the road that
led out of town. As the sound grew, she knew that the more
adult part of her was correct. This was man, not magic.

Esther was jumping up and down on the spot, unable to
contain her excitement.

'Elijah's coming. Elijah's coming. Elijah's coming,' she
chanted, never taking her gaze from the overcast sky. 'Bekah,
Bekah, Elijah's coming.'

Her sister shook her hand to get her attention.

'Shh, quiet, Esther, it's not Elijah, it's coming from down

3

the road. Can't you hear? It's getting louder. Don't make such a noise. Don't draw attention to yourself.'

She was fully the responsible older sister now, wary of the looks passers-by were giving them. Being noticed was not safe. Mother and Father were always warning them not to get themselves noticed when they were out of the house, and especially when they weren't in their own district.

Esther pushed her bottom lip out in disappointment, as if it were Rebekah's fault that the angels were not coming. As if she, one of the grown-ups, like all the grown-ups, wouldn't allow the magic in. They were always talking about Elijah, praying and singing about wonders and signs of God's love. But, when Esther wanted to know when she would see him, and when the magic would come to her part of the world, they shook their heads and said she didn't understand. They talked instead about being quiet and careful. Everyone seemed to know that magic was needed. All the prayers and the rituals told of times when magic and wonders had come, and begged for their return.

Even with her short, four-year-old memory, Esther could recall the time, not so long ago, when everyone got sick. There had been terrible wailings and weepings from the grown-ups. Her friend Tilly had got so sick that she was never coming back. Lots of people she knew had gone, including her older brother Jakob, who had just been barmitzvahed, and Sara, who was engaged to the rabbi's assistant. But he had gone, too, soon after Sara. Esther thought they must be together, wherever it was they had gone to, though no one ever seemed to explain very well where that was exactly. But, really, it was Tilly, her friend, she missed the most. Then Mother got sick, and there was an awful hush in the house. Great black things appeared all over her, and a terrible smell had come from the room they put her in. Esther had been ignored for days in the rushing about and praying that went on. She had sat in a corner, her bottom lip stuck out, and wished and wished for her friend Tilly to come back so she'd have someone to play with. She didn't, but Mother didn't go, she got better; and then fewer people got sick and there were tremendous prayings in the synagogue.

Life couldn't have been less magical. Esther thought that if the grown-ups really believed in the magic, believed so hard that every bit of their bodies were squeezed tight with belief, then it would happen. She blamed them for not believing properly.

Now she relaxed all the excited muscles, deflated yet again by adult disbelief, and looked in the direction that Rebekah indicated. Anyway, even if it wasn't Elijah, it was *something*. It was music: drums and pipes, and singing; a strange chantlike singing that drifted heavily through the air and seemed to curl around her small limbs like wisps of smoke. Something was happening. Was it a fair, or a band of entertainers who would juggle and tell stories, and make everyday magic in the town square?

But as the sound got closer it lost the gaiety that Esther had thought she heard. The chant was more of a moan. The drums beat with an ominous regularity. The noise, as it got clearer, began to darken the day, so that it seemed the light was failing.

The two children were not alone now. Several people had stopped and looked in the direction of the only road that led into the town. This was the route by which people returned home if, rarely, they had ventured out; the route by which strangers arrived, passing through, sharing news, and moving on after a night's rest.

Esther began to feel frightened. She thought she wanted to go home and press herself against Mother's skirts and breathe in her safe, warm smell. Now she squeezed her sister's hand with fear. Rebekah recognised the different quality of the pressure.

'It's all right,' she whispered down to her sister, feeling braver through Esther's fear. 'It's just a procession. Pilgrims. We can watch them. It's all right.'

It was market day. Rebekah and Esther loved to walk into the centre of town and watch the comings and goings in the square. It was so busy and bustling, and the smell of produce and livestock mingled with the cries of the sellers and the creaking of the wooden wheels of the carts. There was nothing that was not for sale or barter. Sweetsellers offered honeyed delicacies, and travelling traders arrived with cartloads of trinkets, bolts of cloth, tools, and noisy pots and pans that they banged with wooden spoons to catch the attention of passers-by. Some had no cart, their wares invisible. They sold words: prophesies, stories and songs, and passed a cap among those who had gathered to listen. But everything, even the stall that sold only mounds of turnips and swedes, was exciting on market day.

The young men and women of the town sauntered in their best clothes, getting themselves noticed. The young men competed against each other in trials of strength, and girls sniffed at scents and examined potions that the apothecaries assured them would have an instantaneous effect. It was all so lively, so gay, and, although they couldn't eat any of the food and had no money to buy it, anyway, the two girls couldn't resist the pull of market day. They would be severely punished if their parents found out that they had left their district. Rebekah and Esther were not supposed to be there, but who was going to notice them? And they always turned their cloaks inside out, before they got into town, so that the sewn-on yellow Star of David was invisible. It didn't seem to matter. What difference did two little girls make in such a hubbub?

Now, on the outskirts, they stopped, and Rebekah turned her cloak and helped Esther with hers before walking on into the square, where everything seemed at first to be as usual. But not for long. The jostling and noise began to die down as the dark figures coming down the road grew close enough to see. Gradually, an eerie hush came over the market, so that soon even the few voices that continued to call out to friends, or curse when their carts stuck in the mud, were stilled. Only the sound of the tabors and pipes, and the sorrowful chant of human voices carried through the air. Esther found herself shivering; she knew about solemnity from the prayers and rituals at home, and some special part deep inside her always quaked at the sight and sound of it. This sound and sight, being unfamiliar, was all the more frightening.

The figures materialised. There must have been over a hundred, over two hundred, Rebekah thought. Esther thought that all the rest of the people in the world had arrived in their town. But none of them had faces. They wore dark rough robes that fell to their bare dusty feet, with sleeves that hung down below their hands. Their downcast heads were covered with wide black hoods that fell over their faces. Esther noticed a curious flickering that ran, like a shiver, along the length of the procession. When she focused more carefully she saw that they held something in their hands and raised up the arm that held it every few steps so that it lay for a moment across the opposite shoulder. The flickering was this movement repeated up and down the line. Some of the people in the market had run out to accompany them into town, and were marching along by the side of the procession, calling praise to God and welcoming the faceless strangers, who looked neither right nor left, but kept their eyes on the earth in front of their feet. As they came into town, people parted to make way for them and flanked the dour column as it headed for the market square.

Rebekah and Esther squatted by an untended cart full of parsnips whose owner had run off to join the procession. When the head of the column reached the edge of the square, it stopped and waited for the rest to arrive.

'What are they going to do?' asked Esther. 'Who are they?'

Rebekah told her to shush, that they would see. The two of them waited, wide-eyed, still as mice watching a passing cat, as the end of the column arrived in the square. The townspeople moved back to give them space, and formed a surrounding circle. Rebekah and Esther crawled through a forest of legs until they found a spot near the front, though not too near, where they could see.

The tall figure who had headed the procession drew a paper from his sleeve and raised his head so that his bleak, angular face peered out from the draped hood. Esther trembled at the sight of him; she thought he was the most frightening man she had ever seen. His eyes flashed a cold anger that seemed to be directed straight at her, though she couldn't know that everyone in the crowd thought the same. His face was thin and bony, like an awful dream. Esther closed her eyes and held her breath in the hope that she would become invisible to him. He called for silence, but it was unnecessary. Esther, almost as curious as she was scared, opened her eyes just as he pulled the yellowed parchment from his sleeve and began to read in a threatening monotone. It seemed to be a letter. It was addressed, he said, to the corrupt flesh of the world, sent by the Lord to his messenger, so that the sinful might take heed, before it was too late. Esther had a lot of trouble following it. It was full of grand words. But it seemed to be about how wicked people were, how ungrateful for some sacrifice that God had made for them, and it was full of warnings. All sorts of terrible things were going to happen, some of them that were too hard for Esther to understand, but the sound of the reader's doomladen voice, the compelling rhythm of the words, and those eyes holding hers, as they held everyone's, sent horrible shivers down her spine.

'We shouldn't be here,' Rebekah whispered nervously, breaking the spell of the man's voice over Esther.

'Why not? We can tell Mother and Father about all these things that are going to happen. We don't want them to happen to us. They'll know what to do, and how to be good so they won't happen.'

'Stupid,' Rebekah hissed. Her fear made her angry with Esther's innocence. 'It's not for *us*. Can't you understand? Don't you know *anything*? It's *us* they're blaming. He said it was our fault.'

'He said it was the devil and . . . the Anti . . . Anti . . . and the Heebs . . .' Esther whispered.

'Antichrist, stupid. The Hebrews . . .' Rebekah jerked Esther's wrist painfully to punish her for being so ignorant.

'Stop it, you're hurting me. I'll tell Mother. Well, what's the He . . . brews got to do with us?

'We *are* Hebrews. That's what they call Jews. We're Jews, aren't we? He said the Devil and the Antichrist, and the Jews were all the same thing. That we caused the sickness by poisoning the wells.'

'We *didn't*. I didn't, and Mother and Father wouldn't have done a thing like that. They wouldn't have made Jakob and Sara sick. Was it someone we know? Was it Moishe's Bubba? She's always cross and shouting. But she wouldn't do *that*. I'm frightened, Bekah. Let's go home and find Father and tell him what they're saying about us. I haven't done anything.'

As they were about to crawl away, the reading finished and some of the men in the procession formed a circle around their leader. He called, 'Repent! Repent!' and the men in the circle threw off their robes, revealing the leather scourges with vicious spikes at the end that had been concealed by their sleeves.

Naked, now, except for a length of cloth around their loins, they began to chant, picking up the cry of 'Repent!' until the air rang with the sound, mournful and threatening. Then they started to move in a slow circle around the square, and flung the scourges hard across their shoulders, causing the spikes to enter the flesh of their backs so that they had to be jerked free before they could repeat the action. The two children were hypnotised. Neither of them moved.

'Why are they doing that? They're hurting themselves,' Esther asked, horrified. Rebekah was too frightened to answer.

Suddenly, one of the men fell to the ground, spreadeagled in the mud, and called out, 'Punish me, punish me, Master. For my sins, for the endless sins of the world. Beat the flesh into obedience to the Lord.' The man in the middle of the now static circle took the scourge from his hand and beat him again and again until his back was criss-crossed with thin streams of blood that ran down his sides and trickled into the mud.

'Please, please, please, I want to go home!' Esther began to cry. 'I don't like this.'

Rebekah seemed to shake herself awake, and grabbed Esther's hand, pulling her back through the maze of adult legs, as the voices above them called praises to the Lord, and cried out, 'Repentance!' and, 'Vengeance, sayeth the Lord! His will be done! His *will* be done! Repent! Repent!'

At the back of the crowd, Rebekah and Esther scrambled to their feet, and ran, muddy, Esther sobbing, Rebekah panting and pulling her little sister behind her, back towards the safety of their home.

2

ESTHER WOKE AT seven after a night's troubled sleep and waited for her thoughts to run their allotted course. For the first few moments, as she floated up and away from sleep, she inhabited a border territory, a vegetable existence with no knowledge of who, or even what, she was. She was without form or identity; nothing more than a weight on a surface. Only the force of gravity connected her with the waking world. She would have kept it like that, but the weight of her body demanded that her sleep-soaked mind begin the struggle to fix herself in reality. It strove urgently for a name, a setting, a history – a place in the world.

The information came, inescapably: the weight defined as human shape, then the bed, the room, until the final question of who and what she was. Esther. Not enough. Who was Esther? Where did she belong? Which Esther? For an indeterminate period the world was fluid; time, geography, identity ran together like pools of colour on damp paper. She was Esther, but that was the only certainty. The finger of identity vacillated over a choice of souls, a multiplicity of Esthers whose *when*, *where*, and *who* differed tantalisingly. Which Esther?

Oh, yes, *that* one. Who belonged – *here*. For a split-second she was flooded with the relief of a lost child seeing its parents run towards it with open arms. She was solid. Real.

But the second passed, and Esther's life seeped in around her. The relief faded, to be replaced with the heaviness that belonged to the newly earthed Esther. Annoyance joined the heaviness: once more there was the need to start again. The routine of waking and beginning another day. The mechanics of the body to be dealt with. The repetition, the arithmetic of living, day after day of waking in the morning. Beginning always with

10

this first minute. Every morning the same unchanging process: confusion, struggle, relief, and the weight, as she remembered herself.

The next thought, too, was part of the unalterable routine of waking. The question: What was that blankness between oblivion and daylight that wanted so desperately to be filled in? What if she managed one day to resist its demands? She would die, she supposed. Perhaps that was what occurred when they spoke of people dying peacefully in their sleep. Perhaps they simply refused to establish themselves one morning, and that was that. But how could there be resistance to the need to re-establish yourself in the world? As soon as resistance was possible it would already be too late; oblivion would have fled. What *was* there to do the resisting, but herself, the very thing she was obliged to find every morning? The vegetable thing ensured its survival by insisting on the struggle for consciousness, and, once conscious, the moment of refusal was lost. You were back, you had found yourself for another day.

Esther sighed, partly at the tedium of having to think these thoughts yet again, and partly at the knowledge that here she was once more, and a new day was waiting for her to get through.

There was no reason to get up; to wash, dress, make breakfast. There was no reason to be awake, even. The phone was beside her bed. If it rang – if there was news – she would hear it. Even if the first questions about her identity were compelling in spite of herself, the later ones, to do with planning and purpose, had no power at all. In the end, after an unsatisfactory hour staring at the ceiling in the vain hope that boredom would return her to oblivion, the dryness of her throat and the pressure on her bladder forced her out of bed.

It was some days since she had felt it necessary to be up and washed, ready to leave at a moment's notice if she got a call telling her to come. Karen had been shocked to find her still in an old T-shirt of Rob's that she slept in, her hair unbrushed, when she had come to sit with her the previous day. She knew better than to say anything, but Esther could tell that Karen thought she wasn't behaving properly. But then, when had

Karen thought otherwise? And, come to think of it, events had proved her right. Not that Karen would take pleasure in that, because she didn't approve of disapproval. It was just that she had seen it coming and wished she could have done something to prevent it. Karen saw nearly everything, because she had lived with Ben for twenty years, and *understanding what was really going on* was something of a religion between them. Ben was a psychotherapist, and brought his work home with him.

Esther sighed and remembered that it was Ben's turn to sit with her today. Karen and Ben took the burden of supporting their unhappy, distracted old friend in turns. Well, that was what friends were for, Karen had told her. Karen whiled away her mornings with Esther making tea and chatting, trying to take Esther's mind off things for a while. On alternate mornings, Ben tried to have the same effect by fucking her. There were some things that Karen didn't see.

Esther winced at herself. She knew her condition well enough. She looked in the mirror with dislike. If this went on she would become a vicious hag. Better, perhaps, to get back to the fear and panic. She looked at the phone beside the bed. It would ring soon. Someone would call, concerned about her, wanting to know if she had heard anything, and she would hate them for it – because of her hope and fear at the sound of the ringing, and the time it took for her heart to get started again after she picked up the receiver and realised that this was not news. And because picking up the receiver forced her to confront a truth that was not comfortable. She hoped to hear that Katya had been found and that she was all right. But, inescapably, she dreaded it, too. She did not want the return of all the anxiety, the responsibility, the not knowing what to do. She did not want to be a woman with a deeply troubled daughter. She did not want to hear that Katya had been found. And, because she did not want to know that that was how she felt, she hated the ringing of the phone.

None the less, a few moments later, as she sipped coffee in the kitchen, the silence shattered. It was Rob.

'Esther?'

Who else would it be? She took a steadying breath.

'Yes, Rob, it's me.'

'Anything?' His voice sounded tired.

'No. I'd have rung you, if I'd heard anything.'

'I was just checking. I haven't been at home . . .'

'Taking your mind off your mad lost daughter with a night on the tiles, were you?'

'No.' His voice was barely under control. 'Felix was taken ill last night. I'm at the hospital. I just rang to give you the number here, in case you heard anything.'

Esther regretted her comment even before Rob answered her. She felt another slice of herself disappear, cut away by her viciousness, and underneath a new sliver of cruelty appear, like a terrible picture, growing, inch by inch, of the wicked crone she would become. Each unkindness, each lunge with the scalpel, took away something human and added something black and awful. When the picture was complete, she would be that black and awful thing, unalterably. She shook the vision away. Stop it, she told herself, you're low, stop it.

'I'm sorry. What's the matter with Felix? Is he all right?'

'Not really. He had a cold. It went to his chest. They thought it was bronchitis, but he was very bad last night and they took him in. It's pneumonia. He's on a respirator, but they think he'll be all right.'

'That's awful. Pneumonia? How did he get it? Do you catch pneumonia?'

'I can't talk about it, I'm too tired,' Rob said, but Esther heard something else, as well as weariness, in his voice. 'I've got to go, I've got to get back to him.'

'Well, wish him better from me. What number do I ring to get you at the hospital?'

Rob gave her a number and she wrote it on the yellow pad beside the phone.

'Don't worry too much,' Rob added reassuringly. 'I'm sure they'll find her soon. I know she'll be all right.'

'Yes,' Esther said, trying to soften her voice. 'Ditto Felix.'

Esther put the phone down and wondered which of them had been the most convinced by the other's quiet certainty.

Esther returned to her coffee and her previous numbness. This was the tenth morning since Katya had disappeared, and – how long? – six weeks perhaps since the trouble, the *worry*, had begun. That wasn't quite true. It was six weeks since Esther had been forced to admit that something was seriously wrong. It was thanks to Karen, of course, that what had been an amorphous nagging somewhere in her bowels had emerged, with good reason, as full-blown anxiety.

3

Six WEEKS BEFORE, Karen had phoned just as Esther was about to get dressed.

'Esther, sorry to call so early, but I wanted a word with you, and I've got appointments all day. Can you talk?'

Karen and Ben were Meg's parents. Meg and Katya had been best friends since they were at primary school together. It was why Esther knew them.

'Katya's still in her room. I was just about to get up,' Esther told Karen, feeling slightly guilty. Karen, she knew, would be up and dressed, the kids already at the table eating breakfast. But then, Esther reminded herself, she worked at home while Katya was at school; there was no need for her to rush the morning. Nevertheless, she felt as if she had been caught out.

'What's going on with Katya?' Karen asked.

A now familiar gnawing low in her abdomen made itself felt at the sound of her daughter's name. She tried very hard to ignore it.

'What do you mean?'

'She's given Meg three pairs of jeans, and taken that God-awful skirt Ben's mother gave her. Did you know?'

'She's only got three pairs of jeans. Well.' Esther thought fast. 'I suppose she's trying out another style . . . you know how they are. I just hope it doesn't last too long, or we'll become the repository for all the granny-crud in the class.' Esther hoped her voice sounded as lighthearted as she had tried to make it. She almost convinced herself. So what? Fourteen year olds do all kinds of things.

'It's not just the clothes,' Karen continued relentlessly. 'She's given Sal all her tapes. I mean *all* of them. And . . . look, I don't want to worry you unnecessarily, but Meg says she seems to have stopped eating. She doesn't go into the dining-room at lunchtime. Is she taking sandwiches?'

Esther lost the battle against her anxiety. Her voice lost its bright, high note.

'No. Karen, I don't know what's going on. She won't say anything to me.' Again a faint hope flickered. 'I expect it'll pass. You know the fads they go through.'

'Well, yes, I know,' Karen answered doubtfully. 'I wasn't going to say anything. I didn't want to worry you, but, according to Meg, this has been going on for a while already. I don't want to make too much of it . . . but . . . do you think she ought to see someone? At their age . . . it's really not good not to be eating, you know?'

'I know.' Esther did know. 'Has she said anything about it to Meg?'

'No, and that's another thing. Meg says none of them can understand it. They're worried, too. Perhaps if you took her to the doctor. He could talk to her. Or there's a counsellor at school. I've heard through the grapevine that she's very good with the kids.'

'I'll have a word with Katya this morning. I know there's something, but – I've been scared to . . .'

'If I can help, or Ben . . . perhaps if he had a word with her?'

'No, I'll do it.' Esther saw the symptoms piling up in the Redfern household. No father in place; the sort of makeshift, rubbing-along-OK kind of life that made efficient organisers like Karen itch to sort it out; an only child who had too grown-up a relationship with her mother. She didn't blame Karen and Ben, she had already made the list herself, without even realising it. She was grateful to Karen for making it clear that things were as bad as she had hoped they weren't. 'I'll speak to her. Thanks, Karen, I appreciate . . . we must have lunch or something.'

Esther had put the phone down, relieved that the call was over, but comforted too that Karen was there to talk to.

She pulled clothes from her closet and dressed quickly. In the kitchen Esther put four slices of wholemeal bread in the toaster and switched on the kettle. She laid the kitchen table with two knives and plates, butter, and jars of marmalade and honey.

When the boiling water had been poured into the teapot and the toast had popped up she waited for a moment, listening, as if to catch a sound that was muffled by the overriding silence in the flat. Then she took a deep breath and called out, 'Kat, breakfast. Are you awake?'

She knew Katya would be up and dressed; it was only habit or wishfulness that made her ask. She still harboured the faint hope that Katya might be sound asleep, or, better still, awake but enjoying an illicit extra few minutes in bed. But the bedroom door opened almost as soon as she had started to call and her daughter appeared in the kitchen doorway washed and dressed and looking as though she had been up for hours. Esther knew she had, and the scratchy feeling in her abdomen broke its bounds. The anxiety was back; worry filled the place in her that was reserved for it, up through her entire torso and swirling around her mind, like damned water rushing through open sluicegates.

Katya smiled good morning at her mother. The kind of smile a landlady might receive from a temporary lodger, Esther remembered thinking. She looked at her daughter pouring hot water over a centimetre of tea at the bottom of a mug and slicing the thinnest sliver of lemon into the anaemic brew. She was pale and there were heavy, dark rings under her eyes. She appeared to Esther very much like the stranger her polite smile suggested she was. Apart from the signs of lack of sleep, Esther's fourteen-year-old daughter was immaculate. Her cheeks were polished pink from a thorough morning wash, and her hair, glossy with vigorous brushing, was pulled back to hang in a single thick braid halfway down her back. Her white blouse, which Esther remembered had been in the drier the previous night, was freshly ironed, and buttoned to the neck, and a neat, dark, pleated skirt just covered her knees. Esther immediately recognised the skirt from Karen's description.

'I haven't seen that skirt before, have I?'

'I swopped it.'

'For what? Who with?'

'Meg. I gave her my jeans. Her grandmother gave her the skirt for her birthday. She doesn't like it.'

Esther wasn't surprised to hear it as she visualised Meg, who, like all the girls in Katya's class (and boys if it came to that), was only ever dressed in jeans and baggy sweatshirts, finished off with baseball boots whose laces were left dangling. Esther had long since learned not to point out that their laces were undone and that they would trip over them. She had understood that they were left undone precisely so that she and her kind would trip over them by remarking on the detail. A fleeting look of triumph would pass between the girls, and one of them would smile politely and say, 'Thanks, we know.'

'Do *you* like it? It's not the sort of thing you usually wear. Which jeans did you give her?'

Katya smiled calmly and took her lemon tea to the table.

'All of them. I got tired of jeans. I always looked such a mess.'

'But it was a sort of creative mess,' Esther protested. 'I liked it, you all looked so stylish.'

'What you wear has an affect on you. The way you think, what you are. It didn't feel right any more.'

Esther had considered what she was wearing; a Fair Isle sweater she had had since she was twenty. It had long since lost what shape it had once had, and barely reached down to her waist. There were undarned holes reappearing in the darned holes at each elbow and the wool was matted like woven cloth with the years of washing. Her jeans were almost as old and even more shapeless, faded to a chalky blue and thinned to the weft at the stress-points of knee and backside. And it was some years since the plimsolls on her unsocked feet had been white in anything other than her memory.

She was conscious that a stranger looking for the responsible member of the family might be forgiven for choosing Katya. She tried a laugh.

'Oh dear, I think you're right. Woolly and full of holes is an exact description of my mind at the moment.'

Katya, who some weeks ago might have enjoyed teasing her improbable-looking mother about her arrested sartorial development, now looked faintly embarrassed.

'I wasn't meaning to criticise you . . . I only meant that I . . .'

'It's all right. I was joking.' Esther sat at her place at the table and drew a deep breath. 'Kat, I can't stand all this politeness.

We've lived together for over fourteen years. Why can't you just talk to me, for God's sake?'

Katya looked down at the untouched toast in front of her.

'I'm sorry, I don't know what you mean.'

'I mean *that*.' Esther allowed the anxiety to sharpen the tone of her voice. 'What's the matter with you? You talk to me as if you were a telephone operator asking if I'll accept a reverse-charge call. As if you lived on another planet and didn't know how things were done down here. What's going on, Katya? Why are you like this? I'm worried. Why are you suddenly dressing like my mother wanted me to dress? Why are you drinking diluted tea with lemon? Why haven't you eaten any of your breakfast? Why didn't you eat last night? What's happening, for Christ's sake?'

'I'm not hungry.'

Esther slapped the table with the flat of her hand.

'You haven't been hungry for days. If you're not hungry, then you're ill. Are you ill? Tell me.' She was shouting now. 'Are you ill?'

Katya put her mug down carefully. It was still almost full. She spoke quietly, using reason to placate and tame the tempest her mother was whipping up.

'Mum, there's nothing wrong with me. Honestly. It's just that I made a promise. I know what you're thinking – that I'm anorexic. But I'm not. Truly, I'm not, it isn't that. You mustn't worry. I'm really all right.'

Esther held very still for a long moment, trying to match her daughter's calm.

'What kind of promise did you make that means you can't eat? Who did you promise? Katya, I think that if a person were anorexic they might not know it. Do you see what I mean?'

'Yes, but I'm not. I've got a reason. I can't tell you about it, you wouldn't understand. But it's all right. I'll stop fasting when . . . when I've kept my promise. Please trust me.' Katya got up and pulled on her jacket. 'I've got to go to school now. I'll see you this evening. All right?'

Esther nodded numbly. She was relieved when she heard the front door close and her daughter's footsteps disappear down the stairs. She had no idea what was going on, or what she could do about it. It was possible, at least, when Katya was out, to dampen the worry to a nameless anxiety. The sound of her voice rising in panic at Katya's implacable calm disturbed her almost as much as her daughter's peculiar behaviour. She pulled Katya's plate towards her and began to butter the cold toast.

4

ESTHER DRESSED AND washed automatically, once she had finished her coffee. The way to deal with a sense of purposelessness was not to give purpose any thought. It was only when she was running a brush through her hair that she noticed, in the mirror, that she was wearing exactly what she had put on all those weeks ago, after Karen's phone call. She wasn't particularly surprised. It had no great significance; this was how she currently dressed for her day.

Esther dressed the way she did because it pleased her to wear comfortable, shabby clothes that had lived through much of her lifetime with her, and because it so happened that the current phase of her life allowed her to please herself in this way. There was a second closet, which these days she rarely opened, containing clothes from other phases in her life when she had been required to make clear signals to the world she was temporarily inhabiting: a couple of proper dresses, one pair of black highish-heeled shoes, a well-enough tailored jacket. Somewhere (at the back of the bathroom cabinet, probably) there was an old sweet tin full of make-up – eyeshadow, mascara, foundation, even lipstick. Most of it dried up, very likely; it was some years since she'd opened the tin. In those periods when she had had to wear clothes properly, as she thought of it – when she was a secretary, and another time when she was front of house at an art gallery – Katya had laughed at the sight of her.

'You look weird,' she'd say, alarming Esther just as she was about to leave the flat.

'Why? What's wrong? Too much mascara? Is this shirt the wrong colour for the skirt?'

'No, you just don't look like you.'

Which was true. Esther was perfectly competent at making-up, and her respectable clothes looked like they were supposed to look, but she was somehow always to be spied *beneath* them. Even someone who had never met her before, or seen how she looked at home, felt that she was 'dressed up', not because she was overdressed, or badly dressed, but because she just didn't, as nine-, and then eleven-year-old Katya so accurately pointed out, *look like her*.

Now that her present life coincided with the clothes she wanted to put on in the morning, she kept the other items in a separate cupboard. But she didn't clear them out. She knew by now that life was a series of phases, only the last of which she could be certain would not require something from the other wardrobe.

Esther thought of life rather as if it were another child she had given birth to. One who didn't grow up, as Katya did, but remained for ever a demanding toddler. Like any reasonable parent who wished to hang on to a degree of sanity, Esther would ignore the demands for as long as possible, while knowing that eventually she would have to pay attention, since, like any reasonable parent, she was aware of her responsibility towards the thing that was, after all, hers.

What can I do? I've got nothing to do, life would ask after a period of quiet. *I'm bored,* it whined. *Let's do something.*

'You have to learn to entertain yourself,' Esther would mutter, content with quiescence. 'Just go and play quietly. Look at all the memories and experience you've been given. Why can't you just play happily with them, like other lives do?'

But life wouldn't accept that for long. And Esther knew that, really, other lives were just as petulant as her own.

I want you to do something with me. I'm fed up. I'm bawwwwwwd.

Nag, nag, nag. In the end, grudgingly, she would give in. Taking life in hand, she would *do* something with it, just to stop it nagging at her.

So, thanks to life's demands for attention, she could look back over her forty odd years and see the pattern of activity and rest that patchworked the decades. There was no sense of development or direction, of starting at the beginning and building towards a climactic end. Each square of the patchwork was independent, while at the same time being part of an overall abstract pattern. Where she was at any given moment was no better or worse than where she had been; it was just different, which somehow (paradoxically, she knew, but it didn't bother her too much) meant it was the same. At least, until six weeks ago. She hastily shoved the last thought out of her mind and headed for the kitchen to tackle the three days' washing-up in the sink.

As Esther squeezed detergent over the dirty dishes, and ran hot water over them, she considered how the flat, but by no means unsatisfactory, pattern of her life differed from the way things had started out. There had been no lack of direction in her childhood.

University in the early Sixties had been a decision only inasmuch as she had decided not to go to art school. She had a talent for painting, but, at the time, reading psychology and German at Bristol had seemed the better way of preparing for a career.

Dinah and Geoffrey wanted the best for her, and more so, perhaps, than if they had been her natural parents. They had never concealed the fact that Esther was adopted. It wasn't their way to lie, and, as they always pointed out at those moments of insecurity that any adopted child must have, she had been *chosen*, and in some ways, therefore, more genuinely loved than the child they could never have themselves. Dinah, being a lecturer in social psychology, was able to monitor Esther's emotional progress, and it seemed that she had accepted the situation remarkably well. It was true that she had night-frights for a few years, and that she did ask, from time to time, about her real parents. This was only natural. Dinah understood, and soothed her anxieties away with the spoken expressions of love and comfort that she knew were necessary. *They* were her real parents, she'd explain.

As Esther got older, she was better able to understand the need for none of them to know who had given birth to her and why she had not remained their child. In any case, she had been made aware, very early, that she was rarely privileged and that certain responsibilities came with it. So much of the world was in want: no food, barely any education, and, where there was some, almost nothing in the way of books.

23

She and Dinah regularly packed parcels of books to send to a school in Botswana. A good education and not having to worry about finding the essentials, the bare necessities, was Esther's fortune. Whoever she had been born to, she was Dinah and Geoffrey's child now, and they must all of them be profoundly grateful for what they had. Education was not to be wasted; the world needed people like Esther, it needed the kind of skills and understanding that her family and her education were able to equip her with.

In the privacy of her own mind, however, Esther had been much more concerned about the issue of being adopted than Dinah and Geoffrey had ever guessed. The occasional questions she asked them were not indications of occasional concern, as they supposed, but eruptions that burst out when her constant wondering demanded a voice. But it was true that *wondering*, rather than deep anxiety, was the quality of her thoughts. At least, as far as she could tell. Who she was, where she really belonged, what part of her was from the anonymous parents and what from her experience of living with her adopted ones, all these were quiet, but insistent questions she pondered throughout her childhood.

Other questions occupied her mind: It was true that Dinah and Geoffrey had chosen her, but how was she to know that they weren't disappointed at how she had turned out? She couldn't ask them; what could they say but that they were pleased with her? She wondered a great deal what they really thought about her; what they thought so privately that they didn't even tell each other. These were things she understood she could never know, but the questions would not go away. Suppose they *did* love her, and she had every reason to think they did, did they love her as much as they would have if she had been their own child? Could they, was it possible? And that question, she realised, was one that even they couldn't know the answer to. Which led to another question: Did they wonder, as she did, privately, secretly, what would have happened if they had chosen someone else, or if suddenly Dinah had conceived and given birth to a child of their own?

That last was one of the questions that she had asked out in the open. Dinah's answer had been something to think about for the rest of her childhood and adolescence. She said that once they got Esther they stopped trying for a child of their own, and that although there were serious doubts about Dinah's ability to ovulate (no biological processes had ever been concealed from Esther) she had none the less been sterilised, just in case.

Still, for all her questioning, Esther supposed that she had been as loved and secure as any other child she knew. The questions arose merely because there was an empty space between biology and nurturing; a no man's land where the soil was perfect for those questions to take root. She didn't feel they had been a torment to her, but, looking back over her four and more decades, it was true that her lack of direction, of commitment to a single goal, was not something she could attribute to her parents' teachings. She was not worried by this trait, this tendency of hers to move on, alter course, have no real plan of action in her life. She took things as they turned up. But this characteristic was not anything that could have been instilled in her by Dinah and Geoffrey. On the contrary. So she did wonder slightly, just sometimes, if this were not a part of her that belonged to her biological ancestry. It would make sense. No one had ever speculated with her about her real parents, but as she grew older she began to recognise that the date of her birth in 1945 coincided with a time when Britain was host to American GIs, and many young women had found themselves with child and without a man. She had no reason to suppose this was the truth of her parentage, but it wasn't impossible, and perhaps a certain waywardness made sense in the light of this theory. It was nothing but speculation, an idle thought she had from time to time. When Dinah and Geoffrey were killed in a car crash when Esther was twenty-three, the urge to find out, which had never been terribly strong, had disappeared. It seemed, somehow, disloyal to search for her real parents now that her adopted ones were dead.

When they died Esther had been working for her doctorate. She had spent a year on research, both in London and Germany, on the psychological aspects of a series of Jewish massacres that had occurred in the mid-fourteenth century. Within a month of the accident, she had abandoned the doctorate. It wasn't that she definitely decided to give it up once Dinah and Geoffrey were gone, she simply discovered one day that she had stopped, that it was in her past. She was not going to pursue a career in clinical psychology, it seemed, and, now that she was no longer doing it, it was as if she had never really believed she would. She wasn't certain about that. Perhaps it was only hindsight. Possibly, whenever one doesn't do something that one might have done or had planned to do, it always appears after the event that there was no genuine belief in the reality of the plan in the first place. She didn't know. But there was no wrench at giving up her studies, and she certainly had no firm plans about what she wanted to do.

This was also true of the men in her life at that point. At university there had been a lover with whom she lived after the first year. When that was over (now she couldn't remember who had left who, or why; perhaps it had just petered out) that relationship had the same improbability as the career plans. A second lover had arrived and gone by the time she stood alone and without plans in the world.

She was suddenly and unexpectedly cast adrift. No family, no planned future. For a time she felt bereft, not just of her family, of people to whom she belonged, but of the world itself. For some months she experienced the kind of heart-banging panic a person might feel if dropped in the middle of a desert without the resources to find a way out.

Eventually, she got a hold on herself and made decisions that, good or bad – it didn't seem to matter very much which – got her life moving again, and the panic began to subside into something intermittent and manageable.

Dinah and Geoffrey had left what money they had had to the school in Botswana. A message to Esther in the will explained that she would understand how they felt about relative needs, and that since she would have the house *and* a firm footing on a career ladder she needed their money much less than others. Esther was content with this arrangement. She knew that this was what they had planned, and approved of their worthy principles. The fact that her earning capacity would not be what her adoptive parents had expected didn't worry her unduly. She sold the house, bought a flat near Queen's Park, with more large, high-ceilinged, light rooms than she currently needed, and put the remaining capital into a building society. She had more to fall back on than most.

26

A little while after she had settled into the flat, she trained as a youth counsellor, almost without knowing why. It had seemed to her accidental, but she was in search of any direction she could find, and she grabbed at the information someone gave her at a party. It had the advantage of seeming to be the right kind of thing for her to do, given her background. She worked, in the early Seventies, in schools and youth clubs with kids whose lives were chaotically problematical. Sex, pregnancy, drugs, family troubles, everything and anything was on the agenda. She talked to them with patience and understanding, and knew where to send them for help when talking wasn't enough.

What Esther knew about life by then was that it was miserable for almost everyone. This was the real legacy from Dinah and Geoffrey. Poverty, injustice, disease, political tyranny; she had been aware of them all from an early age. Geoffrey had worked for UNESCO, and both her parents had belonged to organisations that attempted to work against the natural and political causes of suffering in what was, at that time, known as the Third World. The troubled planet was as much a part of their family discussions at the dinner table as where to go for their holidays. And from Dinah, Esther had received her education about the murky undergrowth of the human mind. It wasn't just poverty and underdevelopment that caused misery. She understood quite early that the pain of the well-fed was no less painful than material want. One did what one could to alleviate suffering wherever it occurred. But the point was that it occurred everywhere. Who escaped? If the Friedmans were exempt from most of it, their pain lay precisely in their exemption and their awareness of the misery of others. They took on their burden, and did what it was possible to do because *doing things* was all there was. They were atheists; there were no hopes for an after-life when things would be better, when wrongs would be righted. Prayer would not fill empty bellies. They were thankful for the good food on the table, but they did not say grace.

Nor did they have an optimistic political creed. They were humanists, or so Dinah would describe them, when Esther asked, insisting on a lower case 'h'. Marxism held no promise for them. It was merely another kind of faith. History replaced

God, but the belief required in the inevitably benevolent out-come of history was not something Dinah or Geoffrey could ascribe to. They believed, if they believed in anything, in themselves as active agents, and in what could be done by the conscious will of those who looked, unblinking, at the world and tried to share some of their advantages with those who had less.

Esther could find no fault with this. It seemed a responsible and proper way to conduct one's life, without the crutch of a belief system that depended on an invisible accountant who balanced up the books – eventually. If something about herself had made her less active, for most of her life, than her parents, it didn't mean that she thought any differently about the nature of her world, only that she felt more helpless, or less engaged, or something. She didn't know why she had less energy (if that was what she had less of) than Dinah and Geoffrey; perhaps it was the times she had lived through, perhaps she just wasn't up to it. Her few years of youth counselling had used up what optimism she had. After a while there were too many of the same problems, too few solutions, and when she began to watch the troubled children bring another generation into the world she had felt, finally, hopeless. She found herself suffocating under so great a weight that none of the small, immediate things she could do to help seemed to get anywhere near the vast, rolling, ever-increasing burden of misery.

She gave up her attempt at involvement and found herself at some distance from everything. This place, rather to her surprise, was not a purgatory of alienation, but so comfortable that she felt she had at last got home. It was as if, after the terror of the unknown drop down the rabbit hole, Alice discovered herself to be back on the lazy Oxford river, with Mr Dodgson telling her entertaining stories of a place whose twists and confusions she was not required to experience.

In the end, what she was left with was a dry curiosity about the race to which she belonged, whose best was a kind of glory, and whose worst was an assault on the mind that tried to think about it. In between there was a chronic muddle which was touching and terrible.

She became an observer, a visitor to the museum of planet

Earth. Her adopted parents' admirable humanism had, in Esther, done a somersault. It was not just her parents to whom she didn't quite belong, despite their protestations to the contrary, but the planet itself, at whose doorstep she had been left a foundling.

Her alienation gave her a certain sort of strength. It had taken her out of the desert that had caused her so much panic, and placed her, if not back on the streets with the rest of civilisation, at least within a few feet of them. Near enough to construct a model of what she saw, in her own space. If it was no more than mimicry, she wondered if perhaps that was not the case for others, too. She didn't let it trouble her.

She met Rob around that time. He was a big, solid man; attractive and kind. He was a painter, a good one, and taught part-time in the art school, where Esther, needing money, and not wanting a regular job, modelled for a life class. She was pregnant within six weeks, and both of them were happy about what they termed 'the accident'. The baby was wanted by each of them, for reasons that neither thought too carefully about, and they were not displeased with the prospect of each other as partners. They married, and, without for one moment being conscious of it, Esther had created the model of the world that she was so nearly a part of. She had invented herself a family. *Her* husband, *her* baby. Rob and the forthcoming child were *hers*, indisputably hers; belonging to her by law and biology.

Esther put the last plate into the rack and dried her hands. She pushed her sleeves firmly up above her elbows, and, with her jaw set, made her way to the studio. Her apathy this morning had frightened her. She knew she had to push herself harder. It was too long since she had done any work. She was determined, suddenly, to try, or, at the least, to be in the place where work could happen.

5

THE STUDIO WAS where she earned her living these days. It was a room that had never been decorated, and its bare wood floor and faded white walls had made it a suitable place for Katya to create as much mess as she had needed when she was a toddler. Later, the large windows on two sides of the room had provided excellent natural light for Esther to work by.

There was a large, old refectory table under one window that served as a workbench, and an easel beside it for preliminary sketches. Under the other window was a kiln. On the opposite side of the room an ancient, purple armchair, overstuffed and large enough to curl up in, stood on top of a threadbare, but nice, Turkish rug. Esther thought of it as her brooding corner.

Everything had come from junk shops, apart from the kiln – and the chair, which she found lying on top of a nearby skip. She and Katya, who was eleven then, had hauled it to the flat and up the stairs, while Katya complained that if any of her school friends saw her, they'd think her mother was a tramp, and why couldn't she *buy* furniture like other parents?

Katya did not share her mother's sense of triumph at finding something that had been thrown out as useless and putting it to good use. Esther would explain that they were a one-parent family, on a limited income, that the money in the building society had dwindled to the point where it was now only a serious emergency fund, and that, considering everything, they lived well enough. Katya was unimpressed. She knew that it was Esther's pleasure to recycle junk. It was not shortage of money that caused every cup and saucer and every plate to be different. Esther *liked* things not to match, to be flawed by time, or other people's use.

It was only when Katya had grown verbal enough to argue her case that Esther stopped buying her clothes in jumble sales and second-hand shops. Some of the clothes Katya had worn when she was little had been beautiful, all of them had had a lived-in look that Esther enjoyed, but Katya had finally got her mother to see that she wanted her *own* clothes, even if they weren't as individual as second-hand ones. Actually, *especially* as they weren't so individual – Katya had the good sense not to make this point in her argument, but what she wanted more than clothes specially bought for her, and previously worn by no one else, was to look like other people. Esther would have given her one of those blank, perplexed stares, if she had said so. But Esther was not so wrapped up in her own world that she couldn't see Katya's point, at least from Katya's point of view. There were no more second-hand clothes after that. The two of them had shared their lives for long enough to have learned to accommodate sufficiently to one another.

Esther sat at the worktable gazing at the paints waiting to be squeezed on to her palette, and the sketchpad and pencils ready for her to draw.

The time marked out by Katya's birth and her entry to secondary school made up a single square of the patchwork of Esther's life. It was one of those times when life sat up and demanded activity. For the first year, while Rob was still living with them, Esther went to evening classes to learn shorthand and typing. It seemed like a good thing to do, since Rob was there to take care of the baby in the evenings. She supposed later that she had been expecting Rob to go eventually, which wasn't so clever since Rob's increasing distance and vagueness even then were too evident not to notice. The combination of secretarial skills and fluent German had assured her of regular work at times that fitted in with Katya's schedule at nursery, and then primary school. By the time Rob left, when Katya was eight, her wages, maintenance from Rob, and the remains of the house money meant she could manage well enough. Once Katya started at secondary school and was more independent, she had topped up the savings enough to allow her to contemplate taking time off. One day she remembered aloud how she had thought once of going to art school, and

Katya had encouraged her to find out if she could study art for a year.

It was during that year that she started painting plates, at first for fun, decorating the plainer plates in her kitchen cupboard, and then, as friends saw them and offered her money to paint plates for them, it grew into a decent source of income. By the time the year was up Esther was supplying several shops in Covent Garden, Chelsea and Hampstead with hand-painted plates, mugs and teapots. Her new and unexpected career flourished, and she enjoyed the chance to work at home at her own pace. Katya's playroom became Esther's workroom, and the respectable office clothes were put in the pending cupboard that smelt of mothballs and lack of use to wait for whatever the future held.

Esther took the sketchbook from the easel and her box of felt-tipped pens and went to her purple chair with them. Half an hour later she held the sketchbook at arm's length and examined what she had done. She hadn't intended to produce anything, not a new design, certainly, but she had drawn a plate-sized circle on the empty paper almost without thinking about it. The design she had made surprised her as much as the fact that she had done anything at all. It was an abstract pattern, and not one of the airy, autumnal or summery-tinted fruit or flower designs she was known for. The colours in this were bright and strong: cornflower-blues, poppy-reds, yellow-brick-road-yellows. When it was a finished object, it would look like a plate that had been made up of shards of other broken plates stuck together to make a new whole. In between the irregular blocks of colour were thin black lines, like grouted joins. She usually gave each pattern she designed a name that was painted, along with her signature, on the underside of the plate or cup or whatever it was. This pattern, she decided, would be called *Waste Not Want Not*. She wrote it at the bottom of the design, dated and signed it.

Although her strange, pale flower and fruit designs were pleasing, both to herself and the buyers, this new, strong-hued, broken pattern more closely represented the workings of Esther's mind. Not that she thought of the plate painting as a means of self-expression; it was a pleasant way of earning a living, and self-expression had never been something she felt any need for. If there was a creative urge it was far down, below the Plimsoll line of her consciousness. But, without her having the faintest idea why, though she wondered about it, this pattern was different. As she looked at it, it seemed vaguely familiar in the way that certain characters or episodes in dreams can seem familiar, yet, none the less, lack any obvious connection to reality that might enable one to find their relation to waking life.

It related most obviously, of course, to the patchwork image she had of her life. The new pattern was a template, a featureless map of how she had spent her time in the world. But there was something else that tickled at the limits of her consciousness. It had, this pattern of flat colour marked out against flat colour, the *feeling tone* of a dream that she knew she had had but couldn't remember. Something that occurred in that period first thing in the morning, between waking and finding herself. She could place the quality of the pattern in that space in her life, but without having the faintest idea why. It was the geometry of another existence, or the pattern of several existences. It was something that hovered over her awareness, a taste, as it were, but totally inaccessible to sense. Somehow, too, it carried the flavour of Katya, but again in no way that Esther could articulate.

She let the feeling of familiarity go, as if it were no more than the shadow of a passing cloud on a sunny landscape. It meant nothing, made no sense, and, once she had shaken it off, she wasn't troubled by it. The pattern became a pattern, good and strong, and an interesting new departure that her buyers would appreciate. It pleased her, there was something about it . . . well, she liked it. She had got herself back to work. That was enough.

Esther sorted out her colours and mixed her paints. But she had thought of Katya, and instantly the worry began to press for its place at the centre of her mind. She kept it at bay by focusing hard on getting the colour tones exactly as she wanted them.

The doorbell rang just as she had finished making up her palette and was wiping the excess turps from the brushes she wanted to use. It was Ben, of course, come to give her his support for the morning.

'You panicked. You let them bully you,' Ben told Esther decisively.

'I suppose so. But what else could I do? She was completely off her head – she's my daughter. I couldn't just let her . . .'

'Let her what?'

'Let her . . .' Esther groped for words to describe what was so obvious that she couldn't find a way to say it. 'I don't know – carry on like that.'

'All you're saying is that you didn't like the way she was behaving. So you decided that she had to be punished.'

'I didn't. For Christ's sake, Ben, how could I let her run around like that? She was *suffering*, she needed help.'

'Well, I agree with that, certainly she needed help. But you weren't helping her, you weren't getting to the source of her problem – you were just drugging her out of inconvenient behaviour.'

'I wasn't! The doctors at the hospital were trying to help her.'

'All right, *you* weren't drugging her senseless, but you allowed it to happen. You have to take responsibility for that, and you won't, because you can't take responsibility for Katya's condition. The doctors say she's got a chemical imbalance, and you grab at that with both hands, because it lets you off the hook. It's not *your* fault, it's an act of God or biology. So keep her quiet and salve your conscience. Go ahead, but one day you'll have to face it.'

Esther groaned and dropped her head into her cupped hands. She was sitting up, cross-legged, on the bed, her part of the duvet thrown aside. Ben lay on his back, his lower half covered by a double layer of duvet, admiring the profile of Esther's naked breast framed by her bent arm, and the curve of her spine, slightly concave at the base and then gently rounded to accommodate her hunched shoulders and lowered head.

'Face what?'

Anxiety lent Esther's tone a snappishness that was only partly muffled by her hands covering her face, but Ben was used to the anger that came from a resistance to the truth, and wasn't bothered by it.

'The fact that you are implicated in Katya's breakdown,' he explained calmly.

Esther took her hands away from her face and turned to look down at Ben.

'And what are you implicated in, may I ask? Or is fucking your clients part of the treatment?'

Ben smiled to himself at the expected aggression.

'You aren't a client. And we began to make love to each other recently because we both wanted to. Didn't we? This has nothing to do with Katya's problem.'

Esther sniffed grumpily, and pulled her half of the duvet off Ben and over her crossed legs.

'Well, I'm glad *something* I do has nothing to do with the fact that my daughter's mad. What a happy coincidence that it happens to be fucking you.'

'Are you telling me you didn't want to – that you don't enjoy it? I think we both knew that we were attracted to each other for a long time. Maybe part of your problem is that you've denied your sexual feelings, and that suppression of emotion naturally transmits itself to Katya.'

'Maybe part of my problem is that I'm not very proud of fucking a man who's married to my daughter's best friend's mother. What's *that* going to do to Katya's psyche?'

'It's got nothing to do with it. What we're doing is something we both wanted. I know there's Karen, but these things happen. It's childish to pretend they don't.'

'Do they happen to you a lot? I don't think Karen knows you're unfaithful to her.'

Ben reached up and stroked Esther's breast.

'Not often. We've been married for twenty years, and it's a good marriage. We respect and like each other. Sometimes – occasionally – there have been other women. But I don't regard my affairs as a betrayal. I love Karen, her position isn't threatened by my making love to you. Human beings aren't designed for lifelong monogamy; it's an accident that everybody lives longer. Until this century, marriages didn't last anything like so long, because people died younger.'

'Women, you mean?'

'Well, yes, more often than men, because childbirth was much more dangerous.'

'So you're just doing what comes naturally?'

'And so are you.'

'But even if we aren't betraying Karen, we're deceiving her, aren't we?'

'It's an unfortunate necessity when society equates trust with sexual fidelity. Open marriages would be much more sensible, but I'm afraid that our conditioning usually prevents them from working. So we have to conceal other sexual encounters. I conceal them from Karen because, in the end, it means she won't be hurt.'

'Unless she finds out?'

'Why should she? We both know what we're doing. I desire you, and I'm your friend. Neither of us wants to break up my marriage, do we?'

'What about Karen? Does she operate on the same principle? Does she have affairs? She keeps very quiet about it if she does.'

Ben looked bothered for a moment.

'No.'

'No? Just like that – no?'

'As far as I know.' His voice had a slight edge to it. 'I'm sure she doesn't.'

'But you wouldn't mind?' Esther enjoyed the sense that she had Ben a little on the defensive now.

'Well . . . It's irrelevant. And so is us going to bed together. It just so happened that it happened now. We're talking about Katya. Katya's well-being is the thing that concerns us. The fact of us making love is something completely different.'

Esther was unconvinced. She began to wonder how good a psychotherapist Ben was if he didn't think there was any significance in her going to bed with him now, rather than any other time. At any rate, she felt it devalued his accusation that she refused to face reality. She, at least, was aware that she had gone to bed with Ben because she was miserable and confused, and she wanted someone to hold her and make her feel less frightened. She paused to wonder, for a second, why she supposed that making love should make her feel less frightened, but let the thought pass. There was enough to think about.

It was true that she had always found Ben attractive; she

liked the way he looked and his confident manner. She envied Karen (although, as far as she knew, without malice) for having someone around all the time who could cope. She was aware, simply, that it would be nice to have another person on hand to share some of her anxieties with, someone who would make them seem less threatening and take some of the weight of worry from her shoulders. Ben was always so certain, cutting his way through details to get to the core of things, and creating a named problem that was likely to have a solution, rather than allowing the day-to-day muddle to overwhelm his capacity to think about what was *really* going on.

Karen was generous with him, at least so far as advice was concerned, but whenever Esther sat at her kitchen table with Ben, discussing some problem about Katya, she was always aware of his thick mane of black swept-back hair, of which he was evidently proud, and the strength and shape of his forearms beneath his rolled shirt-sleeves. Sometimes the sight of his dark forearm and wrist lifting a cup, or reaching comfortingly to take her hand, made her uterus go into spasm, and oddly, as if he felt the movement deep inside her, he would raise his eyes to hers for a moment and make her look at him until the discomfort forced her to remove her hand and look away.

He was right to say that sex had always been a silent topic between them. But Esther had never allowed herself to imagine that they might become lovers. Karen was not a very close friend. Esther always remained, with everyone, not just Karen, slightly aloof from the intimacy that Karen might have been pleased to have; but she was a friend none the less. And, perhaps more importantly, Katya and Meg were best friends, always in and out of each other's houses, so that the two families were a network that Esther didn't want to disrupt by allowing her attraction to Ben to become a reality.

What had happened a few days ago was that when Ben looked into her eyes she did not look away or remove her hand from under his. It seemed they sat and stared at each other for an impossibly long time, and then, in a flashing moment, too short to recall how the move had occurred, their mouths were together, sucking the breath from each other's lungs, tasting and feeding like starved children. How they had got from the kitchen to the bedroom was also vague in Esther's memory. She supposed that the less conscious they were of the manoeuvres that finally got Ben moving inside her, the less likely it was that one of them would think, or say, What about Karen? Forgetfulness was a useful ploy that used desperate necessity as a handy euphemism for sexual incontinence. Or so it seemed to Esther. Ben, apparently, would have no truck with guilt or shame. It would have been against his professional judgement, to say nothing of his best interests.

Esther noticed again how sour she felt. Post-coital *tristesse*, she wondered, and then corrected it to post-coital cynicism.

The real guilt, though, was about Katya. Why had she spent the last two hours crawling all over a naked man, totally absorbed in his sharp sexual scent, the silk-soft muscle-hard texture of his skin, the feel of his cock growing large – *again, again, more* – in her mouth, when, for the past ten days, her only daughter, last seen raving and demented, had disappeared without trace?

These things happen, Ben would say, and she couldn't deny that. But she felt foolishly undeveloped, the very minimum of evolved humanity that had to take carnal comfort where thought and intelligence were the real requirement. Taking sex, and if it hadn't been available she would have taken food, taken drink; sucking in anything to fill the body that felt wounded, stopping up the places that allowed the outside world to become part of her and made her part of it. Plugging the gaps that fuzzed the boundary line. She would have had it all closed off: mouth, ears, nostrils, vagina, anus. She wanted to be sealed. She wanted to be cut off so that her brain was isolated, overloaded with internal sensation, unable to reach out to the place outside and fret over a problem it couldn't begin to understand. 'Fuck me, fuck me,' she had whispered with an urgency that conveyed itself to Ben's genitals. She meant, Make everything go away; do me the service of wiping me out. And Ben had complied, though possibly for different reasons.

But fucking Ben was only a short-term solution. You can eat yourself to death, and drink yourself to death, but no one had ever devised a way of fucking yourself to death, although that was, obviously, the project. She and Ben had done what they could with their bodies. The problem of Katya remained, unaltered. Esther decided to leave what had happened with Ben for another time. Perhaps it would just go away; suddenly, making love to Ben seemed a minor issue.

She got up and pulled on a dressing-gown. Ben watched her body disappear inside soft folds that hinted at the outline beneath. Esther looked at him as she tied the belt firmly around her, and wished that they were both up and dressed. She tried to return to a conversation between concerned friends. Her voice had lost its throaty post-orgasmic quality and reverted to the tones of confusion and anxiety.

'Why is it that I'm an intelligent, educated, reasonably well-informed person, and I don't know what to do about the fact that my daughter's gone mad?'

'Not mad. That's a term that has no meaning. There's no such thing as madness.' Ben got out of bed as he spoke and made for the bathroom. Esther followed.

'Yes, there is. When someone is found standing stark naked in the middle of Queen's Park, trying to gouge her flesh away with her fingernails, and screaming that everyone should keep away because she would make them die if they came close to her, they are mad. And, if you tell me she was just expressing herself, then you're mad, too.'

Under the shower Ben washed away the scent and flavour of Esther while Esther splashed water over her face and put her jeans and another old sweater on. He ducked his head outside the downpour of water.

'I didn't hear you. What?'

'Nothing,' Esther said, drying her face. Ben went back under the shower. 'I just said you were mad,' she explained into her towel.

Fifteen minutes later they were back at the kitchen table sipping coffee, with only Ben's tell-tale fresh-washed smell to suggest that anything other than advice had been given or taken. Ben was his normal, avuncular, psychotherapeutic self.

'When they find her, you have to get her out of, away from the hospital. There's a place she can stay – a house, not a hospital – she can work through her obsessions and there are qualified, sympathetic people she can talk to.'

'There are qualified people at the hospital.'

'Look, you don't know what it's like. They haven't got the time, the patients have got every kind of problem. All they can do is drug them into submission, into a pantomime of normality. You should see those places – populated by zombies. And that's only the staff . . .'

His joke fell flat; usually, it won reluctant parents round because the underlying truth was leavened with the release of humour. Esther was too anxious about Katya's whereabouts for it to work. He let it go.

'They will give her very powerful tranquillisers so that she can't think straight.'

'She can't think straight anyway. That's why she was there.'

'Esther, listen to me, you've got to get her out of there.'

'She is out of there. She's got to be found before I can take her out of there again.'

'Yes, I know,' Ben reassured her, placing her hand on his. 'But she will be. Then you've got to put your foot down. You have no idea of the damage they can do. By the time they've finished with her, it'll be impossible to get to the root of the problem. She'll end up suppressing her inner life with drugs until she's old. You can't allow that to happen to your daughter.' He paused. 'Unless, of course, that's precisely what you want . . .'

'What?'

'She's adolescent, with a burgeoning sexuality. It's classical for a female parent – particularly if there's no father around – to fear their daughter's sexuality, especially as it comes at a time when their own is on the wane and the body is beginning to decay.'

'Thank you very much,' Esther snapped. 'It didn't seem to be so decayed that you couldn't think of something to do with it this morning.'

'That's exactly what I mean. There's no need to be defensive. I'm just trying to get you to understand the dynamics of the situation. You're lovely still, you know that. But there's a family sub-text in all this.'

The fact that they had been to bed together would not go away, it seemed. Esther pushed a stray curl of hair off her face and sighed.

'Ben, I'm sorry. I just don't know what to do. She's always been so sane. I don't know why this has happened.'

'That's what we should be finding out.' Ben took her hand between both of his, and she let him hold it. 'The child is trying to tell you something. You must listen to her. You have to acknowledge her interior life.'

Esther shook her head in perplexity; the curl fell back over her forehead.

'I don't know, Ben. I don't know. Let me think about it.'

As Ben left, Esther remembered the first time they had fucked, the morning that Katya had gone missing. An hour later, Karen had phoned.

'Ben's told me,' she said.

Esther had had a surge of adrenalin that was almost instantly replaced by apathy. She didn't care if Karen knew. Katya was uppermost in her thoughts now. Karen could accuse her, scream at her, hurl abuse, and all she would do was agree and apologise. It didn't matter.

'He said you were in an awful state,' Karen continued, and Esther heard the sympathy in her voice. 'Well, obviously you are. Look, we both think it would be a good thing if you packed a bag and came and stayed here for a day or two. It wouldn't be any trouble, honestly, and you shouldn't be on your own. You must have people you can talk to. Will you?'

Apathy, now that the immediate danger of a confrontation was over, was replaced by guilt, but not so much that she wasn't sure of what she wanted. 'Thanks, Karen,' she'd said, hoping that the relief wasn't too evident in her voice. 'It's kind of both of you. But I need to be alone, I think. I'll be all right. But, thanks.'

She was alone now. A middle-aged single parent, an independent woman with a runaway, mentally disturbed adolescent daughter. With Ben gone, no longer channelling the range of her reactions, no longer observing, she was free to respond to her situation in a natural, private way. She wondered, as she had wondered for the last ten days, what that might be, and considered sitting in the living-room on the sofa, crying, perhaps. She might pace up and down in the kitchen, phone the police every hour, a desperate, anxious parent. Music was a possibility. A walk. Work.

They were all possible and authentic behaviours in the present circumstance. The only one that wasn't was considering which one she would choose. She had no natural response. She had tested the possibility that this was a response in itself, but she couldn't convince herself that it was. Being alone and unobserved by someone else did not alter the fact that she was constantly observed by herself, and therefore there *was* no spontaneous behaviour. She could have worried about this for the rest of the day. It was an alternative to worrying about Katya. But the truth was that the boiling worry about Katya she had lived with for the past few weeks had died to a manageable simmer now that there was nothing Esther could do about it. Katya was in the first place a problem for the police, and then a medical problem that was someone else's area of expertise. She had been released from mother-worry by an official diagnosis that was not her province. Her resistance to Ben's arguments about what to do when (if?) Katya was found was based on this: she didn't want her new-found lack of responsibility spoiled. Ben was essentially right about that. But in practical terms, she thought, she was genuinely confused because she knew she was unequipped to decide.

She allowed that this was merely the same self-justification from another angle, but still, there was some truth in it. She remembered Katya's birth. She had armed herself through the pregnancy with all the information she could find, and got the right terminology under her belt to ensure that the doctors could not override her ignorance with their jargon. She was determined not to lose control of the process. She made sure that Rob knew his stuff, too, in case she wasn't in a fit state to fight for what she wanted. But, when it came to it, Katya was a breech baby, and Esther's pelvis, they said, was narrower than they had thought. Never mind, she had said firmly, she was going to have a normal delivery. The obstetrician immediately came back at her with the well-being of the baby, using her information against her to tell of the risks she was incurring for the infant. She knew she was beaten. She agreed to compromise, she could try for a non-Caesarean delivery, and they would induce labour. But it was too late. The Caesarean was inevitable once she had moved an inch from her previous position. Her own knowledge defeated her – she knew about foetal stress and they made it clear that she could not claim innocence if anything went wrong. She lost.

The uncertainty she now felt was the same as then. Her emotional involvement made her dither between this and that decision, and, in the dithering, she would lose control. Was she going to risk Katya's mind by letting the drug doctors have her; was she going to risk Katya's safety by letting Ben delve into her disturbed and uncontrolled mind? No answer. Except that Katya wasn't with either of them at the present. Still, when she was found, the drug doctors would have her as a matter of practical emergency, so sheer inertia might solve the dilemma. This, it struck her, was what she hoped for.

Esther decided to be a worrying woman who threw herself into her work, and went back to her studio.

6

AFTER HER FAILED attempt to get Katya to tell her what was going on, Esther spent the rest of the day applying colour to white-glazed plates. By the time Katya got in from school a new design was ready.

Katya went up to the workroom, kissed Esther, and examined the new design. It was a painting of a strawberry tart.

'That's pretty,' Katya smiled. 'A plate to eat strawberry tarts off.'

'Exactly,' Esther said, pleased with herself, and with Katya's approval. 'So you'd get more strawberry tart, the more strawberry tart you eat. Having your tart and eating it! How was school?'

Katya laughed at the joke and indicated that school was OK, nothing special had happened. 'I'll be off to my room.'

'What about some tea? We could go out for tea – eat strawberry tart to celebrate?'

Katya shook her head. 'No, I've got things to do. Thanks.' She turned to leave Esther's workroom, smiling.

Esther breathed in the energy she needed to speak to her daughter. 'Wait. Katya . . . why aren't you eating?'

Katya stopped and turned. 'I told you this morning.'

'This morning you told me you'd made a promise. I want you to tell me about it.'

Katya looked uncomfortable. 'It's something I have to do. It's not for any bad reason. Honestly.'

'Are you involved with someone? Or pregnant? Is it exams coming up? Or . . . drugs? They can all be dealt with . . . if you just tell me.'

Esther saw her daughter's face close against her. There was nothing aggressive, just a wall of privacy that went up as Esther listed all the traps that she could think of that lay in wait for adolescent girls. Somehow she knew that she had proved herself as incapable of understanding as Katya had told her she was. She felt obscurely ashamed at her suggestions.

'We could have a cup of tea,' Katya suggested brightly, placating her mother. 'I'll go and put the kettle on.'

Esther followed her daughter down to the kitchen a few moments later, when she had calmed down and determined, with Karen's voice ringing in her ear, to do something about the situation. She wondered, though, why it was that the possibility of eliminating pregnancy, drugs and anorexia left her more worried about Katya than before.

Katya smiled vaguely at Esther. Everything was ready; the teapot and an empty cup waited for her. Katya sat in front of a mug of what Esther wouldn't deign to call tea.

'This is nice,' Esther said, sitting at her place. It wasn't. It would have been if . . . but it wasn't. Katya retained the benign smile. Esther's increasingly sour self described it, silently, as simpering. But there was a kind of wildness in Katya's eyes, a sort of glow (no doubt from starvation, Esther thought) like the accidental residue of something bright and strong that lay hidden behind them. Esther took a deep breath.

'I want you to see Dr Grainger. I'm going to make an appointment with him for tomorrow.'

'I'm not ill . . .'

'Even so. Don't argue, Katya. You've hardly eaten anything in the past week, and I know you don't sleep much. Not eating and sleeping can do weird things to your head. You might think you're all right, but it doesn't look like that to people who know you. If you can't talk to me, then talk to Dr Grainger. He knows you. Will you? Or Ben? You can talk to Ben, if you'd prefer?'

'Mum, I don't want to talk to anyone. I'm all right . . .'

Esther picked up her cup and saucer and dropped them from too great a height into the washing-up bowl in the sink. They didn't break.

'Right. I'll get you an appointment for tomorrow after school. Don't be late back.'

Esther left Katya sitting where she was and went back to her workroom and the strawberry tart design.

*

The diagnoses ranged from anorexia nervosa to adolescent psychosis. One consultant cut through the niceties and wrote 'schizophrenia' in his notes. This was bold: both archaic and before its time. No such thing as schizophrenia, some insisted; others, that schizophrenia was a biochemical disease, a genetic predisposition. Before long, they would add, somewhat irrelevantly to Esther's present situation, we'll be able to test for it in parent and foetus.

Generally, whatever the label offered, physiological causes were hinted at. Hormone imbalance. The dramatic change that occurs in adolescence either triggers a mental cataclysm, or causes it directly. The fault was, essentially, that Katya was fourteen, and, for whatever underlying reason, suffering the mental effects of adolescent chemistry.

Why Katya should suffer from mental symptoms of adolescence, rather than, say, acne, was just one of the mysteries that genetic research was going, one day soon, to solve. In the mean time, happily, it so happened that mental derangement was a symptom that could be controlled, whereas acne was less amenable to pharmacological solutions.

Ben, on the other hand, had different ideas. He was a psychologist of the old school. What was going on with Katya was a response to something that involved the family. The primary relationships between Katya and Esther, between Esther and Rob, Rob and Katya, were an intricate web of pressure that needed unravelling. While the medical men pondered chemistry, Ben, with tact and compassion, talked to Esther about psychotherapeutic solutions.

Esther sat in consulting rooms and listened to the doctors. She sat at her kitchen table and listened to Ben. She was inclined, by her own upbringing and the times she had lived through, towards Ben's view. If something was wrong, it was likely to be because something had been wrongly done. An accident of chemistry, genetic or hormonal as it might be, made less sense to Esther. But she had to admit that the sudden transformation of her daughter into a stranger had a quality of chemistry about it. In another society it would have been called possession, or witchcraft – and those magical explanations lacked only scientific understanding to transform them into chemical explanations. Her upbringing as the daughter of a social psychologist, and her training as a youth counsellor seemed to count for nothing. She was as fraught and confused by her daughter's behaviour as if she had had no past at all. 'Well, it's always different with your own child,' Karen consoled.

7

THE SOURCE OF the frantic pattering that had disturbed Esther's thoughts turned out to be the lamp over the worktable. It was the only light on in the studio.

Esther sat in the fading armchair, in the half-light, taking comfort from the warm glow of the lamp across the room, but not wishing to leave the shadows. Five plates with the new broken-put-together *Waste Not Want Not* pattern painted on them rested on the drying rack. They would be ready for firing in the morning. She was pleased with how they looked, and pleased, too, that she had managed to spend the rest of the day working.

She focused her eyes when she heard the sound; they had been open, but saw only phantoms conjured by memory. The disturbance was a delicate drumming, a desperate tattoo, and it was in the room, although the studio was empty except for her. She traced it to the direction of the worktable and then noticed a flitting shadow that danced on its surface.

Probably, she had solved the problem of the sound before she saw the shadow and linked the tapping to the lamp. It was hardly necessary for her conscious mind to formulate the word 'moth' once the other part of her had answered the question the sound posed. The irritation of something unknown was soothed without the need for her to pay further attention to it. But the shadow and the tapping in the lamp were events, something that was happening in the room and, once she had noticed them, they were, for a passing moment, at the centre of her life.

So she thought: *Moth*. And other thoughts followed.

It was late in the season for moths. Autumn. It must be dying, anyway. Electric light confuses moths, they mistake it for the light of the moon, which they use to navigate. Where do they want to go? Esther thought. Evolution had not equipped them to differentiate between natural and man-made light. No, she corrected herself, that's not right. They do differentiate, choosing the strong glare of the electric bulb over the softer, more distant illumination. What evolution had not equipped them with was the good sense to choose the subtle over the obvious. Nor, if it came to that, had it made provision for the nights when the moon and its light was invisible.

It pleased Esther that nature was imperfect, or at least casual about its aims. It gave its creatures just enough to get by on. After that, it was a case of adapt or die. Which worked well enough for species' survival, and allowed nature to wipe its hands with the satisfaction of a job well-enough done. For individuals there was only the luck of the draw: accident, life or death, what the hell? What could some poor sod of a moth do about the fact that it was programmed to look for radiant light, and human beings had come along and pierced the night with light so powerful that no moth worth its genes could resist it? Nothing. Adapt or die only applied to evolving generations. Nature merely shrugged its shoulders over individual casualties, and would indeed repeat the same gesture if the entire species went the way of the individual. All it could offer were statistical probabilities over long periods of time. Bye bye, moth.

But here, in Esther's studio, was an individual dying moth, beating its wings against the hot glass and the burning metal shade, trying to get somewhere, attempting to escape its insignificant fate, making enough noise to bring Esther back from her reverie to focus on its condition. Not intentional, that, of course. Moth's world had contracted to the space between lightbulb and shade; to the battle between its overwhelming desire for the light and its overwhelming desire for life. Like nature, Esther just sat and watched. Unlike nature, she felt the cataclysm of the individual's struggle. It reminded her of something. And there was another departure from nature, which didn't mess with metaphor.

So she did not shrug her shoulders. But neither did she turn off the lamp.

Esther got up and sat on the chair at the worktable. By now, the moth, already past its time, was exhausted. Although it couldn't stop its craving for the light, the wings beat slower, the drumming became intermittent, no more than an automated memory of the other desire that demanded escape and continuation. There was no more energy. Perhaps the occasional wingbeat it now managed was entirely to do with its longing for the light, the desire for life fading beneath the power of that other, greater obsession. Esther watched, her chin in her hand, as the life in front of her ebbed away.

She picked up the dead moth from the surface of the desk and examined it. The edges of the wings were ragged, though whether this was from its fight for life, the singeing heat of the bulb, or just what happened to moths in old age, she didn't know. It was not a beautiful thing. The torn wings gave it a look of decaying antique lace, dusty and tattered with time, though, unlike old lace, the moth had never been beautiful. She wondered what the difference was between butterflies and moths, biologically. They were all Lepidoptera, she knew, but that was as far as her information went. Whatever Linnaeus had to say about it, Esther's system classified butterflies as beautiful and moths as not. It didn't matter much to the butterflies and moths, she supposed, what she thought of their relative aesthetics. And that gave her another small burst of pleasure.

The dingy moth lay still in Esther's palm, as if waiting to regain her attention. It wasn't anything special. Just a dull grey with a darker marking on part of the lower half of each wing, as if it had been used for practice by an apprentice calligrapher. But the colour and pattern of the moth presumably signalled species or sex or both to others of its kind. They weren't there for her to ponder over. Esther and the moth had coincided by the merest chance, and, while it gave her the opportunity to rest from her previous brooding, it did nothing whatever for the moth, whose day was done. She remembered being told that the vivid colours of creatures in the ocean that astonished her in wildlife documentaries were purely a function of the light used by the film crew. There was no light in the depths of the sea, therefore no colour, except what human observers invented in their attempt to see what things were really like down there. So we never did, actually, see the way things were.

Suddenly, Esther's focus changed. It was perhaps the sight of the six stiffly bent, jointed legs, and the motionless antennae, that should have been quivering and sensing telling indications of the world. Now that she had noticed the stiffness and the stillness that had allowed her to have her meandering thoughts, she became aware of the weight of death on her palm. She was repelled by the dingy grey corpse, the dead thing that she cupped in her hand. She tipped the lifeless moth into an ashtray on the table, where it lay among the remains of two smoked cigarettes. It was curiously well camouflaged against the ash, as though ashtrays were its natural habitat and nature had provided for just such a moment.

Esther went to the bathroom along the hall and washed her hands using lots of soapy lather and hot running water against the prickly feel of death on her skin, that clung like dirt and had to be cleansed away.

Back in the armchair she cast around for the end of the train of thought that the death throes of the moth had interrupted. Where was she? She had lost her place. She had been thinking about – what could be done about Katya. But her mind, relieved at the distraction the moth provided, had shut the door on the darkened room marked 'Katya', and Esther did not have the will to open it again.

It was late, well past midnight. She turned off the lamp, shut the studio door behind her and went to bed.

8

ESTHER AND REBEKAH had run without stopping to their home among the cluster of houses at the edge of the town. Esther's short legs had had to work much harder than her big sister's, and her sobs mingled indistinguishably with the sound of her small, starving lungs gasping in the air. Both of the little girls' faces were streaked by muddy tears that they had spread trying to wipe them away with the backs of their hands. The need to get home, to be engulfed in the familiarity of where they belonged, had made them lose all caution. It didn't matter that they were seen by the curious eyes of old women sitting on stools outside their doorways; it didn't occur to them to wonder what their own community would make of their wild looks. *Being careful* had fled from them as if it hadn't been repeated two or three times a day, like a prayer, for as much of their lives as they could remember.

The two frightened children stumbled into the Jewish quarter of town, their long skirts pulled up and clutched against their waists, their naked legs covered in mud and dung from where Esther had tripped and brought Rebekah down with her, spattering the yellow Stars of David on their cloaks with dark spots. Their long hair was loosed from the modesty of tight caps: Esther's clinging, still tied round her neck, Rebekah's lost and gone for ever.

They didn't pause at the wooden door of their house. For the first time in their lives they failed to press their fingertips to their lips and reach up on tiptoe to transfer the kiss to the *mezzuzah* on the doorframe, before crossing the threshold. There was only their child's terror that had grown with each step. Everything they had learned about how to conduct themselves had vanished as they crashed through the door, panting and shouting.

52

'Mother . . . Father . . . !'
'Father . . . Bubba . . . Mother . . . !'
'We saw . . .'
'Men . . . strangers . . .'
'They said . . .'

Both children stopped at the same instant, their mouths still open to tell their story, but silenced, as if a spell had been cast over them by the sight of their father's incredulous face. He sat at the small wooden table on a stool and looked, for an instant, no more than astonished that such an unseemly clamour could be happening in his house. Then as he took in the state of his two remaining children he seemed to inflate with anger. He pressed his palms against the table and rose up, staring down at them as he drew in a long breath. To Esther and Rebekah it was as if he had expanded to fill all the space in the small, dark room, his eyes glowing threateningly at them from beneath his heavy brows.

Esther trembled, as always, at the sight of her big, bearish, loving father turning, as he did from time to time, into the terrible, wrathful deity of the Torah. Now he was Jahweh, the vengeful God. The long curls that hung in front of his ears that Esther played with when she climbed into his lap, the dark flaxen robe whose folds she hid in when she had teased Rebekah beyond endurance, the skullcap he had gently told her she must not take from his head because it was a sign of humility before the Lord – all these became awesome signs of a mighty anger.

The children saw why as soon as they could tear their eyes away from the altered apparition of their father. He was not alone. There was a stranger in their house, seated at the table. Not one of them. One of the *goyim* from the town. There were papers and Father's casket of money on the table. They had burst in on him while he was conducting his business. Nothing was more forbidden than this. When men or women came from town to borrow or repay loans, the rest of the family, now just Mother, the two little girls and their Bubba, had to take themselves off into the kitchen and speak, if they must, only in whispers. The clients all arrived with a look of distaste on their faces, and something furtive about the way they held their shoulders. They left in the same manner, clutching small bags of coins, having left papers behind with their name or mark on them. Invariably, they stopped for a moment as the door closed behind them and turned to shoot a glance of resentment in the direction of the Jew moneylender's house.

The man now seated at the table pushed back his stool in alarm as the children rushed in, and there was naked fear on his face as he stared at the filthy wild children, who shouted in a language that sounded similar to his own, but was not. He looked nervously about for an exit that was not blocked by the children, little devils if ever he'd seen them, who were now shrinking back, aware of the enormity of their transgression, of making themselves so dreadfully noticed in front of the *goyim*.

The terrible tableau was disrupted by the children's mother rushing in from the kitchen, having heard the noise and calling in alarm to her husband whom she feared was under attack.

'Samuel . . . Samuel . . . what is it?'

She saw the two children, who had turned towards her voice in relief, freed from the fury of their father's eyes, and scooped them to her, one inside each arm, and bustled them out of the room into the sanctuary of the kitchen.

Rebekah and Esther sobbed piteously, burying their faces on each side of their mother's waist, when they heard the door latch lift and fall back into place. She rocked them back and forth, frightened herself by their fear, which was now almost entirely of the retribution that would fall on them when, any moment now, their father arrived in the kitchen.

'Shh . . . shh . . . babies. What's the matter? What is it?'

All three of them were silenced by the sound of the kitchen door opening, and they turned to stare fearfully at the looming figure of the patriarch in the doorway. Esther looked almost comical as she contorted her features, twisting her face as if it were a handkerchief being wrung out, and squeezing her eyes tight shut to keep in the tears and keep out the explosion that was going to burst upon them. What she wanted more than anything in the world at that moment was not her mother's apron that she clung desperately to and its warm kitchen smell, but the strength and kindness of her father's great spreading hands, stroking her hair and soothing all her terror away.

Suddenly she loosed her grip on her mother and flung herself at her father's legs, wrapping his robe around her, still with her eyes shut, seeking the protection she needed from the only thing in her life strong enough to keep her safe from his fury. 'Dada . . . Dada . . . Dada . . .' she wailed, while Rebekah sobbed against her mother.

Samuel clasped Esther by her arm and pulled her off. She stood, quaking, in front of him. He raised his hand in fury against the child. Esther stood still and shook helplessly with fear.

'Samuel, wait! Don't . . .' his wife begged.

But, even as she opened her mouth to speak, he had pictured the terror on his children's faces as they rushed into his room, and had already stopped himself from landing the blow, his anger overcome by the need to know what could have made them behave in such a way.

Samuel knelt down and brought his face to the same level as Esther's who was still making hiccuping noises as she tried to contain her sobs. She opened her eyes cautiously to see her father's brow furrowed with worry, as she felt his hand pulling her towards the comfort of his embrace.

'What is it, little one, what is it?' His dark eyes peered at her, searching her face for the source of the fear.

Then he looked across Esther's shoulder towards Rebekah who stood staring wide-eyed at her father, unsure still of his intentions. He put a hand out to her and she let go of her mother and came rushing to take up the spare place in his arms. The three of them rocked together, and Samuel, squatting beside his daughters, murmured, 'There, my children! There! There!' like an incantation. His wife moved towards the little group and stood above them, one hand against the back of her husband's head, and the other placed on the children as if she were giving them all the *Shabbos* blessing.

Gradually, Esther and Rebekah were calmed enough by the consoling warmth of their parents to tell them what they had seen and heard in the market square. They waited, with some stoicism, to be reprimanded for being away from the Jewish quarter without permission, but no reprimand came. When Esther raised her head to find out what was happening, she followed her father's strange gaze to the eyes of her mother. She saw knowledge and fear meet in the space between the two adults, and the comfort and security they had offered lost some of its power.

What she had seen was not something the adults could explain away. The words that should have accompanied the stroking of their hands ('There's nothing to worry about. You misunderstood. Like a bad dream, it's nothing. Everything is as it was. You are safe. We are all safe, my darlings') were absent. Esther could take comfort from their arms, but there was no reassurance.

'Lock the door behind me,' Samuel told his wife, getting up from his knees. 'I'll warn . . .' He glanced at the children staring up at him. '. . . tell the rabbi. Where's Mother?'

'She went out . . . she's with the baker's wife . . . the child is due . . .'

'I'll fetch her. Stay in the kitchen, don't open the door unless it's me or Bubba . . .'

'What's happening? What's the matter?' Rebekah asked, looking from one parent to the other. Samuel stopped for a moment and looked at his ten-year-old daughter. His wife hugged the children to her.

'Go, Samuel, go quickly. We'll be all right until you come back.'

A look between husband and wife agreed that it was best the children didn't know. Whatever was to happen, the children could at least be spared the fear beforehand. Rebekah was old enough to be alarmed by her parents' reaction, but she didn't yet have the ancient fear, the terrible knowledge that dwelt, deep and dark, within her parents, ready to spring alive on the instant, as it did now.

Esther and Rebekah had never seen the sea, so they did not recognise the growing murmur they heard as the sound of a great wave, distant but moving ever closer. They felt its power, though; the pressure of a great mass, pushing all before it so that the very air seemed to concentrate and thicken in the kitchen, almost suffocating the small group that stood, huddled close together against the wall. They hardly dared to move when Samuel banged on the wooden door, to be let in with the children's grandmother. Then the sounds in their own locality began.

Men called out to their families as they ran for their homes, or from them to find a missing member. Names rang through the air as if they themselves were warnings of danger. The sound of women's voices joined the men's, shrieking terror and wailing lamentation. There was a tone in all the voices, crying, calling, ululating, that was strange; not just the pitch of fear, but a deeper resonance that Esther had never heard, but which, none the less, vibrated in a part of her that still lay dormant and was recognised as despair, as horror. When death occurred, as it had so often during the sickness, men and women had raised their voices in grief, but this noise was different, more terrible; not just the combined sound of individual voices mourning the dead, but a choir of desolation, of hopelessness. The massed voices, not only of the living, but of generations gone and yet to come, cried out to a God whom they knew was no longer there to hear them.

Esther recognised it as the sound, rendered human, of the *shofar* that the rabbi blew in the synagogue on the Day of Atonement. He put the curled ram's horn to his lips and blew a note that pierced the heart. Her father had told her, as he held her up to see above the rocking heads of men praying, that it called to God for forgiveness. But it seemed to Esther that it echoed too closely the chant of human voices, and did not reach to God. She thought it was not loud enough, and had too much sadness in its sound.

Suddenly there was a stillness in the group. The roar of the murderous rage coming towards them broke over the cluster of houses, like the wave meeting the rocky shore, drowning the cries of the inhabitants; but as it did so Esther felt the tremor in those close to her die down. Somehow each member of the family touched all the others. Esther was in the centre; Father and Mother stood, their heads close, their arms surrounding the children and their grandmother like a wall. Rebekah and Esther held each other and rested against the bodies of their parents. A heart beat in the smallest child's chest, but it seemed as if it were all their hearts giving a rhythm to the stillness that came over them.

As the crowd of flagellants and townspeople approached the house their howling peaked. The mob screamed fury at the Jews, who, in every house now, waited, still and silent, and dedicated their forthcoming work to the glory of God. The well-poisoners, the Christ-killers, the usurers, the heathen filth, the slaves of the Devil, of the very Antichrist himself, had failed in their mission to pervert the goodness of the world, and to undo the sacrifice of the Lord's only son, made flesh in the living Christ.

'Repent! Repent!' they screamed. 'If you value your lives, repent!' But their voices were too loud for them to hear if anyone responded.

And then, for Esther, the sound of the tumult outside their door disappeared into silence. Her father's voice was all that she heard, intoning softly, '*Shema, ysrael Adonay Elohaynu Adonay echad . . . .*'

They beat her father first, laying about his head with clubs, knocking him to the floor to stop his voice, but even as Esther saw him lie bleeding and broken and finally still, she continued to hear only the sing-song of her father's prayer, '*Baruch shem kevod malchuto le'olam va-ad . . .*'

Everything else was silence. Her mother's mouth opened, but no scream came that Esther heard.

There were too many people in the small kitchen; the walls seemed to bulge out of shape. From Esther's height there were only parts of people, seemingly disconnected, a confused forest of limbs: legs that kicked, arms that dragged the little group apart. They tore their mother away, although her hand seemed to clutch at Esther's even when she could see her pushed to the ground, and the feet kicking and kicking at her head and body.

Bubba was so small and frail that she seemed to float away on a sea that threw her tumbling over and over into the air, and then back down again, only to be tossed once more against the soundless storm that broke her fragile old bones to pieces.

Esther saw Rebekah cry out as she was finally parted from her, though still she heard nothing. Her sister crumpled, falling along an arm that had held a skinning knife, as if she were leaning on it for support. Her face, Esther thought, looked so grown up resting on its side against the crook of the arm, her dark eyes thoughtful, staring unblinking at the wall, until the arm jerked back, pulling the blooded steel out of her and she folded like a doll of straw to the ground.

Esther stood alone in a pool of silence. A large hand closed around her neck, and lifted her up so that her feet left the ground while a thumb pressed down against her throat. She felt no pain, just as she heard no noise, but she noticed how snugly the hand fitted around her and she liked the feel of warm flesh against her skin, now that there was no one left to hold her. Somewhere across the room, paper was flying about, promises crumpled and torn. People scrabbled on the floor for coins that someone had let fall from her father's casket. She was surprised that they didn't know how cross Father would be. No one was allowed to touch his casket. Then a hand grasped the wrist of the hand that held and squeezed Esther by the neck. A woman mouthed something, and the hand released its grip and let her fall to the ground.

Esther thought that she would sleep because everything was very strange, so much happening, and the peculiar silence. She lay where she had fallen, ignoring the movement of feet around her that were now making for the door. She was tired and she wanted her mother. She put her thumb into her mouth and sucked hard on it. Within seconds she was fast asleep, and completely unaware when the hand that had held her round the neck lifted her up and threw her carelessly over a shoulder.

9

ESTHER LAY IN bed on her side, the pillow beneath her cheek wet from the tears that had seeped through her closed eyelids. She was not asleep, but not yet herself, still in the wilderness that was called Esther, but was not *her*.

The irritation from a runnel of tears along her uppermost cheekbone and across the bridge of her nose brought her closer to the boundary line of everyday awareness. She crossed the thin, dark line between what was and what is. The wetness across her face, and the damp patch under her cheek signalled the present, the reality of her flesh, of cotton, of a sentient body in touch with the material of the world.

Esther. This Esther. Now.

Then relief. Yes, solid. Yes, real. And something more. Not the other one. Thank God, *this* is me. Thank God. Put the terror, the sadness away. Not yours. Not really. That terror, that sadness, not mine. Let it go.

Another day. This Esther of the present. Plates waiting to be fired. A visit from Karen. Katya. Worry about Katya. Call the police.

Esther turned over. The fresh cotton under her cheek dried the remaining moisture. She opened her eyes.

There were noises in the kitchen. Esther got out of bed, her head still fogged, her body rocky; her biology, at least, not quite separated from the place between oblivion and now.

Rob was in the kitchen, making coffee. Esther stood in the doorway clutching her dressing-gown to her breast, bemused at the sight. He turned and saw her.

'I've come straight from the hospital. Is it OK if I make some coffee?'

Esther made a gesture, turning one hand palm-upwards and

waving it vaguely towards the coffee machine.

'Mmm. How did you get in?' she asked, trying to make herself come properly awake.

'I've still got a key. You don't mind? It was just that . . .'

Esther interrupted him.

'It's OK. How's Felix? You look terrible, have you been there all night?'

'He's passed the crisis. He'll be all right, but he's very weak. Any news of Katya?'

Esther shook her head, and got two mugs out of the cupboard. Rob sat hunched over his coffee.

'If . . . when they find her, what will happen?'

'I don't know. We have to decide. It depends on what kind of state she's in. I suppose she'll have to go back into hospital . . .'

'I wish I'd known . . .'

Esther snapped.

'You *did* know. At any rate you were told. I *told* you. I kept telling you that she was acting strangely, but you were too busy to see her. You've hardly done more than speak to her on the phone for weeks. I told you she wasn't eating and how worried I was, and you said don't worry, it's just a phase, but you didn't have to live with it. And it wasn't just a phase . . .'

'All *right*,' Rob said impatiently. An old, married tone was appearing in both their voices. 'There's no point in going on at me. It's too late now. Felix was ill. I had enough on my plate.'

'What, three months ago? Felix was ill three months ago?'

'He's been ill off and on for the last six months.'

'What?'

Esther noticed again how awful he looked. Esther's anger at his withdrawal from parental responsibility disappeared beneath worry for the old friend that he was.

'I just wish you'd told me how serious it was,' Rob said.

Friendship disappeared and old fury re-emerged in Esther at the unequal emotional division of labour.

'I did. Katya needs a father. *I* need Katya to have a father.'

Rob's shoulders sunk under the pressure. He fought back.

'Maybe you shouldn't have been so demanding.'

'I'm *not* demanding. I always offered her choices. I let her make her own mind up about things.'

'Exactly. Maybe you gave her too many choices. You demanded that she chose. She's a child. Even when she was still a baby you were making her choose. You never just put food down in front of her, you offered her a choice. Do you want egg or porridge? Children shouldn't have to decide so many things.'

'Children are people,' Esther said angrily. 'People need information about what's available, and to make their own informed decision. Katya's very grown up for her age. She thinks sensibly about things.' She remembered. 'She used to think sensibly . . .'

'She was too grown up. She had too many choices and she finally went crazy with them. Food is one thing, but you were always offering her this or that view of the world. *Telling* her everything, not waiting for her to ask, and giving her more information than she wanted or could handle. You never gave her a straightforward "this is it".'

'How could I? Nothing is *it*.'

'That's your problem, you don't have to impose it on your child.'

'Our child.' Esther stared fiercely at her ex-husband. 'And if we're talking about confusing choices, how do you think she felt about her late-developing father deciding that he was gay and moving in with a male lover when she was eight years old?' Her voice rose as she spoke. Suddenly, she shrieked, 'What's wrong with Felix?' her voice crinkling at the edges with panic.

Rob stared at her for a moment, but it didn't seem as if he saw her. The silence bellowed after the noise of their shouting stopped. Rob dropped his head into his hands and began to weep.

Esther kept very still. She heard Rob sobbing and her own heart racing. For a long time she said nothing, keeping her palms flat on the table and staring at the top of Rob's head. She noticed how much his hair had thinned.

'You?' she said eventually.

Rob lifted his head, his eyes damp mirrors of despair.

'I'm OK, at the moment,' he said grimly.

Esther began to see another enormity enter the outskirts of her life.

Rob shook his head, as if disposing of a parasite.

'Let's just leave it, now. OK? About Katya. Is it the right thing to let her go back to the hospital?'

Esther forced her mind back.

'Not according to Ben,' she sighed.

'Oh yes, Ben must be having a field day.' Rob smiled. 'Katya's the victim of our neurotic behaviour, I suppose? He may be right. You may be right. It does begin to look rather as if the sins of the father are being visited on – everyone in sight, doesn't it? In public I fight it like hell, but sometimes, when I'm not concentrating hard, the word "punishment" creeps to the tip of my tongue.'

'Don't.'

'I try not to. I'm tired.'

They sat on in silence. The new disaster took over the remaining space in Esther's mind. The neat compartment that was reserved for anxiety, and that she had thought filled to capacity with worry over Katya, turned out to have adjustable walls, like a Japanese house. The perimeters shifted now to take over the space that was left, the space that had allowed her some relief and given her the possibility of thoughtlessness – a capacity to drift and stay quietly in the moment. Now there was nothing in her mind except Katya, Rob and Felix, or rather (and more alarmingly) the terrors they now represented: madness, disease, helplessness and death.

She felt she had to hold on to the actual names, the precise people, because the generalities were too dangerous. To allow foolish impossible questions to run freely through her mind would be to let all sense slip away. The dangerous question was: *Why?* There was no answer to it; there couldn't be an answer that didn't lead to another, deeper, more dangerous *Why?* She tried to hold on to the concrete *What?* and apply it to actual people and specific problems. What was to be done about . . . ?' But, at present, she couldn't do it. *Why?* kept erupting and spilling, slow and deadly, like lava, to fill her mind with what gradually solidified into horror. Usually, she had managed with the practical *What?* to make her life seem more or less workable. Problems were resolved, things went roughly as might be expected. Decisions had results that were not astonishing, not something that nobody had been able to imagine. It was an ordinary, easy story: Esther adopted, Esther educated, married, pregnant, divorced, working, managing well enough. And still, even now, looked at in one way, Esther was still all right, working, managing well enough.

But everybody else was not all right.

Suddenly, as she sat, being quietly overwhelmed over coffee at the table with Rob, a question came into her mind, one that she seemed never to have thought before, blanketing, though not dispersing, the mass of growing fear of things entirely out of control.

She spoke the question aloud.

'I wonder what my real name is.'

Rob blinked.

'What?'

'My real parents would have given me a name when I was born, wouldn't they? Dinah and Geoffrey told me that they called me Esther, when they got me. I never thought to ask them what my real mother and father named me.'

Rob knew Esther well enough to understand that, however it may seem to him, this was probably not the irrelevant, frivolous question it appeared. On the other hand, he was a practical man who looked for workable answers to problems.

'It doesn't matter,' he suggested through a haze of worry and exhaustion. 'You've been Esther for all but a few weeks of your life. You're Esther.'

Esther had married Rob for his practical solutions as much as anything else. For his birthday, not long ago, she had made him a plate that had 'I wouldn't worry about it if I were you' painted in the centre, with a rambling yellow rose entwined in the lettering. *I wouldn't worry about it if I were you* was Rob's answer to all anxiety about what might happen, but hadn't happened yet. Esther had put a good deal of effort into trying to learn to use his response, to put worry into abeyance. All very well, but, more often than not, the problem Esther had foreseen did actually come to pass. All right, Rob would say, but at least we haven't had to worry about it until now. Well, *he* hadn't had to. Esther saw the advantage of this, but wondered if something, at least, might not have been averted if they had given some thought to the possibilities before they became reality. And anyway, Rob's capacity not to worry was, she reckoned, organic. If he *were* her, he would have worried. And Esther did worry, quietly, achingly, guiltily, although she had to admit that what might happen usually seemed to happen anyway, so Rob was basically right.

'I suppose so,' Esther said, still trying to see it Rob's way.

But after Rob had gone, and she went up to her studio to begin firing yesterday's crazed plates, Esther was left with a gnawing sense that if she could just know her real name, everything else would work out all right.

The doorbell rang just as Esther had finished the last of a series of sketches that seemed to be a development of the *Waste Not Want Not* pattern that was baking in the kiln.

Karen came bustling in with an armload of groceries that she put away in the fridge and kitchen cupboards while Esther made some coffee.

'Are you working?'

'Mmm, I've got a design going. Well, a series, really. It's different from the stuff I usually do.'

Karen was delighted to hear that Esther was working. She thought it was the only way she could keep sane.

'Can I see them?'

Esther led Karen into the studio.

'I don't know how the design will develop beyond this. Perhaps it won't. But those are the next ones I'm going to make.'

She indicated a line of painted sketches ranged along the back of the worktable, propped against the wall. They all used the same colours as the original pattern, bright-blue, red and yellow, but the shapes and sizes of the segments of colour and their black boundaries differed. In one drawing, the sections around the edges were quite narrow compared to the blocks in the middle, as if they were being pushed off the edge by pressure from the centre. This was taken up in the next drawing, but there were only three large sections on the circular plate shape: blue, yellow and red, just one of each, side by jagged, black-outlined side. But the red section was smaller than the other two, pushed over, marginalised. And in the third drawing, there was no more than a sliver of blue, most of the plate being divided between the red and yellow. In the fourth drawing, it was the yellow that was marginalised. Taken together, it looked as if the colours were struggling for their place on the plate. Sometimes one colour predominated, sometimes two shared the larger space.

Karen admired the colours.

'Which one are you going to use?' she asked, after examining them for a few moments.

'All of them. I'm going to make a dinner service. Large plates, side plates, and soup bowls, using all the different patterns.'

'Different patterns for each kind of plate?' Karen tried to imagine it on a table.

'No, I'll use the patterns at random. It should be quite effective.'

'You'll make everyone too dizzy to eat.'

Esther shrugged and smiled.

'Well, the food on them will just have to be good enough to compensate.'

'What if someone wants just one of the patterns for their dinner service?' Karen wondered, still doubtful about their saleability.

'Not allowed. It's all or nothing.'

'Why?'

Esther turned to look at Karen who had sat down in the purple armchair.

'I don't know,' she said.

10

FOR AS LONG as she could remember Elizabeth had woken in the morning, not to a new day, but to a new death. As the dawn broke and the light began to irritate her brain into consciousness, the bad dream came. Not that she could ever remember anything about it but the final seconds, when a great pressure stopped up the breath in her lungs so that her chest expanded and expanded with the trapped air desperate for escape, fighting for freedom and finding none. The agony stopped abruptly and there was blankness, oblivion, a time – a dream time, without duration – of nothing, until her eyes opened and saw the dim grey light of what she understood was death.

Every morning she woke to a new after-life, and waited, searching for something that was never found, until the sweet, fetid smell of the warm straw pallet beneath her, and the sound of the animals waiting with increasing impatience to be tended told her it was morning, and not death, and that she, Elizabeth, had better get up and on with the day.

The *something wrong* of every morning was not exactly righted by her daily realisation of who and where she was. The mystery of what was never found in those early seconds was not resolved by the coming of reality. It was not a solution to the problem, only a practical necessity that pushed the earlier discomfort into its daytime corner of her mind. That she was Elizabeth, and had to get up to milk the goat, and feed the hens was not an answer, although it did provide her with the knowledge that she was not dead. A sense of strangeness permeated her day, but, knowing that this was how it had always been for her, she supposed that this was what it was like for everyone, and this gave her a sense of normality.

Strangeness, familiar to her as life itself, became life itself, and the fact that the other people in the town gave no indication of feeling it only reinforced her sense of its everyday ordinariness. A sense of not *belonging* made her certain that she belonged. This was the nature of the life she woke up to every morning, as, she was sure, did everyone else.

She imagined her mother waking to see her father snoring next to her on their pallet on the other side of the upstairs room where they all slept, and blinking with surprise to see him, wondering who he was and how they came to be lying so close. Her father, snoring awake, would have the same confusions. And then recognition or resignation would make them grunt a greeting or complaint to each other. The same for everyone. When little Christian snuffled and moaned awake, either on their parents' mattress or hers, depending on where his nightly stumbles had finally landed him, she supposed that he, too, gazed for a brief second with surprise at the world to which he found himself waking. Perhaps he was too young yet, at seven, to know that what he was feeling was strangeness; certainly it didn't appear to worry him, but Elizabeth couldn't imagine that there was any other way.

This morning Christian was beside her, huddled for warmth against her rough woven blouse and skirt. His face was pressed against her chest and she could feel his warm, damp breath through the layers of cloth against her skin. She looked down at him and began lazily to pick a louse or two from the wayward blond curls that hid his face. She stopped after a moment, because she didn't want to wake him. She preferred to get up before the others and do her morning chores in peace and quiet. When Christian woke early he would follow her about, whining and bothering her with questions to which she didn't know the answer. She liked to have some moments to herself at the beginning of the day. Later on, when she tried to find some time on her own, she would be disturbed by her mother or father, or Christian, calling out to her.

Elizabeth? Where is that girl? Why is she never here when there is work to do?

Elizabeth, where are you? I've an errand for you.

Lizbet, I want you. Tell me a story. I'm hungry. Show me the fish in the stream.

Elizabeth pushed back the sacking that covered her, and gently, so as not to disturb Christian, she got up and pulled on her woollen stockings against the chill of the morning. She could see the still-sleeping forms of her mother and father in the half-light as she turned to face the crucifix above their pallet, lowered her head and made the sign of the cross over her torso. 'Name of the Father, Son and Holy Ghost,' she muttered hurriedly under her breath, then picked up her thick-soled leather sandals, and climbed down the rough wooden steps with them in her hands to the room where the family did most of its daytime living. She put her shoes on and splashed some water over her face from the bucket that stood by the still-smouldering fire, and carefully unlatched the door as the church bell began to clang its tuneless declaration of morning.

She might have been the only person awake in the world, for all that she knew that in every house in the town and surrounding countryside people were walking and sleepily beginning their day. It was still not properly light; a grey mist hung in the air and the ground was chill and damp from the night and the morning dew. Elizabeth smelt moist hay, and the peculiar special scent of the day almost ready to begin. She wondered always what happened to that smell once the sun had risen fully. It disappeared into the rays of the sun, perhaps, drawn up like the souls of the dead to heaven. That was the story she told Christian when he woke early and insisted on sharing her morning. The scent of dawn was the waiting spirits of all those who had died in the night, gathered in the blades of grass, longing for the tolling of the church bell and sunrise to guide them home, upwards to the warmth of the new sun. And when the ground dried out and the smell had gone, so had the souls of the dead, and the day belonged once more to the living.

'Yes, but what about the souls of bad people? What about the ones that don't go to heaven?' Christian had demanded.

'They have to gather somewhere else,' Elizabeth would tell her little brother. 'They hang around the bogs and mires and murky dark places where the rays of the sun never reach. The stink you can smell is their rotting souls, trapped in the shadows and the filthy stagnant water.'

'Why don't they go to hell? Father Anslem says the souls of bad people go to hell.'

'That *is* hell,' Elizabeth would answer, more absorbed in holding the goat still so that she could milk it. Then, growing interested in the thought and reversing her abstractedness, she would allow her fingers to squeeze the teats automatically and give her main attention to expanding the explanation. 'Bad souls have to stay here, in the worst places on God's earth. That's why God made them, that's what they're for. Why else would there be stinking bogs, silly boy? You know that everything God made is good. Why else would He have made bad places, if not for bad souls?'

Sometimes Christian allowed this explanation to convince him. Elizabeth was as good as grown up and so should know what was what; and it sounded right to him. But sometimes he knew there was something wrong with her story. For one thing, it wasn't the same story as anyone else told him about God and souls, and heaven and hell. It troubled him that it should be so different from what the priest and his mother and father told him. It bothered him, too, that there should be such a mingling of live and dead here in his everyday world, when he felt such different things ought to be separated by great unimaginable spaces of sky and underworld. He did not like the idea of sharing his daily life with wicked souls, even if they *were* all packed together in the smellier parts of the earth; there were enough smelly, stagnant places near by to make it impossible for him to avoid them entirely, even in the course of a single day's roaming about. Far too often, he would crash through some wooded place to find himself face to face with exactly the kind of stench-ridden hole that the wicked dead lurked in. He felt the sharpness that filled his nostrils as the fingers of the dead, pulling him towards the dark still water, trying to make him one of them. He would gasp and make the sign of the cross while pinching his nose closed with his fingers, and run as fast as he could to the safety of the sunshine and fresh air.

He didn't even, if the truth were known, very much like the idea of the good souls who waited in the morning for the sun to lift them up. He was always careful not to go out early without Elizabeth as his protector, and worried very much about treading on a soul or two.

'What if I squash one?' he asked anxiously, stepping carefully, but how could you step carefully enough not to tread on invisible souls? 'Will God punish me? Will I have to go to the smelly places when I die?'

'Don't be silly,' Elizabeth would say impatiently, returning her concentration to the milk dripping into the wooden bucket, and the fidgety goat. 'Souls are ethereal. How can you tread on something ethereal?'

Christian didn't know what ethereal was, but didn't ask in case he managed to work out a way of treading on them anyway. He accepted Elizabeth's disdainful answer to his question and allowed his ignorance of its meaning to comfort him. None the less, he was inclined to look where he walked, and tread cautiously until the sun was well up and the day bright and warm.

This morning Elizabeth thought she smelled fox, a high note in the usual dewy smell, and went straight to the hen house to check that all was well. The chickens clucked busily at her and seemed no more than hungry, so perhaps the fox had found her prey elsewhere that night, and only passed by, assuring herself of the availability of another meal when it should be needed.

Elizabeth collected the warm eggs, and threw the hens the scraps left over from last night's meal, and a little maize. She milked the goat in the growing light, resting her head against the wiry belly swollen with soon-to-be-born kid. She listened with one ear to the internal rumblings and heavings of the pregnant goat, and with the other to the waking birds calling from the nearby woods and warning off intruders from their patch of the world.

It was all fresh and new, this day, life waking and asserting itself, and Elizabeth, out there and part of the beginning, was almost entirely persuaded that this was where she belonged. The feeling of strangeness lost its definition and hid away for the time being. Just occasionally, for a second now and then during the day, there would come over her a pang, like a small gust of warm wind, a passing breeze, that denied her place in the world and gave her a momentary familiar sense of wrongness. She would straighten up and stand still, feeling an odd hollowness within her, as it seemed to pass through her and disappear into the air from which she was sure it had come. She never thought about it as something particularly to

71

do with her, but rather as a side effect of God's will which she could hardly expect to understand. It was just part of the mystery and oddness of the world. But, for all her acceptance, she had moments when she wanted to be sure that she was just like everyone else.

'Do you sometimes feel – as if you weren't *you*?' she once asked Christian while she was scrubbing turnips and carrots for the soup pot.

Christian had looked up from the stick he was shaping into a spear and said, 'What?' with a look that said that girls, grown-ups, his sister in particular, or a combination of them all, were very peculiar.

Elizabeth tended to try out dangerous questions on Christian first, to get a reaction, because he was clever for his age, and yet young enough not to brood or discuss the things she said with anyone else. It was almost like talking to herself, except that she could hear the words, and that, in itself, was useful. As soon as she had asked the question about feeling like oneself, and heard it put into words, she knew not to ask anyone else. It sounded silly actually spoken, and there were enough differences between her and the others of her age in the town without drawing more attention to herself.

She had friends, of course, who she met and spent some of her spare time with, though there was precious little of that, and she did like to be on her own quite often. But there was a distance between them and her, even lately with Greta, who she was closest to.

She didn't look like anyone else in the town. Her dark looks set her apart: the thick eyebrows that almost met across the bridge of her nose; eyes of such a deep brown that it was only by peering up close to them, and then only in the brightest light, that you could see that they weren't quite black, and did, in fact, have pupils. Her mouth was wide, with a slight fuzz of dark hair over the upper lip; her thick, coarse-curled long hair escaped even when she pulled it tightly back and covered it with a scarf. Everything about her was different from the other young people who were sturdy variations of blue-eyed blonds, the eyes sometimes shading into grey, the hair now and then a mousy light-brown. Elizabeth's looks were other, and there were some who kept well away from her. Sometimes, when she was younger, children would huddle in groups as she passed with her parents and baby brother, and whisper together. Elizabeth never knew why, except that she understood that she looked different. As the years passed (she was fourteen now, virtually a woman) the whispering got less, either because people had said whatever it was that they had to say, or simply because time and the familiar sight of her, year in and year out, had made them forget what there was to whisper about.

Her parents couldn't answer her questions about her colouring. They would chase her out of the house impatiently, telling her that they had better things to do than concern themselves with silly questions from a vain girl. But there was something troubling in their eyes. Elizabeth was not sure, but it seemed to her that there was something troubled about their eyes whenever they looked at her, as if her own black eyes bothered them and made them want to look away. Even when they looked directly at her, she felt in some way that they avoided her eyes. There was a kind of awkwardness, a shiftiness even, in their dealings with her that she never observed when they spoke to others.

She felt from an early age that they did not love her, although they never said so. It was not a time or place for extravagant, open affection. Life was too hard and short for that, but still she had seen in the faces of other mothers and fathers a look of pleasure, a kind of light, as they watched their little ones or spoke of them. She saw nothing of this in her own parents, except in their dealings with Christian. Elizabeth simply accepted it and grew to understand that this, too, had to do with her unusual looks. She felt that she embarrassed them, and she was sorry for it. But the lack of warmth was reciprocated. Elizabeth did not feel close to her mother and father, although she was a dutiful and hardworking daughter.

Apart from Christian, whom she loved despite her parents' obvious preference for him, there was only Greta, who was the same age as her, the daughter of the woodcarver who lived in the next house. Greta's father made wooden dolls for his daughter, and the two girls, when they were little, would spend hours dressing them and inventing stories about them. Greta always wanted them to be a family and made them lead the life she knew about from her surroundings, but

73

sometimes Elizabeth tired of this, and made them wanderers and adventurers who went far afield, sometimes to the city, unimaginable miles away, where no one in reality, except the priest, had ever been. Later they talked about the future, as their bodies developed, Elizabeth's a little before Greta's, and shared in the strange business of becoming a woman, of growing breasts and hips and hair in places that had been naked, of bleeding monthly and accepting the dragging pains that were not signs of illness but their lot as women. They spoke of these changes and what they portended with a mixture of fear and excitement, disturbed that their bodies carried them in directions over which they seemed to have no control, and yet feeling strangely powerful and secretly special that such dramatic, private things should happen to them. Greta had been a loyal friend who stood by Elizabeth, different as she might be. When the boys whispered and pointed, and sometimes called out names at her that neither girl understood, Greta would take Elizabeth's arm and steer her firmly away, calling names back at the boys, and lifting her head high against their stupidity.

But recently a new reticence, a discomfort, had crept in on Greta's part. Elizabeth understood what it was about. Greta was a strong, good-looking girl; her eyes were a sharp blue, and her hair thick and fair. She smiled easily and was competent at all the tasks girls were required to do within the family. For the last few months she had been an object of interest and some rivalry among the local youths. For a few weeks she walked back from church on Sundays with Pieter, the barrel maker's son, then others had taken his place. She had taken to dressing in her best cotton blouse and Sunday stockings for market days, and Elizabeth noticed a new swing to her hips when she walked in public, and a busyness about her eyes that seemed to try and take in, without seeming to, much more than just what was in front of her. Tomas had become a regular visitor, and walked with Greta in the fields outside the town. Sometimes Greta went at midday with bread and goat cheese to the fields Tomas worked with his father. She had far less time for Elizabeth.

But there was more than just a lack of time about the new distance between them. There were no boys visiting Elizabeth's house. No strong, work-hardened arms offered to her after church. Elizabeth's body had changed. Although it was more rounded, it was still slim. Her breasts were small with long dark nipples, her legs narrowed down to delicate ankles. Her bones defined her shape rather than her flesh. She did not have the sturdy voluptuousness of Greta and other local girls that suggested a strong arm and a capacity for hard work, abandoned sex and vigorous childbearing. There was a grace, a fineness about Elizabeth's body that gave her an elegiac quality. Her sexuality was contained: dark, delicate and promising, offering a mystery that would require a long, delicious unravelling by someone interested in the subtle pleasures of discovery. Such people were not to be found among the sons of the neighbouring artisans, and local farmers' boys. Courtship was tied to the needs of survival. Young men who sought bawdy fun with girls with strong arms and thighs to wrap around them found it, and, at the same time, tested for wives with the right qualities for the hard struggle of production and reproduction. Most of the girls were pregnant when they married, and, if the Church called it a shame and the young men and women hung their heads dutifully, the reality was that men wanted fecund women who would provide them with strong sons to work for them, and marriageable daughters to make useful alliances with other families. A pregnant bride was evidence of a right enough choice.

Elizabeth was, moreover, clever. Rumour had it that she could read, and it was true. She had begged the priest to teach her when she saw him one day poring over a manuscript. It seemed, even at ten, a precious piece of magic. That someone, miles or years away, could make marks on parchment, and that she, here and now, might take a meaning from it, might actually be able to see into someone's thoughts who was not present, could only be magic, and she wanted this power for herself. When, after much pleading, the priest had agreed to give her lessons (though he insisted that they must be secret), she learned something even more extraordinary and exciting: not only could she learn to read other people's marks, but, once she had, she too could make her thoughts fly across space and time. She could learn to write as well as read. It was, however, to be kept a secret, and she must never be seen reading or writing. It was unthinkable that someone of her condition, and a girl, should have such an ability. In fact, it was remarkable that the priest himself should have it. Most local priests were sons of the area with hardly more education than their parishioners. Father Anselm was a stranger. The gossips said that he was the son of a noble who had trained in Rome itself and was expected to gain high office – a bishopric at least. But something had happened, though no one knew what, and he had chosen to be a local priest in a small market town with a church whose bell was cracked and tuneless. No one had any facts, and no one knew anyone who had, but the story got around and stuck, just as, in spite of no one ever witnessing Elizabeth's reading skills, word had it, though no one really believed it, that she could read and write, and therefore the damning label of *cleverness* had become attached to her and made her all the more unmarriageable.

Greta's new distance from her friend was not out of spite or contempt, but from discomfort, now that her life was taking its proper course and Elizabeth's, plainly, was not. Greta might protect her friend from the malice of others, but, now that she was being fully absorbed into the world of the others, she had to leave Elizabeth behind. She still remained friendly, and they visited each other and shared some of the daily chores, but much of Greta's life now was experience of which Elizabeth knew nothing. Greta felt the lack of huddling with another girl of her own age and giggling and whispering about this boy or that, about what he had done to her, and had her friend's lover done that, too? This conversation, that they had had not so long ago about their changing bodies, was no longer possible with Elizabeth. Greta did not dismiss Elizabeth from her life, but she found other girlfriends to talk to about what mattered most.

Elizabeth did not mind very much about not being courted, and she understood that her new distance from Greta was inevitable. But she was lonely, and started to wonder more if her sense of strangeness *was* actually what everyone else experienced. She began to redefine the word, to give it, in fact, its real meaning, and see that perhaps *she* was strange, and not at all like everyone else. Partly, this was a comfort to her, but deep down she was frightened by a vision of loneliness that stretched out, not just into the future, but appeared to have been the reality of the past, too. The certainty that her inner feelings were no different from other people's began to crumble, and left her not just a stranger in a community she had spent all her life in, but a stranger, too, to herself. The re-evaluation of herself was painful and deeply frightening.

There was only Father Anselm to whom she could speak of her fears. They had never spoken of such things before. He had schooled her in letters, but maintained a distance from her that precluded intimacy. Of course, she went to confession every week, but since Father Anselm was hidden behind a grill she never felt that she was speaking to *him*. It was also the case that what she confessed to were never the things that really troubled her about herself. Although her, 'Bless me, Father, for I have sinned,' prefaced the list of laziness, spiteful thoughts, omissions of duty, and distractedness in church she offered each week, the truth was that she never really believed in them as sins. She knew these things to be human frailty, weaknesses, but she couldn't think of them as offensive to God. For one thing, why should God bother himself with such petty failings? But, more than that, the God Elizabeth envisaged was not alienated from her because, in a careless moment, she had knocked over the bucket of warm goat's milk. The lost milk mattered, because the family relied on it. But the actual sin, the thoughtlessness, did not seem to Elizabeth something she had to atone to God for. She would accept a beating from her father, and the shrill anger of her mother; she could quite see why these things happened. But the penance she was told to make during confession did not seem sensible. God didn't care about the milk, and her carelessness, being a worldly matter, was best left to her parents to deal with. She couldn't believe that God could stop loving her for that. If He could, He would hardly be any different from her parents, and what was the point of that?

The things she thought might most alienate her from God's love were those she was least able to offer to Father Anselm behind the grill. Most difficult were precisely her thoughts about confession. How could she use it to tell Father Anselm that she didn't believe in it? She worried, because although she had an inner certainty about it, she knew that if she was wrong she was doomed. There was only her own image of God to go on; the Church didn't make the distinction between sins against the parent, or the goat, and sins against God. These were things she longed, not to confess, but to ask about, and there was no one to ask except Father Anselm when he wasn't hidden behind the grill. But Father Anselm made it clear that their discussions were to be about nothing more than the arrangement of letters on parchment or slate. It was as if he were holding himself back from a great danger, that she herself was a danger to him, even though their meetings were confined to the teaching of reading. It made her uneasy because she couldn't understand why he should think her so dangerous; how could she be, and if she were (and she supposed Father Anselm would know better than she) did this not suggest that she *was* wrong about God's anger, and she was indeed sinful, her everlasting soul at risk?

So each week she offered the shadowy figure of Father Anselm her misdemeanours, collected through the week, indeed somewhat cherished, because if she had not forgotten this, or done that, or spilt the goat's milk, she would have had nothing to confess, and in the silence might have blurted out the things that really worried her. For example, that she no longer believed with any certainty that she was like everyone else. That in her vital core she did not love her parents, and, perhaps, did not care very much for anyone, except, possibly, Christian. That she woke each morning believing herself to be dead. These facts about herself, unwanted, but increasingly pressing on her daily existence, were, she suspected, serious sins of the heart. If God could be moved to anger, this absence of feeling, surely, this sense of herself as essentially different and solitary, would be what provoked His rage. Her arrogance would be intolerable to Him, and her doubt even more so. She knew that, if she doubted such basic things as her evident place in the world, then God would understand what she didn't dare to admit often, even to herself, let alone whisper in the confessional, that the doubt was deeper still. She proved with her worldly doubts that she was capable of doubting, and, by extension, of finally denying the Church, and even God Himself. God, she thought, would not forgive His own extinction, even in the heart and mind of a young girl of no significance in the world. And she was back again to another terrible sin. These thoughts themselves were, of course, sinful. That she could even think that her own belief could endanger God was so mortal a sin that she began to feel that thought itself was the original sin that she had to deal with.

But still the thoughts came and came, as she went about her chores, doing her everyday work. Nothing seemed to stop them developing and circling back upon themselves to become greater and greater degrees of wickedness. The concern she felt about her secret feelings, and the loneliness she saw stretching ahead of her like a desert frightened her. She longed to have someone who *knew* explain to her that all was well, that she was, after all, like everyone else, and that God loved her, which was proven by the acceptance of her thoughts as not terrible or dangerous, by – whoever it was that she told. But there was no one. Who could she speak such things to? Who had the time for her nonsense? Who would understand the words she wanted to use? Or worse, who would not feel, physically different as she already was, that she had the Devil inside her to talk so? Even if she were still close to Greta, she could not have said such things. Greta would have blinked as if there had been only silence, and started to talk about how many children she might have, and who, of the various possibilities, their father would be. There was, Elizabeth knew, only Father Anselm in the whole town who would begin to understand what she was saying, but he was a priest, a man of the Church, so how could he be understanding of the terrible things she longed to say? And anyway, he made it clear that he did not want her to confide in him outside of confession. He looked at her sometimes, a sidelong glance as they were bent over a manuscript they were deciphering, and she felt rather than saw his wariness of her. Perhaps it was her strangeness, she thought, that made him feel distant from her as it did everyone else, or perhaps he suspected the wicked thoughts she harboured, and refused to give her the opportunity to speak them.

The feeling of belonging, of normality, that she had tenuously achieved this morning, had gone. She took the wooden pail of goat's milk inside the house and swung it on to the table. It was time to get fresh water from the well.

The morning's chores were not a list of things that had to be done and could be ticked off as each task was achieved. They were not separate things that needed to be sorted out before she could get on with something else and different; they, along with her tasks for the rest of the day, *were* her daily life, and there was no other kind of life than the daily one. This was true for them all, for everyone she knew and had ever known. The feeding of the animals, milking, fetching water, cooking, carding and spinning wool, rendering down fat for the dim illumination of long, dark winter nights *was* living. But now the oddest thought came into her mind. It was a question about the business of the day which, until now, had required no more thought than the fact that she slept at night. As she let go of the handle of the pail and began to move towards the water bucket by the hearth, the question came into her head as though someone else were speaking it.

It was: *What for?*

It might have been Latin for all the sense it made. *What for?* was without meaning. There was no *What for?* You woke up and did what was necessary to keep you and your kin fed and warm for the day, hoping, perhaps, that a small part of what you did would spill over and go a little way towards maintaining the situation for the future, which was defined, simply and vaguely enough, as tomorrow. You fed the chickens in the unconsidered hope that they would be alive and laying the next morning. Perhaps *What for?* belonged to the realm of feeding the chickens. But, in reality, it belonged nowhere. That they needed eggs tomorrow went without saying; why should anyone think about it? The priest promising good souls a reward in the hereafter might suggest the answer to *What for?* but, in reality, the hereafter just *was*, and nobody actually thought about it, except, possibly, at the Sunday mass, when the host was placed on the tongue to connect you, earth thing, to the everlasting. But even that was no more than something you did; a Sunday task, another practical necessity, so embedded in life that it carried the same weight as pulling parsnips for the soup. No light thing, the preparation of sustenance, or the requirements of the priests, but not weighty, either; necessary, but nothing to ponder over.

But Elizabeth had dredged up this thought, this *What for?*, or more correctly had found it floating in an empty space in her head, and the mere fact of the existence of this space, let alone the nonsensical question that filled it, made her fear for her normality. To be not-normal, to the other, was to be a fool or mad. There was no third possibility. If you didn't see things the way they were, the way everyone knew they were without having to think about it, there was no place for you other than at the edges of the town, roaming, muttering nonsense, dependent on the gruff generosity of the townsfolk who might look the other way as you scrambled under stalls for scraps on market days, or throw you a crust of bread so long as you went on your way soon enough, back to the perimeter, where you belonged. It was a way of life that was outside life, that was not about continuing to perform the daily work that was living, but that depended on others to keep you alive, and absorbed so little of your time and effort that the madness ran rife in the empty spaces of your existence. At best there was pity for these poor souls, if souls they were. What other alternative was there to work, from morning to dark, except to wander, mad and mendicant, at the mercy of thoughts that could not be thought by anyone but the inadequate and soft-headed?

There was nothing for Elizabeth's *What for?* to attach itself to. No problem that required such a question to be asked. Yet, she asked it, or it asked itself. And, as it was asked, between the getting of the milk and the fetching of the day's water, it created a fissure in the day, or, as it might be, in Elizabeth's life. A before and after was brought into being that could not exist in her world. The distance between the milk and the water was not measured by distinction, not defined by before and after, but by continuation. There were no such distinctions in life, no disjunctions, but only the comfortable, solid certainty of perpetual similarities. But now a line was drawn, a crack opened, and *What for?* stretched itself languorously into the future, and changed everything by creating future itself.

It was too late for Elizabeth to shake the question out of her thoughts, like the bugs that fell from the mattresses when she shook them out by the front door. *What for?* was there, and clung, and before she knew it there were two Elizabeths.

One of them seemed to be her, a continuation of the fourteen year old whose hands had just released the handle of the milk pail. But it was the other one who got on with the day's business. Elizabeth-who-was-herself watched as the other one crossed the flagstone floor and picked up the water bucket. She even had time, before the busy Elizabeth walked through the door and slopped the stale water on to the kitchen garden, to think that she had never seen herself from behind; had never, actually, seen herself in full, from head to toe. This thought should have terrified her, perhaps, and made her doubt her sanity as she had only a moment before. But it did not, because the Elizabeth who thought it was in no doubt that *she* was herself, and, in any case, the mind-rocking thought *What for?* had rendered all others, it seemed, thinkable. So, all unperturbed, she followed the other Elizabeth out and watched her go about her daily business; that other Elizabeth being untroubled, also, because the one who had had the impossible thought was not her.

11

ESTHER CAME AWAKE to find herself sobbing again. It was a few moments before the pressure of tears lightened enough to allow the sobbing to die down. She lay still in the exhausting aftermath of grief and wondered, opening her eyes to the dawn light, what she was grieving for. Whatever it was, she couldn't grasp it, only acknowledge that such a powerful sorrow had to be about *something*. There was something wrong, her mind told her, as if at the first statement of the syllogism. Some loss, a tragedy. Yet so weighty a loss had to have a name.

Her eyes, although open, were still half-seeing, focused on the space between the pillow and the duvet, a shadow place where she saw no more than if her eyes were closed. It came to her, the name. *Esther*. She had lost Esther. Close enough to being fully awake, she knew there would be little struggle finding herself this morning. There was only one Esther, no doubts, no choice.

They called me Esther, she thought to herself, and that's what I am. Only Esther. Esther the only one. One. She wanted back the confused space between oblivion and waking, for all the disturbance the confusion caused. Her grief was for the other, unknown thing that made her waking moments painful, a struggle into the daylight. She lay, almost fully awake, putting off the far too simple task of coming through to ordinary daylight.

Elizabeth, Esther thought for a fraction of a second. *Elizabeth?* she wondered. And then the name, *Katya*, and full consciousness came at the same moment bringing relief and desolation in equal parts. There was the grief, that was the name. All the rest, the strange searchings and lost fragments, were nothing more than evasions of the awful moment when she must wake (far too early, of course, to be able to do anything, if there *was* anything to do) and remember that Katya was missing, sick and missing, and anxiety had come to take its triumphant place, dead centre in Esther's life.

12

ELIZABETH'S MORNING HAD gone well. She had finished her chores before Christian and her parents woke, and breakfasted in silence, breaking chunks of bread into a wooden bowl filled with still-warm goat milk.

At some moment, while she raked the cold cinders from the fire and blew the remaining embers back into life, Elizabeth rejoined herself. But the split remained. The Elizabeth who was herself settled back into the space that *What for?* had created without actually losing her sense of separateness. Once she understood that she was free to come and go as she wished, while the more corporeal version of herself would continue to behave as if nothing special had occurred, she was happy to return. Elizabeth would do what she had to do, but now there was another part of her that stood to one side, or hovered two or three feet above her head watching and asking inconceivable questions, who began not to think of herself as Elizabeth, although she didn't know why, since it was precisely that part that was who she was.

She didn't worry. She felt extraordinarily light, as if the pull of the earth itself had lessened its grip. The question that this morning had seemed unaskable and had caused her to come into existence, nameless, watchful and incorporeal, was now something that could not only be asked, but could also have an answer. She didn't know what the answer was, but she knew there was an answer and that she could find it, though she wasn't certain how. *What for?* was the reason for her existence, and in some sense she understood that, in her new determination to ask the impossible question and discover the answer, she had answered it already.

What for? was no more than a beginning. In the space where the real her existed, the ghosts of other questions jostled for recognition. A vague muddle of query grew like a fungus on stale bread, its spores hovering in the air, recognising a host on which they could thrive. They settled in the place where *What for?* had grown and waited for their further development.

Father Anselm's face grew dark when he saw Elizabeth slip through the side door of the church. He was kneeling in front of the rough altar, his head bent, when he saw the movement from the corner of his eye. He crossed himself and stood, turning towards Elizabeth who had stopped when she saw him at prayer.

'I'm sorry, Father. I didn't want to interrupt you.'

Father Anselm's thin lips elongated slightly into something like a smile. It was not a greeting to Elizabeth, but a private, wry smile to himself, as if he had been caught red-handed doing something distasteful and were acknowledging the fact of his discovery. The sour smile lasted for no more than a fraction of a second before his long face became serious and fell back into its usual wary look.

He stared solemnly at the child in front of him, taking in the strange glow of excitement that lit up her eyes. They had always been intelligent, those eyes, long, almond-shaped, dark-lashed as if they had been painted, and so dark it was scarcely possible to look at them without a feeling that one was being drawn into their depths to drown in their blackness. The glow, however, was new and seemed to make it even more difficult to avoid their demanding stare.

'Elizabeth, my child, what is it? Has something happened?'

She shook her head vigorously, wanting to dispel the alarm she saw in his face.

'No, everything's fine. There's nothing wrong. I just wanted to talk to you.'

Father Anselm did not look relieved to hear that all was well. His eyes darted directly at her once or twice, and then returned to their more usual gaze to one side of her face, seeming to look at something standing behind her shoulder.

'Can't it wait until tomorrow? Weren't you going to come and read tomorrow morning?'

'Yes, I was . . . I will. Only, I wanted to talk to you.'

Reluctantly, Father Anselm took her by the arm. Only his fingertips touched the coarse woollen stuff of her sleeve just above the elbow. He guided her to a rush stool and sat down himself on the edge of one just across the narrow aisle. He was a thin man in his middle thirties, and tall compared to the more stocky local people. As if this worried him, he affected a permanent stoop, which had the effect of making him seem older and also somewhat furtive, as though he were concealing something with his rounded shoulders and lowered head. His prominent, almost pointed, cheekbones gave his eyes a sunken, dark appearance, and a square jaw and chinbone made his long face seem to slope outward from his wispy-haired flat brow to the protruding chin, almost like the head of a horse. His habitually sombre expression complemented his unprepossessing looks, as if, here at least, nature and physiognomy were at one.

He was not loved by the townspeople, who were conscious that he was not one of them, but they respected his gravity and appreciated the odd moments when he would raise his eyes and speak firmly of the duties which God's love placed upon them. Though the local people did not go about their daily tasks fully conscious of their Maker and the sacrifice He made that they might live, they felt it right and proper that the representative of His Church should remind them of what they admittedly immediately thereafter forgot – not because they did not believe, but because they believed so implicitly that conscious acknowledgement seemed, for the most part, superfluous.

There was also the mystery of Father Anselm's origins, of which he never spoke. Indeed, although he ministered to his congregation, and was with them during those singular moments when a man or woman feels the need for more than the satisfaction of food in the belly – times of birth and death and unaccountable misfortune – no one knew anything private about *him* at all. Not much in a priest's life could be private, but the older inhabitants remembered the last priest, the son of a local fishmonger, whose everyday life had required many a blind eye to be turned towards him. If people muttered about corruption and sins of the flesh, it was also true that they had a fondness for the old cleric, and protected him when the Bishop's envoy arrived to investigate an anonymous complaint of fornication. The fact that two young women had given birth to children whose father's name was no more than a whisper allowed the local population to click their tongues behind their teeth, and mutter harsh things about the Church, but in the daily world of make and make-do everybody knew how people had to have allowances made for them, and hypocrisy was no more than a grand word which did not seem to apply to the priest who had been born and grown old amongst them. Moreover, there was something like admiration, unspoken, but evident in a humorously raised eyebrow or two, that their doddery, wine-sipping old priest should manage such a feat with not one, but two of the more luscious members of his flock.

Such allowances were not so easily made for Father Anselm, however, being a foreigner and so much more a representative of the Church than a familiar. But there was nothing except his oddness of physique and close nature that gave anyone grounds for complaint. He walked alone amongst them, doing his duty, and seeming to have no ordinary interests apart from sitting cooped up in his room burning quantities of fat to enable him to read and write late into the night. The light flickering in his window gave passing members of his congregation a view of him bent over parchment, running a forefinger down his long nose, and then picking up the quill to make marks late into the night. This was an activity that no one, however suspicious they may have been of such behaviour, could find any actual fault with. It may have been without value in their own lives, but reading and writing did not seem actually corrupt or sinful. So the townspeople let it pass.

'Father,' Elizabeth began anxiously, trying to make his eyes meet hers so that he might see the importance and sincerity of her question. 'Is it wrong to think?'

His hooded eyes slowly lifted, the bulbous lids peeling back until his deep-blue irises stared straight into Elizabeth's. For a second he said nothing, but simply held her eyes with a dolorous stare. Elizabeth felt uncomfortable, as if she had said too much, had said everything and none of it could be taken back. Finally, he spoke, soft and serious.

'Think, my child?'

The spell broke and Elizabeth was freed from the sense of him prying into the furthest corners of her mind.

'Yes, Father. To have questions.'

Father Anselm remained impassive.

'And do you have questions?'

Elizabeth nodded.

'Yes, Father. I have one question. There may be more.'

'Is this not something you should speak of in confession, my child?'

Elizabeth shook her head uncertainly.

'No. It's not a confession, or, at least, it isn't yet, because if there's an answer it can't be wrong to ask it, can it? Can questions be sins?'

'Oh yes, certainly they can.' Father Anselm briefly smiled his private smile, and then straightened himself, though his shoulders were still curved in towards his chest, and placed the flat of his hands along the skirt covering his thighs. 'What is troubling you, Elizabeth, what is your question?'

'*What for?* My question is: *What for?*' Elizabeth lowered her head as she spoke, and waited.

Father Anslem's face hardened so that tensed muscles appeared above his jaw.

'I don't understand, my child. What is *what* for?' He seemed to hold his breath after he spoke.

'What is it *all* for?' Elizabeth's voice grew strong with the power of her question. 'What is the point of all the things we do, everything – working, getting up, going to sleep, marrying, having children, being me? What is the point of being *me*, particularly? Why?' Elizabeth gasped with astonishment at what she had said. She heard that it was nonsense, that it was not possible to think or ask such things, that no thoughts such as these had ever been expressed. If they were wicked, they were as wicked as it was possible to be. Could she be the wickedest person in the world?

The heavy silence grew. Elizabeth heard the sound of deep, regular breathing, but she could not tell if it came from her or Father Anselm. Eventually, the silence was broken.

'The question is sinful, my child, because it is one that you have always had the answer to, since the day of your birth. To speak it means that you have forgotten what you cannot help but know. It is a most serious sin, it is the sin of doubt.'

Elizabeth's worst fears were confirmed by the tone of Father Anselm's voice, and the look on his face, as much as by his words. But her confusion was greater than her fear. How could the question have been born in her if she knew the answer? What had happened to her, that she no longer knew what Father Anselm said had been known to her since she was born?

'What have I forgotten, Father, what?'

His lips tightened into a cruel line.

'All that we do, everything, from birth to death, is for the glory of God.' He spoke angrily, as if even having to utter such a statement filled him with disgust, so self-evident a proposition was it.

Elizabeth was familiar with the form of the words he spoke, and she trembled with the understanding that Father Anselm was right. If she questioned that, what was she? If this was not the answer before the question was ever formulated in her mind, had she taken leave of her senses, was she overcome, invaded by wickedness? But the terror did not reach every part of her, and could not prevent the Elizabeth curled up in the place of questions from speaking out, through the fearful mouth of the other one.

'What we do every day isn't glorious. Why does God need us to get up at dawn and do chores till the light fails? Why does God want our backs sore and our bellies hungry? What's the glory in that, for Him? And why does God need . . .'

'Be quiet!' Father Anselm bellowed, cutting her off. 'It is not for you to ask such things. How can you know of God's purposes? How dare you ask these questions, a child, an ignorant child?'

Elizabeth heard his anger, but something in her stiffened against it. She spoke as angrily as Father Anselm.

'I dare ask these questions, because I *thought* them.'

'You have no right to think them.'

They were both shouting now, each at the other, leaning forward across the aisle.

'But I *do* think them. I can't stop thinking. And if I'm the child of God and He made me, and I think, then it must be good, mustn't it, because He made me able to think.'

'That's enough, Elizabeth.' He stood up and towered over her, his face grey with wrath. 'I am a minister of the Church, it isn't for you to debate with me. This is more than intellectual arrogance. These are wicked thoughts that question the teachings of the Church. You cannot think them, there is no place for them. We are all children of God, there is nothing else we can be.'

'Then how can I have such thoughts? What's wrong with me?'

Father Anselm's anger seemed to leave him and be replaced by a great weariness. He sat on the edge of the stool in front of Elizabeth and rested his head in his palm, rubbing his temples with this fingers.

Still with his head buried he said quietly, 'You are not one of them, Elizabeth.'

'What do you mean?' Elizabeth was more frightened by his sudden attitude of despondency than by his earlier anger. 'Not one of the children of God? Do you mean that?' She waited, but there was only silence. 'Tell me! What do you mean? How can I not be a child of God? What does that mean? What am I?'

'Different,' Father Anselm breathed rather than spoke.

'How can I be different? There is only the Church and God. If I don't belong . . . do you mean that I am a child of the Devil?' There was no other answer, but just saying it made Elizabeth colder than she had ever felt before.

'In a manner of speaking.'

'Why me?' she asked, horrified.

'Because you are different. You are not what you seem even to yourself. Doesn't the fact that you have had these thoughts tell you that? Who else do you know who asks such a question?'

Elizabeth knew the truth that Father Anselm spoke. That the impossible question had come to her unbidden. Nothing she had ever seen or heard could make the question possible. If they were ungodly thoughts (and who else was to judge but a priest?) there was nowhere else they could have come from but a wicked heart that listened to the voice of the Devil and allowed him in. She clearly saw the logic. There was no other answer available. But still the question was there,

91

lodged in her mind, and, even if she chose not to think about where it might lead, it was clear that Father Anselm understood the mortal danger she was in. But still, when she searched her heart she could find nothing she could recognise as truly devilish, nothing that felt actually evil. Except, the thought suddenly struck her, she did not care very much for her parents, and she realised that this was also a great sin. Perhaps not her lack of feeling (who knew what other people felt or didn't feel?) but her *awareness* of her dislike for her mother and father, who were no better or worse than any other parents as far as she could see. A mind that could not stop thinking thoughts that nobody else seemed troubled with, and which could not know it was thinking them could well be a mind that had been taken over by the Devil for his own evil purposes.

'Am I evil?' she whispered, in despair of the answer she knew she must receive and of her entire existence. 'Will they burn me? Must I burn in hell?'

There was another long, unbearable silence. Eventually, Father Anselm turned to face Elizabeth, and let his hand fall so that he looked directly at her. He spoke carefully and deliberately.

'The Church would say yes. It would tell you that you have committed a grievous fault. It would say that unless you do great penance, and erase your questions entirely from your mind, you *are* of the Devil. Some would say you had been possessed for such a question to enter your mind. Yes, if you did not recant, you would burn, and yes, your soul would suffer eternal damnation. Your one question is not a single question, and I believe you know that, even if you have not yet thought out what the rest are. But you, my child, are questioning the goodness and even the existence of God. That is what you would come to eventually, if you followed your question along the path it would make in your mind. The Church would excommunicate you, cast you out. And outside the Church there is nothing, nowhere, and nobody.'

He finished talking and then sat very still, staring intently at her, while Elizabeth absorbed his words.

'But *you* are the Church's representative. What do you mean, "The Church would say"? Is that what *you* say?'

Still Father Anselm did not move; he had not so much as blinked an eye since he began talking.

'Will you recant? Will you go to confession and do penance for wicked thoughts, and then put them out of your mind for ever? Will you?'

Elizabeth dragged her eyes from Father Anselm's and looked about her, hearing the echo of his last words returned to her by the stone walls. There was nothing especially beautiful about their town's church. It was not beauty that gave it its power. But it was strong, as the whole Church was strong, and inside it was always cool and dark and quiet. A wooden statue of the Virgin gazed down at her from one side of the altar. Greta's father had made it when her brother was born and given it to the church. The Mother of the Church looked out at the individuals who entered the confines of the stone walls, her eyes seeming moist with pity. She, who had most to be pitied for, gave it instead, and offered the comfort and promise of her intercession with her son, the Christ, on behalf of the weak and helpless of the earth. Within the solid, stone walls of the church, echoing its priest's prayers back at the people, within the arms of the Virgin, all pity and all forgiveness; where else was there to be? What could a world be without those things that no one was ever without, like air, like water, like the love of God, like the teachings of the Church of God? The very structure of existence, of the body as well as the mind, was held together by the truth that the Church gave to all human souls. What shape could there be, what would hold one's body, mind, or the world itself together, if that were gone?

Elizabeth longed to throw herself into the outstretched arms of the Virgin, waiting, overflowing with forgiveness for the sins of the imperfect soul. She wanted to be comforted and forgiven. But *What for?* had taken root in her, creating the other Elizabeth, still the *real* Elizabeth, who could not be removed, not even for the love and comfort that she longed for. How can I not think what I have thought? the real Elizabeth asked the one who longed for the arms of the Virgin. And the dumb, penitent drudge had no answer.

'Elizabeth?' Father Anselm waited for her reply.

She brought herself back, and looked hard at the priest.

'I would sincerely confess and do sincere penance for having wicked thoughts, Father. But I couldn't stop thinking what I think.'

'You won't recant? Do you understand how serious this is, Elizabeth? You would have no one, no home, no family. You would be alone in the world. There would be a world of believers, and there would be you, with no one to help you or support you. You would have to live as best you could, and, yes, my child, the Church might see fit to put you on trial, if you attempted to speak your thoughts aloud. Will you repent?'

'I do repent, Father, I wish more than anything that I had never had the thought. I'd give up everything, even my life, if I could make it so that it had never happened. But the thought is there. I still have a question that hasn't been answered.'

'But it *has* been answered. I told you, it is for the glory of God. Can't you accept that and let the question go?'

'I would let it go, but it won't leave.'

Father Anselm took a deep breath.

'Recant, my child.'

'I can't,' Elizabeth said with finality. 'I'm sorry, Father, but I can't.'

13

EVENTUALLY, SOMETIME AROUND dawn, Esther had slept again for a fitful hour or so. She woke, troubled, with Katya brightly neon-lit in her mind; a child in danger, lost, and cut off from those who cared for her, alone in the world. She felt the pain of isolation as if it were her own; an ache, more agonising than pain, an anguish of desolation. She lay for a time with her hand pressed firmly against her solar plexus, the radiating centre, as if pressure could contain it. It was Katya's pain, and Esther's pain, and more. She pressed down harder and flexed the muscles around her ribcage, urgently needing to keep it within bounds. She didn't want it. She wanted a practical solution to the problem of her lost daughter.

At eight-thirty she was relieved to answer the phone and hear Ben, as practical a person as she knew.

'Have you heard anything?'

Esther pulled herself up to sitting position.

'No. Still nothing. I don't know if there's something I should be doing. I don't feel very useful just waiting, and hoping that nothing – awful has happened.'

'I'm free until after lunch. I'll come round.'

For a fuck, Esther thought, though she supposed that he was sure that sex was just what she needed to distract her. And, as if to wipe the small smile of irony from her face, a pulse of desire throbbed momentarily in the pit of her stomach, doing away, briefly, with the anguish that gnawed at her. Well, perhaps distraction *was* what she needed. This morning, until after lunch, desire and anxiety could do battle with each other.

The battle raged for an hour or two. There were a few moments when her body, marvellous machine, blotted out everything but its need for the weight and texture of Ben's body, and the obliterating moment of penetration. The worry, though, would reassert itself, returning suddenly and causing a noticeable loss of concentration.

Ben's tongue, flicking delicate passes along her clitoris, paused, and he lifted his head from between her thighs to look quizzically at her. Her building moan had stopped and she stared with wide, anxious eyes at the wall to her left, where a photo of Katya as a toddler hung. Ben pulled himself up to bring his mouth against hers; to wake her, as it were, with a kiss. For his trouble, he received an acknowledging smile and her fingers combing through his thick hair, more maternal, perhaps, than sexual.

'Esther?' he said softly, and adjusted himself again to take her nipple between his lips. He sucked with gentle satisfaction. And it was desire's turn, once more.

The alternating roles of lover, child and mentor, did not worry Ben; on the contrary, it was an exquisitely delicious game.

Afterwards, with her head resting on his shoulder, and his hand working stray curls back from her face, Esther broke the post-coital silence.

'I'm having strange dreams.'

'I'm not surprised,' he murmured back, immediately settling comfortably into his role as mentor. 'You can't imagine that your psyche won't be affected by all this.'

'All *this*? Us fucking?' she queried vaguely.

'Katya,' he reminded her, reversing his former task of distraction.

'Oh yes. I suppose they did start around the time that Katya stopped eating. Or I think they did. There's something . . . as if I've always been dreaming this dream.'

'Tell me,' Ben urged, still stroking.

'I can't. I don't really remember them. Just fragments and – I don't know – a flavour, an atmosphere. When I wake up I can't find myself for a while. I get as far as my name, Esther, but it's not exactly me, it could be someone else, but it's not *not* me either – another me . . .'

'And where's Katya in this dream?'

'She isn't. Well, the Esther, the one I'm not, for a moment

when I wake, reminds me of Katya. There's a feeling of her, but it's not her either. Something terrible happened to Esther. I wake crying – screaming sometimes.'

'Something terrible *has* happened to you and Katya.'

'Yes, but it's not as simple as that. It's not just a kind of metaphor for what's going on in my life. It's as though there's another life, completely different from mine in some ways, but it's my existence, too.'

'What happens?'

'I told you, I don't know. I can't remember properly. As soon as I'm awake and myself, I can't get any more than the emotional flavour.'

'Which is what?'

She thought back, almost getting the taste of the dreams in her mouth.

'Terror. Loss. Loneliness. Confusion.'

'All things you and Katya are experiencing,' Ben said with the satisfaction of a professional hearing exactly what he would have predicted.

'Yes, but it's *itself*, Ben. It's another reality.'

Ben was slightly surprised at Esther's psychological naivety.

'Well, of course, dreams give us messages in a way that make them safe for us to absorb.'

'No, I don't think it's that.'

He felt irritated that Esther was resisting so adamantly. He understood the need to resist correct interpretations, but it was an awful waste of time.

'I mean,' Esther continued thoughtfully, 'if it's just my psyche telling me that I'm frightened and confused and so is Katya – well, I know that, already. Why would my psyche bother to invent a mysterious dream about something that couldn't be more obvious to my conscious mind? What for? It's pointless. Why isn't it telling me something I need to know, and don't, like what I ought to do?'

'There's not much you *can* do until Katya's been found, except, perhaps, work on your own feelings. That's what the dream is telling you.' Ben looked at his watch as he spoke.

'Well, I think there is something to understand about the dream, if I could only remember it. I *know* there's something

– not more, but *else* – only I can't grasp it. I wake and the other Esther disappears like a ghost. But she's real, Ben, I swear she's real, and different. Only this morning – well, last night – I woke and Esther wasn't there, not even for the usual split-second. There was someone called . . .' Esther reached for the name, '. . . Elizabeth. But she faded, too, before I could . . .'

'Could what?'

'I was going to say *talk to her*. But I suppose you'll think that stupid.' She lifted herself up and looked at him, all ready to be annoyed by the answer he would give, but the sight of him, relaxed and naked in her bed, gave her instead another twinge of desire.

Ben took a deep breath.

'Not stupid,' he said, getting up and making for the bathroom. 'It's a way of avoiding something painful. You're externalising your fears – if you make this character in your dream real then *her* problem isn't yours. It's avoidance,' he told her categorically. 'And look what you've done with it – you've even made her change her name, so that she is further removed, not you and not even your name any more. Nothing to do with you. The mind is very devious.'

Ben disappeared into the bathroom to have his shower.

'But that's what I'm saying,' she called out to him. 'She *is* something to do with me. There *is* a vital connection – or there was with Esther. She's different, but I know she has a bearing on all this. I have to know her.'

'Look.' Ben appeared in the doorway, looking serious. 'You're under tremendous stress. There is a danger that you might split, escape, as it were, into fantasy. Some people are prone to doing that. I think you should see someone. Will you let me get in touch with a man I know? He's good, and he'll see you as an emergency.'

Esther stared hard at Ben, her lover turned diagnostician.

'You mean I'm schizophrenic?'

'No, of course not. There's no such thing as far as I'm concerned. But there are tendencies to react in particular ways to stress. From what you're saying, and what I know about you generally, I think your way might be to retreat into a fantasy world. But it doesn't have to get to that point.'

'Don't patronise me, you bastard. I thought we were having a conversation, not a consultation.'

Ben knelt on the bed. His eyes softened and he looked at her with warmth and understanding. He took her hand and stroked it.

'Look, love, it won't help to take your aggression out on me. You really need to see someone. Let me call Jonathan – he's very nice, you'd like him.'

Esther withdrew her hand and got up.

'Why a man? Why not a woman?'

Ben twitched his head impatiently.

'This isn't the right moment for a debate on psychotherapy and feminism. As a matter of fact, I *do* think it should be a man. Your attitude to men is something that I think you need to work on.'

Esther, still naked, stood and looked at Ben for a long moment. She turned and reached for the robe hanging on the bedroom door.

'Get dressed and fuck off, Ben. I'm not interested in what you're selling.'

She threw on the dressing-gown and left him to scrub himself clean of her.

For the rest of the day Esther sat facing a line of plates, on the floor of her studio, with a sketch pad on her lap. On the floor beside her were three coloured, thick felt-tip pens: the blue, red and yellow that were repeated over and over in the plates that leaned against the skirting boards in front of her. She stared at three sheets of paper that lay side by side on the floor boards at her crossed legs. On each she had drawn an empty circle in black pen.

She picked up one of the sheets and clipped it to the wooden drawing board resting on her thighs. She reached for the red felt-tip and began very deliberately to colour it in, working around the perimeter carefully and then filling in the rest of the white space with firm strokes all in the same direction. When the circle was completely red, she placed it back on the floor board and picked up the next sheet. This one was all blue. The third yellow.

She looked at the three coloured circles for a while and then wrote the number '1' with the black pen at the bottom edge of the sheet with the red circle; '2' on the blue sheet; '3' on the yellow. A moment later she put the drawing board to one side and got up to reach for a bottle of Tipp-Ex on her worktable. She sat down again and brushed the white liquid over the numbers she had just written. The sheets of paper were blank again except for the circles. Esther put out her hand hesitantly and let it hover over the red circle as if she were uncertain whether to pick it up or not. Finally, she did, and now sat with the black pen poised over the paper on the drawing board. She wrote 'ESTHER' in plain elegant print around the upper semicircle inside the black rim. The blue circle was also 'ESTHER'. The yellow, 'KATYA'.

Esther picked up her sketch pad after inspecting her work and made another empty black circle, then looked down at her coloured pens. After a moment she tore off the sheet and crumpled it in her hand, throwing it towards the wastepaper basket by the worktable, but missing. She took up the red circle inscribed 'ESTHER', and in the bottom semicircle printed 'ELIZABETH', drawing the letters close enough together to leave a small gap between the two Es and the R and H that began and ended each name.

The sketch of the red 'ESTHER' plate was finished. 'The 'KATYA' sketch she finished by printing 'ESTHER' around its bottom half. Then she stared hard at the blue cirle on which 'ESTHER' was inscribed. She swivelled the red 'ESTHER-ELIZABETH' plate sketch around 180 degrees. It only worked one way, of course.

Esther crumpled the blue 'ESTHER' sketch and threw it towards the wastepaper basket, this time scoring a bull's-eye. She began a new blue circle and, when it was coloured in, wrote 'ELIZABETH' in the top semicircle and 'ESTHER' around the bottom half. Then she put it back in the gap between the other two sketches.

For a long time Esther stared at the three drawings, searching them, it seemed, but then she shrugged her perplexity, and got up. For a moment she continued to look down at them, as if perhaps greater distance might make sense of what she'd done. She thought that they were probably right; they *felt* right, but she couldn't for the life of her say what they were right about.

The phone rang, releasing her from the sketches. It was Rob wanting to know if there was any news. She told him she hadn't heard anything, but that she would let him know, of course, as soon as anything happened.

'I'm at the hospital,' Rob said, 'Call me there. I'll be in Randolph Ward.'

'How's Felix?' Esther asked, remembering.

'Better today. They might let him come home in a couple of days if he goes on improving.'

'Good. That's good,' Esther said, almost plaintively. Somewhere in her head, in the part that thought unwilled thoughts, she had a peculiar equation. Felix was on one side with a minus and an X; Katya was after the equals sign. She didn't like it, and pushed the thought away firmly to a place where it wouldn't trouble her.

'Send him my love. Rob?'

'Yes, thanks, I will. What is it?'

'Where could she be? Do you think she's all right . . . I mean, safe?'

In bed that night Esther remembered when she and Rob had driven to the hospital to see the consultant psychiatrist, the day after Katya had been admitted.

As she drove towards the car-park, Esther had to stop behind an ambulance that was stationary at the emergency entrance. Its doors were open and the ambulance men were carrying a stretcher down the steps. Esther and Rob sat in silence while they waited. At first, Esther thought it was a child on the stretcher; the tiny body wrapped in a red blanket took up hardly any space on the narrow canvas. Then she looked more carefully and noticed that the face, surrounded by a white head-covering such as Muslim women wear, was not that of a child, though it was hard to make out an age. It was the colour that puzzled her most. The woman's skin was dark, yet not the tone of Asian skin, but grey. The word 'ashen' came to mind and again she noticed how small the woman was, bird-boned, barely fleshed, a minute old lady, or a child, she still couldn't be quite sure. The ambulance man holding the far end of the stretcher looked straight at Esther behind the windscreen. As he reached the tarmac his face suddenly broke into a vicious grin, and with slow pleasure he ran his forefinger across his neck, from ear to ear, while Esther registered his meaning. The sneer was sexual. Esther knew that, as he mimed the joke of an old woman's death at her, he got erect, filled with sexual excitement at her distress. Esther gripped the steering wheel until her knuckles went pale, and stared back at the man almost questioningly, only half-believing what she saw. As he pushed the stretcher past the car towards the emergency entrance, he turned his head sideways to look at her face-on, and gave her a long, slow wink.

Rob who had also been paralysed by the pantomime suddenly came to life.

'Jesus! The bastard!' he exploded, his face creased with disgust. He reached for the door latch, about to launch himself out towards the ambulance man.

'Don't, Rob.' Esther shook her head. She slammed the gears into reverse, and backed away enough to drive around the open door of the ambulance with no more than a couple of inches to spare. They turned into the car-park and cruised in silence around the rows of cars until they found a space.

Dr Khan was patient, but decisive. She answered Rob's questions and assured them that Katya was having the best treatment possible. At present she was quietening, the drugs were beginning to take effect, and there was no need for any other kind of restraint. Her psychosis was manageable, but it was best, for her own safety, that she was legally detained for the time being.

Esther took some comfort from Dr Khan's efficient tone, and the short white jacket she wore over her sari. But still, she found herself asking a question that she knew had as many answers as there were philosophies of the human condition.

'Was it something we did? Was it our fault?'

It was Dr Khan's job to give reassurance where possible. It was also her belief, as a medical psychiatrist, that it was fruitless delving into past history when there were immediate chemical solutions which suggested strongly that the problem was chemical too. She explained kindly that she didn't feel any other approach was very helpful, and that studies into the relative efficacy of psychotherapeutic as against somatic treatment showed that her way had a substantially better cure rate, particularly in cases such as Katya's.

'In any case,' Dr Khan explained, 'I've been in this business for twenty years, and in that time, my dear, I have seen many very ill people whose family histories couldn't have been more different. If you look at any family you can find reasons for psychiatric illness, but then . . .' Dr Khan spread her hands philosophically. 'Why is it that some people do *not* develop it? We do know that certain drugs return people with certain illnesses to a normal life. This is knowledge. We must use our knowledge to help people. We cannot speculate when there is a cure available. We will make Katya better,' she concluded on a vigorous, positive note. 'That is the important thing.'

Esther and Rob looked at each other to see if they could take comfort from this. As Dr Khan watched and allowed time for her words to be absorbed, the phone on the desk rang. The doctor listened and then asked a few terse questions into the instrument, glancing up at Esther and Rob from time to time.

'Yes? When? No one noticed? She just . . . ? Never mind, get on to the police. No, they're in my office now.'

She put the phone down softly, and clasped her hands in front of her on the desk before she spoke.

'I'm very sorry, but I'm afraid that Katya has disappeared.'

Esther brought herself back to the present and recalled that she had spent the morning fucking Ben. She tried to do something with it, extracting it from the desperation that swilled around inside her. She wanted to take moments of body on body, and reanimate them for her private pleasure. She remembered the sexual event clearly enough, and could mark the moments that she would have chosen to savour: When Ben's fingers found her cunt, slippery with readiness for him, and *her* fingers, simultaneously, curled around his straining cock, and they both stopped, held the moment, and smiled into each other's eyes, pleasuring each other with anticipation. When Ben pushed her hair away from her face and whispered, 'Esther,' into her ear in a voice that made him entirely new and unfamiliar, so that she had to look hard at him to see who he was. The mingling of their sweat, the confusion of scent, and his sharp, surprised cry when he came, as if he had not been expecting such a thing to happen. His arm tightening around her as she came, not allowing her to pull away into private sensation, keeping her climax theirs.

But they were tableaux, *natures morts*, not vivid memories that surged through her body allowing it to retrieve the sensations. She wondered at her emotional distance from the sexual events of the morning, and told herself that it was because she was distracted by the problem of Katya.

But it wasn't that, and she knew it.

It was because she didn't like Ben. She had wanted him, and all the pleasure had been there at the time, but it had no staying power, because she really didn't like the man. In particular, she didn't like Ben because he had fucked her instead of saying no and explaining to her that she would have wanted anyone at the moment. She didn't like him because he should have put her daughter first, even if she didn't. What she thought about Ben was that he was a self-serving little shit who happened to have dark hair and a pair of forearms that she fancied. So there was the reason why her mind refused to co-operate with her body's desire to remember. It simply didn't think that Ben was worth the effort.

She turned on her side and curled up, ready to sleep. Just before she dropped off, she opened her eyes briefly and told herself the truth: It was herself she didn't like, and, what was more, she hadn't the faintest idea what the truth was, about anything at all.

TWO

*F*reud's fanciful pseudo-explanations (precisely
because they are brilliant) perform a disservice.
(Now any ass has these pictures available to use
in 'explaining' symptoms of illness.)

– Wittgenstein

*Religion as madness is a madness springing
from irreligiousness.*

– Wittgenstein

14

KATYA AND THE policewoman sat in silence in the interviewing room. They had given up trying to get her to talk, but it would be only a matter of time before they found her name and description on a missing persons list. It would take a while before they connected the description her mother would have given the police to Katya. Her ten days on the run had turned her, physically, at least, into someone else. But, eventually, Katya knew, they would put two and two together. She certainly looked different, but she didn't know how she had altered inside, where it mattered. If she had, she wouldn't know, because the altered her would *be* her, and all she would feel was like herself.

This was the first time she had considered the changes that had been wrought in her. But she dated the events, not from when she had left the hospital, and not, as her mother did, from the time Esther had first challenged her about not eating, and changing her clothes, and made the appointment with Dr Grainger, but from a week before that when she had received grace.

Or that was what she had thought it was. That was the word that came to mind when she tried to find a way to describe to herself what had happened that night.

She had been asleep and had woken suddenly in the early hours. She heard the wind whistling through the branches of the trees in the park opposite the house. Rain tapped furiously, driven against her bedroom window. It was a raw, winter night in the suburbs. Then, as she lay listening, thinking of nothing, half asleep, a silence had fallen, as if a great blanket of snow had settled over the world and stilled all its noise. But that wasn't quite it, because the silence had come from inside her. The wind and rain continued, but a rushing, roaring silence in her ears overcame sound and hushed the noise outside. For a moment she wondered if she had gone deaf, but then the silence grew in her, racing all through her and making her an empty shell. Its force hollowed her out and then, like a hurricane, like a torrential waterfall, a *force* had entered through the top of her cranium and filled her with – with the indescribable. With fullness. With . . . *grace*.

She lay as if paralysed, or rather, as if all her fleshy boundaries had dissolved and there was only the thing that filled her, a fluid rush that eventually broke through her skin and joined her to the universe. All the objects and shapes of the world dissolved too, into their constituent particles. A great unformed mass of her, them, it, danced a shimmering dance in space, except that space danced also, along with everything, as part of everything. She was it and everywhere. Katya and everything, all together, all one. Katya lost in the mass of everything. Katya found and touched by everything.

It had lasted – she couldn't have said – but, when the whirling had died down, dawn had already broken and the day begun. Things, the world, the sound of wind and rain, branches and trees, window panes and rooms, objects and herself, wound back into their original forms and returned to their places, becoming themselves, ready for the new day. It was a gradual and peaceful return that left the world looking the same but utterly changed. Katya had seen, had experienced what it really was, and, like the toys she had imagined as a child, dancing in the night, she and the world returned to being what they were expected to be. Only now, even in the daylight, even the next day, even a month later, she knew better. She and the things of the world held a secret, a treasure, a truth. Katya, at fourteen, had seen God dancing in the particles of the universe, and danced along in God's midst.

She had no doubt about the interpretation she put on the experience. All through the following day a voice, soft and beckoning, had whispered her name in her ear. *Katya . . . Katya . . . Katya . . .* it soothed and promised and reminded. Katya had found God, and she hadn't even been looking.

The trouble was that she didn't know what to do about it. She and Esther had talked about the world for as long as she could remember. When she was a baby Esther had told her stories of Lucy, her Australopithecine ancestor, who had all manner of adventures, and of Lucy's children and her children's children, and how they learned first to live on the ground, then to walk on two legs and to make quite new and different uses of their freed front limbs. How they learned to make verbal signals and how they began to use these not just for getting what they wanted – Pass the mustard, please – but for entertainment and lies; how one day Lucy's great-great-great-grandchild had woken up and said, 'Once upon a time . . .' and nothing was ever the same again.

The story of human origins had been Katya's first fairy story, but there were others. Esther also told her about Adam and Eve and the Garden of Eden, and the Big Bang, and Zeus and Hera, and Brahma, and Tirawa of the Pawnees. Katya's childhood proliferated with creation stories. Esther had allowed none more weight than any other. Having been given all, Katya could believe none. If all were told, then none was true, but all spoke of the curious, questioning, problem-solving nature of human beings, and that was what was offered to Katya as the central truth.

When they went on holiday, or visited friends, Esther took her to local archaeological sites: to burial mounds, stone circles, curious monoliths that stood proud in the landscape and had meant something to someone, though who knew what, really? They went also to old churches and cathedrals. Esther had given as much importance to the craftsmen who built and carved the edifices as to their doctrinal purposes. They pressed their palms against cool dark stone, and wondered if they could feel centuries of time tingle on their skin. The houses of God were monuments to humanity. Katya and Esther sat in quiet side chapels and listened from a distance to human voices raised in worship. In great cathedrals they took in the sharp smell of frankincense, and tasted its alkaline tang on their tongues as they sat in the cool and dark under vaulted stone ceilings, listening to the chanted responses of nearby but unseen congregations. The voices raised in concert no longer belonged to individual humans, but to humanity issuing a supplication for mercy on behalf of all humankind. But who or what was listening? Esther allowed Katya to feel her heart thump with belonging and then wondered aloud what the vibration from human voices called up; on what frequency it vibrated. Were we all talking to ourselves, she asked, letting the stone absorb the continual waves of sound and return it gradually, over the centuries, so that its stored humanity seeped back at us and gave comfort? Katya was not deprived of the beating of her heart, but understood it came from common humanity, from the cycle of joy and suffering, from time itself.

Esther had a great respect for time and the way that stone mediated between the centuries. Them then, and us now, connected through worked and weathered stone, and more directly, somehow, than by the written record. The old ones call to the future, and we absorb the past when we place our palms against the cold rough stone. There was no momentous message passing back and forth, Esther suggested, only a mutual nod of recognition, of strangers acknowledging one another on the street. We feel their existence and in doing so confirm our own.

This was as close to the spiritual as Esther got. She offered it to Katya and taught her to hover, if she chose, three feet above humanity and time, and be impressed with it.

Katya was never sure if she really felt what she was supposed to feel, or if she was *really* supposed to feel anything. Perhaps it was no more than a metaphor Esther had made for history and her place in it. But it did seem to Katya, when she left her hand or pressed a cheek against a stone first worked 800 years ago, or a neolithic remnant standing alone in a field, that she felt a tingling, like a mild electric shock, run between her flesh and the hard granite.

This had all been rich information for Katya, as a growing child. It had prepared her for the extraordinariness and innocence of her species, but it had not prepared her for a moment when God, just another notion of funny, needy, touching homo sapiens, like the Devil, had rushed into her heart and made His presence known.

Suddenly all the choices Esther had passed on to her daughter (You are free to think anything, but why not think about everything and be conscious of being part of this dangerous, beauty-making, story-telling, lying, loving, hating species?)

were no longer available. There was one truth, and she knew it, and nothing in Katya's whole life had prepared her for such a moment. Nothing had taught her what to do with *belief* when it had come and pressed on her heart and mind.

So Katya had responded to this unasked for, unfamiliar experience by doing the first thing that came into her head. She had decided to fast. Just as a love-crazed teenager might refuse to wash after her singing idol had kissed her – an act of generosity, but nothing personal – so Katya wanted to abstain from anything that distracted or altered the body which had experienced the gift of grace. To feed it, to satisfy it with food, would be to distance herself from her singular experience. So she made a promise. She would eat and drink nothing except for weak lemon tea for as long as she could endure it. She would keep herself clear of everything that might come between her and the experience she had had, and which, if she behaved correctly, she might be given again. She would be still and wait, and she would make herself good enough to deserve it.

As the days went by it became clear to Katya that making herself worthy enough to receive grace didn't depend on a single, symbolic promise. *Everything* mattered. All the details of her life, how she dressed, the lazinesses, comforts, her attitudes and behaviour towards others, the way in which she approached schoolwork, it all counted. She watched and altered the way she conducted herself because she came to feel more and more that a single wrong note, the smallest degree of inattention, was all that was needed to keep grace away. It was obvious – she didn't need to ask anyone about that; if getting herself right didn't involve immense difficulty, then how could she expect to be given a priceless treasure? Katya had set to, and put her house in order. For seven nights she sat, trying to be alert and open, yet undemanding, staring at the white wall in her bedroom. At one in the morning she went to bed, to take the four hours of sleep that she allowed herself so that she could rise at dawn the following day and begin again the daunting task of making herself better.

Katya had felt her mother's anxiety creep like ground-hugging smoke through the silence of the flat. It distracted her. It demanded her attention when she needed all of it focused elsewhere. She had thought of speaking to Esther, and explaining what she was doing. What she had to do. But she couldn't imagine her mother hearing the words she would have to use and not misinterpreting them. She had tried to think of other ways to describe what had happened, but only the simple, obvious and unacceptable words fitted. So she decided she had to remain silent. Her heart told her she must not speak to people who couldn't understand.

She sat upright on the wooden chair that she had turned away from her desk to face the opposite wall, which was now an empty, white space. Once the wall had been covered with an intriguing collage of images – pop stars and strangely posed fashion shots mingling with news photos of a troubled world. Images jostled, commenting ironically on other images. Sting had gazed knowingly at a publicity shot of an American TV cop, his impeccably Italian-cut trousers falling in elegant folds from the waist, his hand raised to shoulder level supported by his other hand, taking careful aim with a designer revolver at – a nun at prayer, a black and white art photo from a colour magazine. The collage had been built up over months and told much of the story of the wit and confusion, promise and fear of being a bright fourteen year old at the end of the Eighties. Katya had taken it down and put its components into the dustbin one evening a week before. Now the wall was plain and white, and told another story.

Katya laid her palms gently along her thighs and focused on nothing at some mid-point of the white wall. She was praying. Or rather, doing what she thought might be praying. How could she know? No one had ever taught her to pray. Keeping very still was not prayer, but it was a beginning. A place to start. It was all she could do without further instruction: be open, quiet, and wait. She couldn't ask, she had no right to ask for anything. But even her silence, she knew, was a request, like throwing a baited line into a river and keeping still, hoping for a catch. She didn't know how to pray; she didn't know how to be good. And, most of all, she didn't know how not to ask for what she so badly wanted. She had tried to separate the wanting from her attempts at silence, but she knew she deceived herself, and that her efforts to still her desire were just an even more cunning method of making requests. Her lies and pretences were beyond her control. As she watched layer after layer of deceit reveal itself, she knew that the lies were fathomless; there was no end to the subtle twists and turns of her essential wickedness. Now that she knew that there was something she wanted, she was revealed as a self-interested schemer. Before, when she was unaware of what she now knew, she had been so profoundly deceived by herself that her own lies had never occurred to her. She had thought herself innocent, a child with no responsibility for the wickedness of the world. She knew better now, having watched herself grasping at what she could only have if it were freely given.

For several weeks after Esther had put her foot down, Katya had obediently attended the appointments her doctor had made for her. She went with her mother to see the consultant psychiatrist of her local hospital, after having been seen by the GP himself several times. The first appointment had been enough to convince Dr Grainger that something was wrong.

'Your mother says you aren't eating? Is that right?'

Katya remained silent for most of the session. The problem was that he wasn't asking any questions she could answer. It wasn't that she wasn't eating; it was that she was fasting. But to correct him would involve her in more questions that she knew she had no coherent answer for. She hadn't had enough time. The point was that she was at the very beginning of a great journey. How could she speak of it, when she hadn't got anywhere; when she didn't even know where it was she was going?

'You've changed the kind of clothes you wear? You've given away all your tapes? You aren't sleeping?'

Turning these statements into questions by adding, 'Is that right?' at the end of them didn't help to make them answerable. If they were right as facts, they explained nothing of reality. They were peripheral details, hopelessly inadequate attempts to make herself a good person. She didn't see what was the use of answering, although she didn't want to be rude.

After several long silences she attempted an explanation.

'I want to be good.'

This was unsatisfactory. It was no more of an answer than Dr Grainger's questions were questions.

'Do you think that you're bad, then?'

'Well, of course . . .'

'Has someone told you that you're bad? What is it you feel you've done?'

It was no good. The words were right, but the understanding surrounding them was wrong. The feeling was wrong, and it was better to be silent.

Between appointments Katya tried not to try. She maintained her fast, adding a slice of unbuttered toast at breakfast because it seemed to make Esther feel a bit better. She continued her nightly vigil, staring levelly at the white wall and trying to keep her thoughts under control. It was, of course, impossible. The attempt showed her only how far there was to go. Wisps of thought plagued her like vampire bats silently attacking cattle, drawing vital fluid without disturbing and alerting their prey. Only when it was too late were they felt. Katya thought she had been thinking nothing, and then she would come to and realise that her head had been full of nonsense: memories flashing past, plans formulating themselves; twinges of hunger or discomfort. Never for a second, it seemed, was her mind still. She despaired of ever achieving silence.

And increasingly, tantalisingly, a voice in her ear would call her name: *Katya . . . Katya . . . Katya . . .* At any time of the day or night, she might hear the soft, feminine voice, but it said nothing apart from her name. It was a reminder, almost a promise. Something would be said when it could be said. When she had achieved enough silence for the voice to be heard, it would speak to her. Lately, the voice had been almost incessant. Sometimes it would wake her during her few hours' sleep, calling and calling her name; reminding her that she had a task to perform.

What had happened to her that night when she had danced out there among the stars had shattered her life. It had provided her with a certainty for which she had no basis. Sometimes, as she sat in the doctors' offices, she felt immensely alone and frightened. She needed to talk to someone, but there seemed no one who would understand what she had to say. The doctors pryed, delicately, but insistently, trying to make her

114

say things that meant one thing to them, quite another to her. Her friends couldn't help. They found her strange, felt rejected. She spent almost no time with them now. At school, they tried to include her in their activities and weekend plans, but she smiled and declined, not wanting to seem stand-offish, but seeming that way nevertheless. They left her, increasingly, to her own devices. There was Esther, of course. It seemed, sometimes, to Katya, that Esther's attitude to time and history might include something more than human activity. When they sat in cathedrals talking in whispers about the power of stone to connect the present and the past, wasn't there something more than human being spoken of? And weren't their words accompanied by the raised voices of humans asserting their faith in *something else*?

One month after her experience, and several doctor's appointments, Katya tried to talk to her mother. Until then she evaded all questions and had become so vague and polite that Esther, beside herself with worry, and paralysed between the consultants and Ben, feared her daughter might simply disappear, just fade away, so that one day, when a decision on Esther's part would be too late, she would no longer be there.

Katya walked into her mother's workroom after school.

Esther smiled across the room at her. Katya settled herself into the purple armchair and there was an expectant silence for a moment. Katya broke it.

'The promise I made was to God.'

'What?'

'God.'

'Oh . . .' It was more an expulsion of the air that she had held in her lungs since the first mention of God, than a comment.

'I had a sort of experience.'

Esther experienced a momentary rush of hysteria as a variety of responses came tripping merrily to the tip of her tongue: God who? Why haven't you brought him round to tea? Would I approve of him? Is he good enough for you? You haven't done anything . . . you know . . . gone all the way? Does he come from a decent family? Is he Jewish?

She checked herself, held the hysteria down, and the silence elongated.

'God . . .' was what Esther finally said, and it was impossible for either of them to tell if she was being rhetorical or admitting the deity into their lives.

The burden of the conversation still remained with Katya. She accepted it.

'I'm trying to tell you what happened to me, Mum. Why I've changed. It's not a passing thing, or a joke, it's really important to me. I mean, I don't want you to . . . It's really hard to talk about it . . . to explain . . . I can't tell the doctors, I know they wouldn't understand. I thought you . . . Sometimes, when we've talked about things, you seem to be saying – well, not exactly *saying* – but it's as if you think maybe there *is* something different . . . more than . . . well, just people getting on with things, just staying alive . . .'

Esther looked surprised. 'Do I?'

'I mean, when you talk about human evolution – development, it's like there *is* a point . . . a reason why all those prehistoric people struggled to . . . you know. And those burials, where they put flowers in the graves . . . like they knew there was something else. You've never called it God, but that's what you meant.'

'Is it?' Esther was unable to commit herself to this version of events any more than to Ben or the psychiatrists' description of what was happening. She was sure only that she did not know what was going on or what to do about it.

Katya regretted speaking to her mother. It was a mistake.

'Why can't you understand?' Katya pleaded, as though she had spoken of her regret aloud.

Esther tried to pull herself together, and made an effort to overcome the paralysis which suddenly felt quite comfortable.

'You haven't told me anything. I can't understand just because you use the word *God*. That isn't an explanation. What was this experience you had?'

Katya, curled in the purple armchair and fanfolding the hem of her skirt, gave her mother another chance, and stammered out words that she knew failed to convey meaning as soon as they were out of her mouth. Each correction, each supplementary attempt, took her further away from the memory she was trying to make visible between them.

'. . . it was like . . . being part of . . . everything. It *was* –

everything. Do you see? I was . . . there were no – boundaries – nothing was separated. Not me – or anything . . . anyone. You were part of it, and Dad, and . . . everything. I knew . . . I just *knew* – well, God. It's so difficult to put it into words. It was *knowing*. Everything made sense. Do you know what I mean?'

Esther did not, immediately. But her daughter's words had a familiar ring. Her stumbling description had all the naive wonder and inarticulacy of Esther and her friends, two decades past, trying to explain to each other their acid visions. 'Wow! It's so *real*. I mean, so, well, *real*. You know? It's like . . . we're all part of . . . you know, everything, man!'

So she did know what her daughter was talking about. But what she knew about it was that the human brain, given the right (or wrong) chemicals and conditions, could fabricate a world of mayhem, losing its capacity to draw lines around things, so that everything – yeah, everything, man! – flowed together. And *real* and *knowing* were the words that sprang to mind to describe what was unreal and unknown, because, actually, people had the most tenuous hold on reality and knowledge, and got easily confused. And God, in some rather vague, un-Jehovah-like Eastern formulation, was as often as not invoked, because utter strangeness was terrifying to a basically order-making creature, and divinity was needed to evade the disturbing fact that, when frazzled, the brain short-circuited and made a complete mess of the world the body had to live in.

Esther said carefully, 'Yes, I think I know what you mean.' She paused and searched for a proper response, and then made a decision that finally closed off the route to her daughter. She addressed herself to what she regarded as the rational part of Katya's mind.

'Look, I know these experiences happen. They're very powerful. But you mustn't let yourself get obsessed. When you're asleep, and you begin to wake, the brain's in a funny state. It's got a name. Hypnogogic – no, that's when you're getting off to sleep, there's another word, I think, for when you wake. It doesn't matter, the thing is that it's a known condition. The human brain is very complicated. It can deceive you into believing things are real when they aren't. Do you see what I mean? And, if you don't eat, and you don't sleep, you make yourself high, and get weird. It's like taking drugs. And you start believing things that aren't . . . true.'

Katya stared at Esther for what seemed like a long time. She didn't look angry or upset. She looked, rather, blank, with her neat hair and unmade-up, wide eyes, as if her mother's words moved slowly through the air between them and had still not finished their journey into her brain.

Esther, staring back, waiting for a response, suddenly felt a pang for the daughter she had a few weeks ago: the slightly too young face that wasn't really concealed by slightly too old kohl and mascara round the eyes, and unnecessary blusher on her prominent-enough cheekbones. She missed the carefully scissored slashes in brand new jeans, the five different hairstyles that were tried before the right one was found for spending the evening in her room with Meg and a new tape. She missed worrying, occasionally, if her daughter was finding time outside of her obsessive grooming activities to read a good book, or ponder on the meaning of life.

Katya blinked. The words had been absorbed, their meaning processed. She uncurled her legs and smiled vaguely at Esther.

'It doesn't matter,' she said, as if it really didn't. 'It's nothing.'

15

TWO DAYS LATER the decision between God, hormones, and family dynamics was made for Esther, by Katya herself.

Later, Esther had wondered if Katya had looked especially distressed as she left for school that morning. Was there anything Esther might have noticed, or was she already inured to her daughter's tense, pale face and diminishing frame?

Katya did not go to school, but to the church a couple of streets away. She was used enough to cathedrals and little Norman country churches, but the ugly, nineteenth-century, urban church near by was completely unfamiliar. In any case, she had never entered a church for the purpose for which it was built.

She walked in tentatively, and stood for a moment inside the door. She shivered a little. It was dank and dark and empty, both in the sense that there was no one there, and that it held none of the qualities of time and spirit that she and Esther had usually entered churches for. Perhaps there had not been long enough for time to accrue like lichen within the stone. Anyway, there wasn't any stone. It was brick, solidly built to last into the next century for the glory of – the glory of solid, industrial Victorian man.

A voice startled her.

'What do you want? You're not supposed to be here.'

A priest appeared from the shadows and walked briskly towards Katya, jangling slightly, as the keys hanging from his waist bounced against his skirt.

'How did you get in?'

Katya indicated the door she had walked through.

'It's supposed to be locked. We aren't open until the six o'clock service.'

He was young, thirty at the most, his face plain, unpleasing, Katya thought. His eyes were too small and pale, his mouth too thin. It was a round island of a face, not designed to reach beyond its own boundaries. A functional face with which its owner might see, hear, smell and taste, but not use to express or communicate.

'Are you the priest?' Katya asked, hoping perhaps that he was only a janitor, or an assistant.

'Yes. What is it you want? I told you, the church is closed.' He spoke impatiently, his tone almost petulant.

'Why is it closed? I thought churches . . . I mean, how can a church be closed?'

'It's closed.' His impatience grew. 'Because if we were open all hours of the day and night, I wouldn't ever get any work done. And because of the petty thievery and vandalism that happens round here whenever you so much as turn your back.'

He glared at Katya accusingly, although, with her neat appearance and hesitant manner, it was unlikely that she intended any great damage.

'I wanted to talk to somebody.'

The priest sighed.

'Are you a member of this church? I don't recall seeing you . . .'

'No . . . I don't go to church . . . I don't think I'm a Christian. I mean, my mother's parents were Jewish, but she was adopted, so I don't know really what that would make me. You can't be Jewish unless your mother is. I live near by, though . . .'

The priest stopped her.

'What is it you want?'

'I told you, to talk to somebody. I've got a problem, and I want . . .'

'How old are you?'

'Fourteen.'

'Your doctor's the best person to talk to.'

'But I'm not ill,' Katya insisted. 'I need to talk to you. It's about God, you see.'

The priest looked startled.

'Pardon?'

120

'God. That's why I came here. I want to talk to you about God.'

The small, pale eyes narrowed into suspicion.

'You said you weren't a Christian. Perhaps you should see your local rabbi.'

'But I don't think I'm Jewish either. Why can't I talk to you about God? You must know something about it. I mean, I had this thing, that happened. It was with God . . . and me and . . . well, everything. And I keep hearing a voice. I want to know about being good. How to be good . . . really good. I need some advice. I try to pray, but I can't . . . it isn't right. And I've promised God . . . I'm fasting . . . but I know that isn't enough . . .'

The priest's face finally found an expression, as Katya spoke. Distaste spread over his features as if a devil were whispering obscenities into his ear.

'That's enough,' he almost shouted. 'I'm a minister of religion . . .'

'I know,' Katya interrupted, 'that's why . . .'

'You need a doctor. Go and see your doctor. I'm not qualified to give medical advice . . .' His voice shook slightly.

'But this isn't medical.' Katya was close to tears, pleading with him. 'It's about God, please listen to me, it's about God.'

The busy young priest let out a sigh that verged on a groan. He gave up the battle to get this hysterical girl out of his hair. He must look on it as today's cross, and accept that the minutes of the meeting about the church social would not be finished by lunchtime after all.

'All right, follow me.'

He led Katya through the church to a door that opened into an office. A word processor blinked away on a desk. He indicated a chair and sat down himself in a chintzy armchair opposite. Katya looked at his face, searching it for signs of wisdom now that he had agreed to listen to her. It still looked very ordinary and rather disagreeable.

'Now, what's all this about God?' It was said with little enthusiasm; the distaste on his face had spread to his voice.

Katya described what had happened in the night, several weeks previously, and the reaction of her mother and doctors.

'They think I'm mad. But I *know* I'm not. I *know* what happened to me. It's just that *they* can't believe, so they have to think that I'm inventing it, or crazy or something.'

The priest listened in silence; the look on his face suggested a schoolmaster who was listening to a pupil telling tales on her teacher.

'So what do you think?' Katya prompted. 'How can I make them understand? And how can I be less wicked? I know I can't be really good, but . . .'

'What did you say your name was?'

'Katya.'

'Well, Katya.' He tried for avuncular with only partial success. 'I think you should listen to your mother and the doctors. This hasn't got anything to do with God. In fact, if you were one of my parishioners, I'd tell you that you were being blasphemous talking the way you are. You see, real religious feeling isn't about excitement. It's got nothing to do with miracles and voices. What makes you think that you're so special that God would come personally to you? That's arrogance. Thoughts like that are sinful in themselves.'

'But it *did* happen. I didn't want it to . . . I just woke up and . . .'

'You say you don't know what religion you belong to. You haven't been brought up in any faith. How can you possibly know what is and what isn't a religious experience? You're just an excitable young girl who had a . . . a dream, nothing more. You want to feel special, so you turn a common, everyday experience into a visitation from God.' His voice was beginning to take on conviction. 'Do you really imagine that God has nothing better to do than to make you feel a cut above your friends?'

Katya shook her head from side to side as he spoke, denying the accusation. Her eyes filled with tears that overflowed and slid silently down her cheeks. The young priest's words had been designed to shock her out of her over-emotional fantasies, but they had worked on him too, and he spoke now with genuine anger.

'Who do you think you are?' He leaned forward and peered at her furiously. 'I've been a practising Christian all my life. I've devoted my life to the service of God. I'm not woken in the night with feelings of oneness with the Lord. I just work, day in and day out, leading services for a congregation of half a dozen old women, marrying and burying people who never bother to come to church for any other reason. I type out minutes of endless meetings' – he waved a furious arm at the word processor, still blinking on his desk – 'and bulletins that get thrown away before they're read. It's just slog, day after day, and for a salary that most people wouldn't bother to turn up to work for. That's the religious life! That's what faith is all about! Hard work, and no thanks for it. And you sit there telling me about hearing voices and being chosen by God. Who the hell do you think you are – Saint Teresa or something? And do you know how Saint Teresa begins her autobiography?' He got up, went to the bookshelf behind his desk and found an old paperback. He riffled through the pages furiously. 'Here. The first line is, "If I had not been so wicked, the possession of devout and God-fearing parents, together with the favour of God's grace, would have been enough to make me good." Do you hear that? *If I had not been so wicked . . .*" Perhaps you'd better think hard about your wickedness before you start talking about being good. What do you imagine you can know about it if one of the great saints is in continual battle against her sinfulness? You are an arrogant and silly little girl.'

He stopped, panting slightly and blinking in surprise at the sound of his own rage billowing through the air. Katya had caught her breath and continued to hold it in the sudden silence. Her face bleached with shock at the assault, which felt to her almost physical, as if he had attacked her with his fists. As the priest stared at her, he mistook the sleep-deprived shadows under Katya's eyes for bruises, and for a terrifying moment he believed that he had physically assaulted her. He almost felt the palm of his hand smarting. He made a fist and dug his nails into his flesh to bring reality back.

'I'm sorry,' he stammered, still afraid of his anger, and embarrassed. 'I shouldn't have got so . . . angry. It's just that . . . well . . . it's just not *like* that. I didn't mean to get so upset.'

Katya remained still, but began to tremble with the effort of holding back her tears. The priest saw it, and grew more alarmed.

'Look, Katya.' He got up and moved across the room, stretching out a hand towards her. 'I was carried away. Don't be upset . . . I . . .'

Katya slid under his arm as it reached her and ran, sobbing violently, out of the room and through the church to the door that still stood open. The priest followed, not quite running, calling out to her to wait, to calm down, to come back so that they could talk calmly.

Katya's wickedness exploded inside her head. The priest was right. Her arrogance, her terrible self-centredness. She was a stupid little girl; why would God want anything to do with her? She was small and foolish. A silly girl. How could she have thought God would be interested? It was a dreadful wickedness to have imagined such a thing. She was nothing, less than nothing. And bad, bad, bad. So bad that she had allowed herself to think . . . she had allowed the Devil . . . yes, the Devil, because she *had* had that experience, it wasn't a dream, so what but the Devil could have come to her? She certainly wasn't good enough for God, but she *was* bad enough for the Devil. She allowed the Devil in, which made her his creature. She was the Devil.

She ran along the street, past her house, going nowhere, weeping, and horrified at what she was. She had wanted help to be good, but there was no help for the wickedness in her that had allowed her to think she could be good.

People stopped and stared as Katya ran towards them. One or two would have offered to help, but she was gone before they could speak to her. She ran for a long time, without any idea of where she was going, trying to get away from her wickedness, to leave herself behind. But it stuck to her. She and it were one and the same thing, and, as fast and far as she might run, she would never get away.

She ran into the park, past the playground where a couple of small children sat on safety swings, pushed absent-mindedly to and fro by their mothers who chatted amiably to one another. She ran across a large expanse of grass that had no one but herself on it and, when she got to the centre, far enough from the mothers and children, and the few people who walked the path with their dogs, she stopped and let herself sink to the ground. She caught her breath, and, cut off safely from other people by the surrounding green, allowed the truth to develop fully, like a carrion flower, opening and exuding its stench of corruption through her mind.

The logic was unassailable and terrifying. She was infested with wickedness so palpable that her flesh crawled. It was inside her, running through her veins, a kind of filth, viscous and foul, that absorbed her thin bright blood and contaminated what should have been replenished. It seeped into her viscera, bathing her internal organs and filling them with stinking sewage. She felt it in her throat, choking, threatening to spew out into the world so that it would see what she was. On the surface of her skin, the vileness took another form; a microscopic verminous life was engendered by the disgusting matter inside her, and crawled through her pores, seething over every inch of her skin, too small to be seen, too numerous to be eradicated. She was contaminated by a wickedness; her wickedness, so cunning that it was invisible to anyone but herself. No one would believe her, no one could help her. Even if they wished to, she couldn't allow it, because she was lethal; anyone who touched her would be infected themselves with the loathsome creatures that swarmed all over her, waiting for the human contact that would allow them to disperse and infect – everything – the entire world. She had a vision suddenly of the enormity of it; the way in which the evil would spread. An invisible, inexorable pollution from which there could be no escape. From Katya at the centre touching, being touched by, just one other human being, the plague of evil she carried on her would multiply, infecting first a small group, then larger and larger, carried and passed on by individuals going about their business in the world. She visualised how many people might brush against an infected individual in the course of one day, and then how all of them would touch so many others, deliberately or accidentally. Planes, boats, rail networks, even mail would carry the spores, the virus of her original evil, throughout the world until in no time nowhere was unaffected and everywhere was spoiled and diseased. And it had all come from her.

Katya was the source, and she knew she must be isolated. Her own terror, spreading through and over her, was little compared to the responsibility she had to prevent the contagion from passing to others, and then to everyone.

In the world of people she would have to run, a deadly danger to everyone she passed in the street, to anyone who came near her. She would not be able to stop running and there was nowhere to go to keep others safe.

Katya stayed where she was kneeling on the grass in the centre of the field. She felt that even if people could not see her condition, how dangerous she was to the world, they would feel its force in some way. She felt signals emit from her body, and radiate across the grass: a force field that kept the world safe from her. While she stayed where she was, the danger was contained, the filth and vermin could touch no one. If she was the source of all the evil that could contaminate mankind, she was also mankind's protector. Whatever horror she would suffer was unimportant compared to the catastrophe that she alone could prevent.

When they finally came and took her away to the hospital, Katya fought them off as hard as she could, for as long as she could: a desperate, vain struggle to keep the world safe.

16

Katya WOKE TO the rustling of a peacock's tail. The gentle susurration brought her slowly out of sleep. The peacock was a couple of feet from where she lay, its tail quivering noisily in a great arc of full display. Coming across her, curled up behind a bush which concealed her from the path, it stopped, uncertain if she were a good or bad thing, according to its peacock judgement. She was too still to represent a danger, so it did what peacocks are designed to do, and made itself magnificent, strutting up and down, shaking its dark, jewelled glory at her, just in case. Look at me, look out for me, it warned, with all the beauty and absurdity that so confuses anyone who watches such a display; except, it must be supposed, other peacocks.

Katya lay still, wide-eyed with astonishment at the sight that greeted her. She thought: I have been woken up by the most beautiful thing in the world. But the pompously protruding chest, and its precious pointy-toed strut made a bubble of laughter form in her solar plexus. The most beautiful and the silliest. Going their separate ways, her eyes glowed at the feast they were presented with, and her mouth smiled at the foolishness.

As she sat up, slowly, so as not to frighten the peacock away, she felt the pain between her legs, and the ache low in her abdomen. The peacock, deciding enough was enough, turned its haughty back on her and walked off to a safer distance.

The events of the previous evening, and a night in the park had played havoc with the school clothes in which she had set out the morning before. Much of her hair had escaped the plait that hung down her back, and strands hung, dirty and limp on either side of her face, no longer polished clean. She pushed her hair roughly back out of the way, and looked down at herself. Two safety-pins held her grubby white blouse together where the top buttons should have been. Her skirt was creased and scattered with earth and grass. And she became aware that she had no knickers on.

She didn't mind very much about any of this; the fastidious schoolgirl had disappeared during the events of the previous night. She brushed halfheartedly at the front of her skirt, but wasn't concerned about the grass that remained.

Katya slipped her hand up her skirt and tentatively pressed her fingers to her vulva. It felt sore and uncomfortable, but the real pain was deep inside. When she looked at her fingers, they had blood on them. She wiped them on the grass.

The young man had come up to Katya as she sat over a cup of tea in a café near Kilburn tube. The tea and a sticky bun had taken the last of the money she had had with her when she set out for school. She was still slightly fogged from the pills they had given her in the hospital; underneath the fog there was confusion. It was strange to Katya that so much had happened so quickly; that it had begun because she had had an inkling of God and didn't know what to do with it.

She went through the events, but was unable to make a link between them although she knew they had followed one after another. Goodness, then its underside – how did you tell one from the other? How could you be confused between the two? She had been. Goodness and wickedness for a time were indistinguishable, and then it had come clear and she understood that she was diseased with evil and her task was to keep the world safe from her. Then she was taken away, and the doctors told her she was ill, which she knew. But they said her illness was that she thought she was ill, and they had signed a legal paper to say that she was not allowed to leave, because they wanted to make her better whether she wanted it or not. They knew best, and had her interests at heart, so she must trust them. They gave her pills that made a heavy, mesh curtain fall in front of her eyes. Fear and horror remained, but muted: hard to remember what they were for. The medication didn't weaken the terror, only the cause.

In the morning she had pretended to take her pills – two

small yellow ones, one large red one in a small plastic cup – but she had kept them under her tongue and then spat them out and flushed them down the lavatory. During the morning as the mesh curtain thinned a little, she remembered God and good and evil and contamination. She thought that perhaps the world would be safest from her if she stayed in the hospital, but the voice in her head began again, reminding her that she must get away, from everything, from everywhere. Her flesh started to creep once more; she felt the parasites come out from their internal hiding place in her bloodstream and squeeze through her pores. In a strange sort of way the horror of this was not worse than the mesh curtain and the knowledge of something terrible forgotten. She almost welcomed them back; she was herself again. She wanted to find goodness, a cure for evil. She had a journey to make. So she left, quietly, while the nurses had coffee, secure in the knowledge that the ward was well enough policed by the morning's medication.

Once back out in the world, she didn't know what to do, or where to go. She had no money and she couldn't go home, because that would only land her back in hospital. But then, over her cup of tea, she decided that she was, after all, in the right situation. She should wait and see what happened. Good or evil, God or the Devil: they could fight for her, in her, out in the world. Whatever happened to her would be the will of . . . whatever she really was. There was a plan, there was intention. Accident no longer had any meaning. She would allow herself to find out what there was to find out. She was in the palm of fate. So she sipped her tea and finished her bun and waited for it to happen.

The man in his early twenties, in jeans and jeans jacket, and an ear-ring, asked her if the place opposite her was free. She said yes, and knew it had begun. He sat down and stirred his tea. What he noticed about Katya was the difference between her eyes and her clothes. From the state of her pupils he reckoned she was on something, but he hadn't seen her around, and the pleated skirt and white buttoned blouse was a new one on him. She was sixteen or so, he thought, and he liked her hair. He didn't know any girl who wore plaits. He imagined his hand curled around it at the thickest part, by her neck.

'I'm Kit,' he said.

Katya smiled, shyly.

He told her that he worked in the record business. At the moment he was an assistant in a recording studio, well, a sort of dogsbody, but the experience was great, because he wanted to break into the record business. He'd actually cut a demo disc after-hours in the studio, and the manager of the studio thought it was good enough to send to the record companies.

Katya listened and made polite noises. If this Kit didn't look much like an agent of God or the Devil, she knew he had to be. He looked actually rather ordinary. His skin was bad, but his hair was carefully cut into complicated layers and sharp edges. He spoke London with a transatlantic drawl.

'And you?' he asked. 'Tell me about you.'

'I'm at school.'

'Not now, you aren't,' he said.

'I'm . . . off today,' she told him.

'You're truanting. You're a wild little schoolgirl, aren't you?' Kit grinned at her. 'What are you on?'

'What?' Katya didn't understand.

'It's OK,' he said. 'I'm safe. I'm not going to make trouble for you. Want some coke?'

'No, thanks. Tea's fine.'

Kit looked at her carefully. She was playing dumb deliberately, perhaps. A tease. Or maybe not.

'Where do you live?'

Katya shrugged uncomfortably.

'Have you run away?'

She didn't answer. She was an innocent, he decided. Come to London for a little excitement, or after a fight with her family.

'I like the way you do your hair. It's old-fashioned, but it's good.'

He looked at her with sleepy eyes intended to show appreciation.

'Do you believe in God?' Katya asked, trying to find out what fate had put this man her way for.

'In God?' he asked, and started to laugh. Then he stopped when he saw the look on her face. She meant it. She was crazy. Drug crazy – brain crazy? He didn't mind.

'Oh, sure – God. I meditate twice a day. You into God?'

'I don't know. I'm not sure if it's God or the Devil . . .'

This was good.

'That's it, baby. God or the Devil. But they're indivisible, you know? They tell you about the Devil and evil, but that's just to keep the secret all to themselves . . .'

'Them?' Katya knew she had found someone. She saw intention.

'Yeah, *them*. To keep you in line. Going to school, the office, the factory. Being a good serf until you die. But it's crap. You have to know the Devil, you have to confront the evil, and then you discover there is no good and evil, there is only a oneness, and the source. You know Aleister Crowley?'

Katya shook her head. She knew nothing, but she was going to find out.

Kit continued. 'They don't want you to know about it, because it makes you your own person. You follow your destiny.'

'Yes, that's it. How do you know all this?'

'I told you, I meditate. I've studied. Crowley, Jesus, the Buddha. I go into the realm of spirit and replenish myself. I can show you.'

'Will you? Please.'

'Sure. Listen, why don't we go to the studio? You want to hear my demo disc? I'd like you to hear it, tell me what you think? OK? And then we can go back to my place and have something, and I'll teach you to meditate. OK? What's your name?'

'Katya.' She had found the beginning of destiny. She knew that this was right.

Katya . . . Katya . . . Katya . . . the silky voice whispered in her head. *Yes*, it said. *Be open, Katya. Listen and learn. Go with your destiny.*

'Yes,' Katya said. 'I'll go with you.'

The studio was in Notting Hill, in a basement. Kit opened the door with a key.

'It's OK,' he told her, standing back to let her walk in. 'It's not being used this evening. There's nobody here.'

Katya walked into a room, one wall of which was glass. Behind it was the recording equipment. The room was thickly carpeted, with mikes overhead. There were two long, low sofas against the walls. Kit shut the door behind him, and she heard a key turn in a lock. She swivelled round.

'What are you doing?'

Kit put the key in the back pocket of his jeans.

'What are you doing?' Katya asked again, as Kit grinned at her. He liked the wide, alarmed look in her schoolgirl eyes.

'I don't want you to lock the door.' Suddenly, she was frightened. She had come here to a strange place with a complete stranger. It hadn't occurred to her before. 'Let me out. I want to go.'

Still in front of the door, and still grinning, Kit said, 'Where to? Where are you going to go?' He patted his back pocket. 'You stay here with me, and we'll have some fun.' Katya's frightened eyes began to irritate him slightly. 'Don't bother screaming, little schoolgirl; this is a recording studio – it's soundproofed. No one will hear you, and no one is going to be here, except you and me, until tomorrow morning. It's all ours, baby. Make yourself comfortable.' He indicated the sofa.

There was a small fridge in the corner of the room. Kit went to it and brought two cans of lager to the sofa, where he sat down with a satisfied sigh.

'Now then,' he said, pulling the ring-top off one can, and handing it to her. 'No? OK. What about this?' He pulled a tin out of his jeans jacket and put it on the low coffee table in front of the sofa. He took off his jacket and threw it on to the floor. Katya noticed that he had well developed muscles under his black, short-sleeved T-shirt. He was strong. Kit set to work, spilling a little white powder on to the table from a small plastic bag. He took a razor blade from the tin and arranged the pile into two thin lines. Then he reached for his jacket, took a five pound note from his wallet and rolled it into a thin tube. He handed Katya the rolled note. She shook her head. Kit shrugged his indifference, and inhaled both lines of cocaine himself. Then he breathed in deeply and sniffed hard a couple of times.

Katya watched this in silence. His back pocket, the one with the key in it, was inches from her hand. But she knew she wouldn't be able to get it, let alone unlock the door and get away. Her heart pounded, but she was stilled by the knowledge that there was nothing she could do. She was locked in, no one could hear her or help her. She waited, fearfully. Kit looked at her, and grinned as he sniffed again.

'OK, now we have some fun.' He reached for her, finding the thick plait and gripped it tightly.

'Don't, I've never done it. Let me go, please. I don't want . . .'

'Come off it, baby. You're a teasing little bitch.'

'No.' She shook her head, pulling away from him, but he tightened his grip on her hair until it began to hurt. 'I swear . . . I'm fourteen . . . I'm a virgin . . . please . . .'

She began to cry.

'You're a liar.' He brought his face up close to Katya's. 'But if that's the way you want it . . . so, I've got a delicious virgin. What a lucky guy I am. I didn't think there were any left. Kit's lucky day. You're going to make my day, and I'm going to make yours.'

He kissed her full on the mouth, pushing his tongue through her tensed lips. Katya hiccuped tears of fear and misery. He pulled back and looked at her.

'Please, please, let me go,' she wept.

He let go of her hair and pulled her blouse apart, sending the top buttons flying across the room, while Katya whimpered and struggled. He bit her breast, pushing her down on the sofa with the pressure of his mouth, and pulled up her skirt. He had her knickers off and threw them on the floor, unworried by Katya pushing him away with the flat of her hands with all her strength. It made no difference. He enjoyed it all the more.

As he entered her, his mouth all over her, his hands pushing her legs apart, Katya heard the voice through the sound of her tears.

Katya . . . Katya . . . Katya . . . It was not whispering now, but roaring in her ears, making his sounds disappear. *Good and evil. Good and evil,* it shrieked at her, like a demented parrot. *Bad girl. Contaminated girl. This is the road to knowledge. Good girl, bad girl. Take the road. Submit. Follow your destiny. You cannot choose. This is experience. You are being punished for your wickedness. And he is being punished. He will be contaminated with the evil that crawls over your body.* And then laughter. Howls of mad laughter rolling around her head.

133

The pain was excruciating as he entered her. She screamed, but the pain went on as he pumped away at her. Shooting pains radiated through her body. She had never known pain like this. She cried out, 'No,' against the pain, no longer concerned with the man who was doing this to her. It was as if he had disappeared. She couldn't see or hear him. There was only tearing pain that went on and on. She wanted nothing now except that it should stop. She thought she would die of it, that experience had brought her death. She didn't mind, so long as the hurting stopped.

Eventually, it did. It ended. And time didn't matter. How long the pain had lasted didn't matter. There was silence, a weight on her, and a dull bad ache low in her abdomen. The world returned.

Kit withdrew his penis and stood, pulling his trousers up and taking a swig of beer from the can on the table.

He looked down at her as she cautiously sat up and pulled down her skirt, her cheeks stained with tears.

'You had a good time, huh? You couldn't stop coming, huh?'

She didn't know what he was talking about, but he didn't seem to care if she answered him. She tried to do up her blouse, but found the buttons missing. She held the two halves together with one hand, and tried to push back her hair with the other. Kit put a hand possessively inside her blouse, pushing her hand out of the way.

'Nice, yeah? Have a good time?'

When she didn't answer he shrugged, and took his hand away, finishing the lager.

'Here, baby.' He went to a pocket in his jacket and threw three safety-pins on to the sofa beside Katya. 'I save them, you never know when they'll come in handy.'

Katya used two to keep her blouse together. She reached for her knickers. Kit snatched them up first.

'No. They're mine. I've got to have something to remember you by. My little virgin.'

He stuffed the knickers into his waistband.

'You want to hear my demo tape, now?'

Katya shook her head.

'Please, let me go.'

Kit shrugged again and dismissed her.

'So go – have a nice day.'

He unlocked the door and went into the recording room. Katya left quietly while he was winding a tape on to one of the machines. He didn't hear her close the upstairs door.

Katya was out in the world again, her first taste of destiny completed. She felt nothing except for the physical ache inside her. She was not horrified at what had happened to her. The invasion and violence done to her body did not touch her mind. She did not feel abused. If she had thought about the man who had raped her, and his intentions, his pleasure in using her, frightening and hurting her, humiliating her, she would have felt disgusted. But not at herself, at him, at his lack of humanity. But she was not concerned with the meaning of what had happened for anyone else but herself. She did not care about the man; he wasn't a person, but a channel. Being raped had been part of what she must understand. She had witnessed viciousness and cruelty with no obvious purpose. A person who was not a person. This was something to be learned. A first lesson in the course on wickedness. You sat in a café and, the way the world was, a bad thing had happened. It was a strong statement about the world.

It was also a strong statement about her. She had, after all, attracted wickedness. Sitting there, it must have been possible that someone good could have come up to her instead. Or perhaps nothing at all might have happened. Her voice explained this to her. Like attracts like. But Katya knew that she did not want to inflict fear and pain in the way that that man had. Oh, but evil has many forms, her voice told her, and goodness is one of them. Katya did not understand, but she knew that she was only at the beginning.

'You won't go away?' she asked her voice.

Not on your life, it answered. *Not unless you let them silence me with their drugs. And you won't do that, will you, because you need me to tell you the truth.*

'Who are you?' Katya asked.

The Truth, she was told.

'Don't you have a name?'

Many. Truth is one of them. Others are: Lies, Half-truths, Silence, Friend, Enemy, Madness. Take your choice.

'I'm not mad,' Katya said.

No, but I am, depending on how you look at it.

Katya wanted to know how a voice could be called so many things. The voice tinkled a merry laugh at her.

All this supposing that something that sounds like one thing is one thing, is supposing wrong. Listen to me, girl, you're a mess. If you don't want to stay a mess you can try calling me a name. Others will call me another name. That man who hurt you had a name. What difference does it make?

'What about God? What about the Devil?'

What about them? Just stick them on the end of the list.

17

THE ONE THING that Katya didn't want was comfort. She didn't want to go home and have the hurt and fear she experienced that evening soothed away. She found herself in Holland Park, just as the light was fading.

Peacocks and rabbits trod the grass. She settled down for the night. The man from the café had disappeared from her experience. It became a story to be wondered at. She saw her body as if it were one of her mother's plates. A blank thing to be painted on. Patterns would develop as the world made its marks on her. She was quite distanced from feeling anything personal. There were things to note. Such people, such things. This was wickedness, the casual tricking and hurting of a complete stranger. But was it evil, she wondered? Was it human wickedness or was its source evil? Perhaps there was no difference. That was important; if there was no distinction between the two, what about goodness, and kindness to others? Goodness and godliness, were they different? She hadn't encountered goodness yet. There was so much to know, so many ideas she didn't understand. And she was tired, sore and confused. It didn't even cross her mind to worry that she was sleeping rough, and was probably being looked for by the police. In a surprisingly short time she fell into a deep sleep behind her concealing bush.

Katya remembered that she had passed a café in the park last night. She got up and headed in its direction. The peacock was out of sight. She looked at her watch and saw that it was nine-thirty. She was surprised that she had slept for so long. There were quite a few people about. She noticed, after a while, that no one looked at her when she passed them. And then that it wasn't so much that they didn't pay her any attention, but that they actually looked away as she drew close.

She had no money, she suddenly remembered as she neared the café, and she realised that she was hungry. Apart from the sticky bun, she hadn't had anything since – she couldn't recall when she had last eaten. She stopped in the middle of the path and stared down at the asphalt, not knowing what to do. When she was little, Esther had told her that, if she lost her bus fare home from school, she should tell the conductor and give him her name and address. But it wasn't a ride she needed, it was food. She doubted that the café would let her have food, and anyway they might phone the police or something. She remembered that recently, in the underground, and several times on the street, people, women and children, mostly, had come up asking for money; not because they'd lost theirs, but because they didn't have any. That was now her situation, she thought, still looking down at the ground.

She heard footsteps behind her and turned round just as a middle-aged woman reached her.

'Excuse me . . .'

She got no further with the sentence. The woman made a wide arc around Katya, and quickened her pace without glancing at her. She tried again as a man in a track suit puffed towards her at a slow jog. He broke into a run as soon as she lifted her head and turned her eyes in his direction. He was gone before she could even open her mouth. The third try was equally unsuccessful. So far she had not even managed to get the words out, let alone achieve any money. She wondered at this, because, normally, if she wanted to ask for directions or something, people at least stopped and listened. Then she remembered that she didn't look her normal self, and glanced down. She was dirty and untidy, she could see, though she didn't know what a state her face and hair were in. But somehow she knew that the real difference was made by the two safety-pins holding her blouse together. The loss of two buttons made the difference between someone who merited assistance and someone to be avoided at all costs. Dirt and untidiness could be excused, or, at least, deserved a hearing. The safety-pins signalled danger that had to be skirted round and run from.

Katya was not concerned that she was begging, just as she was not bothered by her desperate-looking condition. That was yesterday's Katya. It all fell away so easily that she didn't even notice it had gone. She felt herself. And she had her voice whispering a sneering sort of encouragement.

Go on, Kat – if at first we don't succeed. Are we downhearted? No! And we're hungry, aren't we? Come on, dearie, look winsome, or something.

Katya walked up and down the path in front of the café for an hour. Once someone stopped; an elderly woman walking a dog, and without ever looking at her, fished about in her purse inside the bag she held close to her bosom and came up with ten pence. Katya was about to say thank you to her, but she moved on, seemingly fascinated by a tree off to the right of the path. She still didn't have enough for even a cup of tea.

Eventually, her legs got tired, so she stood still at the edge of the path, a couple of feet to the right of the doorway. It meant that she missed out on people entering the café from the left, but she was too exhausted to care. She stood with her head dropped, and one arm at her side. The other she held out, with her palm upwards, making a shallow, empty cup, for as long as she could, until it ached too much and she had to change arms. This turned out to be more effective. Several people who had to pass in her direction put their hand in their pocket as they approached, and found a coin or two to drop gingerly, careful not to make skin contact, into her waiting hand. Keeping her head down, though, was essential. If she looked at them as they came towards her, or were finding change, they would pick up speed, and pull a hanky or a packet of cigarettes from their pockets instead of money for her.

After an hour of standing there she had £1.25; enough for tea and maybe a sandwich. In any case she couldn't wait any longer: she didn't think she could stay standing up.

She found an empty table in a corner of the café. Several people looked at her warily as she passed them, some recognising her from outside, willing her not to sit at their table. It was clear to them that she didn't belong; it was something of a shock that they had paid money to enable her to come inside. They were nervous that she might interpret their generosity as some kind of fellow feeling and demand more than they were willing to give: an ear to listen to her troubles, a bed for the night – God knows what. Some of them regretted their charity; others just hoped she would know her place.

She had enough money for a cup of tea and a cheese roll; the sandwiches were too expensive. Katya was ravenously hungry. The cheese roll was finished in a matter of seconds, and at last she felt something personally. Tears came to her eyes because of the hunger that wasn't assuaged, and at how difficult it had been collecting even enough for what she had had. Several tears slid down her face, streaking the dirt into channels. The pain in her abdomen was no better, either.

Punishment, her voice told her briskly.

'Why? What have I done?' Katya asked pitifully.

People looked sideways or glanced quickly backwards at the young girl who had been muttering aloud to herself for several minutes. Some of them concluded that they had been right to avoid her; others felt a stab of concern for her, hardly more than a child and in such a dreadful state. They had read about runaways, homeless kids on city streets, and seen them, too, most of them. Pity, at least for some, was mixed with revulsion at what should not be, or at any rate, not be seen. The pity, the revulsion, and the mix were evidence in Katya's search for understanding, but missed by her. She was not even aware that she was talking to herself.

Katya looked up to see a woman standing at her table. She was in her early fifties, perhaps, and was staring down at her.

'You should go home. You're just a child,' the woman said.

'I'm being punished,' Katya said. The woman was surprised to hear a middle-class accent.

'But your parents wouldn't want you wandering around in this state, whatever you've done. Why don't you go home to them, dear?'

'It's not them,' Katya said unemphatically. 'It's God. No, the Devil. Well, that's what I don't know. She says I'm being punished but she won't tell me why. Do you know?'

The woman registered the 'she' who was not there, and wanted to leave, in spite of her distress at the child's condition. She opened her bag and put a five pound note on the table.

'Please, get yourself something to eat. You must go home – your parents will be terribly worried and you need help.'

Katya looked down at the note and smiled. Something good had happened.

'Thank you,' she said to the woman who looked as if she wanted to say something else. She began to put a hand towards Katya, but then stopped, and with a look of pain hurried out of the café.

Katya bought herself a ham sandwich and another cup of tea. When she finished them, she counted her change. She had £3.10. She left the café and made her way out of the park.

She had no plans, of course; she simply walked without noticing where she was going. She had been brought up in London, and much of the route she walked should have been familiar to her. But the city became anonymous, just as she seemed to have done. To be in familiar territory in a completely new way rendered her a foreigner. Having no money and no direction, the streets, Notting Hill, Oxford Street, Soho, that she knew by their architecture, shops, atmosphere, were alien landscapes. Just walking, one foot in front of the other, made the city a desert without an oasis; no landmarks, no comfortable recognition. People who passed her were on the inside, local, safe, with somewhere to go. She was on the outside, not belonging, not inhabiting the city that she had lived in for fourteen years: the experience all gone in a day. And not surprising, really, since Katya herself had disappeared. There seemed to be little left of her, no more, perhaps, than her name. That remained, unforgettable, since the voice, when it was not accusing her, or laughing at her, murmured continually, like a light wind riffling over a calm sea: *Katya . . . Katya . . . Katya . . .*

But her name, too, seemed devoid of meaning. She heard it as sound, and knew it referred to her, but there was no accompanying image, just some hazy sense of something gone, and something new.

In Soho she was invisible, no one either looked at her or avoided looking. People stood about and did business on the streets, or wandered in and out of doorways that Katya passed, from which snatches of music blasted incoherently, as one fragment gave way to the next, doorway by doorway. None of it had anything to do with Katya, until she paused outside a particularly noisy entrance. It was an amusement arcade, full of machines. The usual over-amplified music mixed with the sounds of electronic bleeps and shrieks. Katya walked in. It was a kind of hell of sound and vision, like a modern war: metal, unnatural flashing light, and a cacophony of noise which bled together to sound, to Katya's ears, like diabolical laughter. Or heavenly laughter – she couldn't tell the difference. Something in the large mad room of machines was hugely amused.

A bored-looking woman sat behind a grill under a bright-green neon sign that said 'Change'. Katya put her £3 on the counter, and the woman slid the three coins under the grill without looking at Katya, and replaced them with three piles of ten-pence pieces.

Katya played the fruit machines. She lost the first two ten-pence pieces, or, at least, nothing happened as a result of putting them in the slot and pulling the handle. She fed in another. There was no interest or excitement on her face as she waited for the windows to become still. It looked as if she were doing a chore that neither interested nor distressed her. A loud triumphant squawk emitted from the machine as the last window came to a stop, and a deluge of coins tumbled out. Like a silver waterfall, or gilt vomit. Katya stood back to allow the machine to finish gushing its jackpot out at her with the same look of indifference on her face. The woman behind the grill came awake at the noise and pushed a small basket through the gap, calling, 'Here y'are, dear, use this.'

Katya scooped up the money and took it to the woman who exchanged the tokens for a five pound note. Katya thanked her and went to the fruit machine next to the one that she had just played. She fed three more coins into it and pulled the handle. This time the machine sang its frenetic jackpot tune after the fourth coin. She changed the winnings into another five pound note, and went on to the next machine. She won on the third coin. After half an hour she was holding £40 in five pound notes crushed in one hand, when she found herself back at the first machine. She hit the jackpot with the first coin she put in, but this time a man came up to her as she waited at the window for the tokens to be changed. The woman was no longer bored and expressed it with a single raised eyebrow. Her interest was not so much at the run of good luck, as at Katya's impassive, unsurprised face. It had come to something when kids weren't even excited at winning half a week's wages.

'That's your lot, kid,' the man told her. He was tall and thin, and wore incredibly tight leather trousers. He leaned over her threateningly. 'I don't know what you're playing at, but go and do it somewhere else. Got it?'

Katya looked down at the winnings – £45 in five pound notes – in her palm and said, 'It's grace,' in a quiet, explanatory voice.

'Don't know her. Just get the fuck out of here. Go on, get lost.'

Katya left and went on walking. She came to a church and went in, sitting on a small rush-seated chair in the back row. She was as unsurprised as she had looked. The five pound note was a gift, an act of goodness, of grace. Last night she had been raped, this morning a woman had given her, unasked, a five pound note. The note, she knew, was a channel, a focus for goodness, electric, as she had taken it into her hands, with the grace of God. It tingled under her fingertips. It was a sign and she knew from the moment she received it that there was something she had to do with it. People were channels for grace, not really recipients of it. When she saw the amusment arcade and heard the coarse laughter, she knew what had to be done. Her voice reinforced her understanding.

Go on. Do it, it told her.

She was completely sure that she could only win with this money, and, when she did, she was not in the slightest bit surprised. She knew that she would have gone on winning on the fruit machines with the coins that were left from the original five pounds, just as, if she had bought an oyster with the money, it would certainly have contained a pearl. It was not a matter for doubt.

Katya rested quietly for half an hour, and then got up. She had not attempted to pray, she knew that she didn't know how, but the voice let up a little there, and she enjoyed the silence. On her way out of the church she stuffed the screwed-up notes into the collection box by the door, giving God His winnings. She had £3.10 left from the original money the woman at the café had given her. She dug into her skirt pocket and looked at the four coins in her palm. She shrugged and put them, too, into the collection box.

The trouble with leaving life up to fate was how much walking you had to do in between its interventions. And, apart from being footsore, Katya decided that walking might, after all, be taking her away from, or towards what ought to be coming to her. What if something had not happened, because she wasn't keeping still? Fate might be half a mile back down the way she had come, and missed her because she had moved on. Her voice called her an idiot. Did she really think fate so gutless that it could be subverted by mere time and place? Katya felt humbled at this, but decided that, if that were the case, then it didn't matter if she stopped walking; she could trust fate to find her and give her feet a rest at the same time. She came to Soho Square and sat down on a bench, telling herself that this bench or that made no difference. But, nevertheless, she shifted from the first one she chose to another diagonally across the Square. She didn't know why. Why not?

It was lunchtime and the day pleasant. The Square thronged with people enjoying lunch in the open, but Katya sat on alone on the bench. All the other benches had two or three people on them. Several people who would have preferred not to get grass stains on their skirts, or trousers, sat on the grass anyway, rather than join Katya whose face was now grey with ingrained dirt to match her once pure-white blouse. Somehow, things that had fallen from a high point of order – a blouse that had been white and crisp and was no longer, hair that had been neatly plaited and was now disarrayed, a pleasant face that had been scrubbed, but was now filthy – these things were more disturbing to people than a grubby T-shirt filthier than ever, matted hair that hadn't seen a brush in years, or a face that it was impossible to imagine ever having been clean. In any case, people simply didn't sit next to strangers who carried on a sub-vocalised conversation with themselves, and scratched obsessively at unmentionable parts of their body, even if they were little more than a child.

Katya, sitting alone on her bench in a crowd, had let go of her broodings about fate, as she noticed, once again, that people were keeping away from her. The quiet certainty that had accompanied her brief encounter with grace left her abruptly, as she remembered her condition, and the terrible knowledge of her evil infestation took over all the space available for thought. They could all sense her condition, and knew that to go close to her would mean certain contamination. She thought there must be something about the air around her that warned people off. A shimmer perhaps. When she focused on the air there *was* a kind of dancing curtain of light enclosing her. A warning, like a beacon, to tell people that they must keep away. Try as she might she could not see the tiny creatures that crawled over her, waiting their opportunity to spread themselves through the world. She tried cunning, looking suddenly, taking them by surprise, pulling up her skirt; or carefully, so that they could not notice, pulling her blouse away from her skin to peer down inside it, trying to catch a glimpse of what she knew and felt crawling over her thigh or down her chest towards her belly. She almost saw them, but never quite, never with certainty. They always managed to scuttle away, but left a kind of shadow, a teasing sense of something that had been there, but always too quick for her. Every inch of her itched, now here, now there, all over. Felt, but never quite seen. She rubbed and scratched at her flesh wherever she felt the things, unselfconsciously putting a hand down her blouse or up her skirt. She existed again in a nightmare; feeling the uncountable, unseeable parasites creeping all over her flesh, feeding on her. She knew absolutely that they were there, yet she could never actually see them, or never be quite sure whether she had seen them or not.

Suddenly it was dusk. Impossible, because moments ago she had sat down and it was lunchtime, although not for her. No one was left sitting in the Square. Now there were people cutting through it, this way and that, on their way home from work. The failing of the light threw shadows over Katya. A dread settled in. Dark fingers of hopelessness crept through her. Night coming again. Nowhere to go. For a moment she was a child again. She was alone, with no one to take care of her. She wanted her bed, her room, her mother stroking the terror away. Someone to say, It's all right, it's all right. But there was no one except her voice who told her that it was not. That she was cast out, alone, separate. It tormented her in a quiet insistent tone, the jocular note gone. She was wicked, this was the condition of wicked people, to be alone, to have no one to turn to. She remembered Kit and she understood that. If he practised his cruelty on other people, that was his only prize, the pleasure he got from it. He would be alone, tricking, lying, hurting. He would be alone at dusk, too. But she had not hurt anyone; she didn't think she wanted to. Still she didn't understand where her wickedness lay. The voice rather testily explained again that her inability to comprehend her own wickedness was part of it. Look at it hard in the face, know it, be it. Here she was alone, with night coming in. Wasn't that proof enough?

The part of Katya that couldn't credit her own wickedness argued back. What about the five pounds? And the proof of grace? Hadn't she won against impossible odds with the money?

Bored, the voice explained what was obvious. The woman who had given her the money: she may have been good – only *may*, mind you; who knew what motive was in her heart? But supposing it was true, the grace stuck to the money. It was not magic, it was goodness. Give something touched with grace to the blackest, most evil thing on earth, and the goodness would work because the *thing* was suffused with it. But it was like a great river; goodness falling into the hands of those not worthy of it created a side stream, the force of the central flow kept it running for a time, but eventually the channel narrowed and encountered desert sand. The trickle died, soaking into innumerable arid grains. The money had held some of its goodness, but so what? What good came from it then? What work had it done?

'But I gave it to the church.'

The voice laughed, rasping in Katya's ear. *So what?* it asked again, and Katya had to admit she had no answer to that.

There was another question, though, that occurred to her. 'But what is it for, then, this grace, this goodness? What for?'

The voice took on a sullen note. *May as well ask what evil is for. Stupid question*, it told her in the tones of a sulky child.

Katya gave up arguing. Her situation, after all, told her enough of the truth. Why else was this happening to her? The voice was right. It made no sense, probably, to ask questions about evil. If it was, it was. All the answers in the world couldn't change anything, because after the very last answer to the very last question, evil existed, and that was that. The real question was: What was to be done about her life? She was bad, a desert where nothing would grow, and only things adapted to aridity and emptiness could exist. It was hopeless. That was the nature of badness. She saw her folly in waiting for anything to happen, in imagining that fate would take her on a journey of understanding. Her wickedness wasn't about anything. It was not a road to anywhere. It just was. Like daytime, night-time. There was nowhere to go, and the light was dying.

Katya, fourteen years old, fearful and lonely, destitute in a matter of hours, had argued and lost, excavated for hope and found none. All that was left was the fact that there was nothing. Nothing behind, nothing ahead. She couldn't move. There was nowhere to go.

18

'WANT A MARS bar?'

Katya opened her eyes and saw a skinny black dog with one brown ear staring up at her.

'Here.'

A Mars bar landed in her lap. She looked in the direction it had come. A skinny boy sat looking at her curiously at the other end of the bench, his knees tucked under his chin.

Katya moved further back against the arm of the bench, ignoring the Mars bar.

'Don't come near me, you mustn't touch me,' she frowned at him.

'All right, I won't. Why not?'

Katya looked at the Mars bar in her lap. Her mouth filled suddenly with saliva at the thought of chocolate, of the sweet stickiness she remembered but could now actually taste at the back edges of her tongue. The taste memory lacked only the satisfaction of the thing itself melting in her mouth.

'Go on, eat it. It's all right, I've got more.'

The boy hauled a plastic carrier bag from the ground on to his lap, dropping his feet to the ground. The dog whined gently and wagged its tail as the boy took another Mars bar from the bag and broke it in half. He gave one piece to the dog, and ate the other himself. Katya could smell the chocolate in the air that wafted to her across the bench.

'Don't touch me,' she said again and closed her fingers around the Mars bar.

The boy shrank back in mock terror and raised his palms.

'All right! All right! But if you don't want that, we'll eat it.'

Katya snatched up the bar and tore the paper, sinking her teeth into the chocolate and toffee and soft stuff in the middle.

She could hardly wait to swallow one mouthful before she bit off the next. The smell and taste, and the fullness of her mouth made her feel almost faint. No food had ever been so perfect, so exactly what her mouth had watered for. She finished it and felt as if she had eaten an enormous, delicious meal.

'More? I've got one more. I'll share it with you.'

Katya nodded, and he broke another Mars bar he'd already taken from the carrier bag. The dog wagged its tail again, and moved forward for more.

'No,' the boy said firmly. 'It's not for you. You've had yours. Sit.'

Reluctantly, it did. The boy held out the half-Mars bar to Katya. She shook her head, staring at his fingers on the wrapping paper. He saw what she was looking at, and, raising his eyes to heaven in mock impatience, gently threw the bar so that it landed on Katya's skirt.

When it was finished Katya said, 'Thank you.' She felt over-full now, but it was a good feeling. She turned her attention to the boy on the other end of the bench. He sat tight up against the arm, mirroring Katya. The dog stood quietly with his chin resting on the boy's knees. He was older than Katya, perhaps nineteen or so. He wore a dirty white T-shirt with holes in it and tight jeans, also with holes. He lifted his legs back up, crossing his arms over his knees, and gave Katya a long, assessing look.

'I'm Sam,' he said, without changing his position. 'And this is Biology.' He indicated the dog, which had settled under the bench with just its head poking out where its master's feet had been.

'Biology?' Katya blinked at the dog, which turned its eyes towards her, hearing its name.

'Biology,' Sam repeated without explanation. 'And you?'

'Katya,' she told him warily, sliding her eyes away from him. He was very pale. His light-straw hair was cut short and ragged as if he had taken the scissors to it himself; his chin sprouted wisps of something too fine and uneven to be called bristle or beard. He had a long face, almost fleshless, the cheeks hollowed, the eyes deep set, pale also, and surrounded by blond lashes. He looked overall as if someone had forgotten to colour him in.

'So why can't I touch you? Can't we even shake hands? Hello, Katya.' He extended his arm towards her and Katya shook her head vigorously.

'No, you mustn't.'

'Don't you trust me? I shared my Mars bars with you.' He looked disappointed and rested his chin disconsolately on the arm that lay on his knees.

It was almost dark. The streetlamps had come on.

'I'm infested. You'll catch it,' Katya told him.

'No I won't. I'm immune.'

'You don't know what I've got. How can you know you're immune?'

Sam grinned.

'I'm immune to everything. So that's all right.'

Katya stared at him. There was something odd about him. Although nothing she could put her finger on. A strange lightness, an absence of something, but she didn't know what.

'No, it's not. Don't touch me. It's not an illness, it's things, creatures . . . Can't you see them? Everyone else can. Or they know they're there, anyway, because no one comes near me. Look.'

She pulled the neck of her blouse apart, up to the first safety-pin, and leaned forward a little to let him look. He craned his neck forward and peered down the front of her blouse. Then he shook his head.

'I can't see anything. What do they look like?'

'Insects, sort of, I think. They're almost too small to see – you have to be quick, because they go away when you look, and the light has to be right. But they're there. If you touch me you'll get them all over you, living on you, and then anyone you touch will get them And . . .'

'Like fleas?'

'Yes. No. They're terrible things. They bore into you, into your skin, underneath, and you can never get rid of them. They live off your insides. You'd better leave me alone.' Katya turned her head away, and waited for him to go. He was quiet for a moment, but Katya could see from the corner of her eye that he hadn't moved.

'Well, never mind. If I promise I won't touch you, then can we be friends?'

150

'Why?' she turned to look at him suspiciously.

'Why not? It's getting dark. Can you cure it?'

'No. Not by medicine.' Suddenly, the reasonable description of her condition seemed totally inadequate. 'I'm not ill. I'm bad.'

'How do you know?' Sam asked, unsurprised.

'My voice says so. I thought I was good and then everything got confused. It all got out of control and then these things . . . and the voice tells me . . .'

Sam stood up and stretched.

'I'm off,' he said, looking down at the dog. Biology came out and waited. Sam picked up his carrier bag and began to walk away. Katya watched him go and felt the fear of the night ahead creeping back into her. After a moment Sam turned but continued walking, backwards.

'You coming?' he called.

'Where?' Katya frowned, but the fear retreated a little.

'With me. You aren't going to stay here all night, are you?'

Katya wasn't going to stay there all night. She got up and walked slowly towards Sam who turned round and carried on along the path to the gate of the Square. The dog followed at his heels, and Katya a little way behind them. She didn't mind where they were going. She didn't care what he might do to her. The darkness had fallen and she didn't want to be alone with nowhere to go. Now, she wasn't alone, and she was going somewhere, even if she didn't know where that was.

Sam didn't really have anywhere to live either. At the moment he was staying in a derelict house that had been bought by a developer and then boarded up because the money had run out. He'd come from somewhere up north and lived as best he could until he'd met up with Biology, also a stray, and then they had both lived as best they could. Sometimes Sam washed up in cafés for food and a little money; sometimes he found things, on skips, or just around, as he put it, and used them or sold them, depending. He'd lived like this for four years, since he left school at sixteen and decided that he didn't belong where he was, and ought to go somewhere else. For a while he hitch-hiked around Europe, getting as far as Morocco; living what was no more than a folk memory – a latterday hippie, his time all wrong. Then money and friends ran out and he went to the British Embassy who shipped him home telling him that they'd had enough of that sort of thing in the Sixties and it was all different now; he'd better get a job or register for youth training, because there was no room in modern Britain for lighthearted shiftlessness.

When he got back he joined up with a group of travellers and roamed the West Country in a convoy of clapped-out vans and buses. He learned a lot about mechanics – the day never passed when there wasn't the opportunity to lie under a chassis or explore beneath a bonnet. He had a natural talent for making engines work even when they shouldn't; and a way with children, who liked the way he managed to treat them with respect and take care of them at the same time. He also learned a lot about the Goddess and joined in a life dedicated to celebrating her. They went from ancient site to ancient site, giving nature her due, scorning the material world. It seemed to Sam to be as good a way of conducting his life as any other he had known.

But eventually the group broke up. A respect for and dedication to the natural world didn't solve all the problems of living together. There were squabbles about money, power and sex. Anger and jealousy wandered from sacred site to sacred site with them, breaking out here and there, while those not involved tried to appease whatever it was that was responsible. Then, of course, those currently gripped by unregenerate emotions turned on the ones who still clung to notions of love and community. Tiny fires flared, now here, now there, but no one noticed that for some time the whole community had been ablaze with everything that each of them despised. When Sam realised, he decided to leave, and arrived in London without a plan. He was sad because they had become his family, as his real one somehow had not, but soon Biology turned up, following him until it occurred to Sam that he had a new family; who said that families had to consist of people? And Biology never had arguments about organisation and who should take responsibility for what.

But, although he liked his unordered life, Sam missed the sense of *something else* that he had had with the travellers. It was hard to hold on to the sacred on concrete pavements

152

and dark, damp basements. But in another way the very deadliness of the city – its functional, denatured streets, the almost ironical squares of green dotted here and there, the solemnly comic half-dead saplings planted in concrete tubs – provided a constant reminder of what was absent. It was like a person who had had a stroke, so that one side of the body was paralysed; the lack of feeling on that side would be a reminder of what was lost, but the feeling side would be more crippled really, aware constantly of its own limitations.

Sam felt a bit lost about life. He couldn't imagine his own future, and although this didn't bother him now, he had an inkling that one day it might, and this worried him from time to time.

Sam yanked back the two lower planks boarding up the basement window, and lowered them to make a gap for Katya to crawl through. Two scruffy kittens galloped towards her, mewing. The larger of the two beat the other to Katya's ankles and wove around them, as much to keep the smaller one away as for its own pleasure.

'Philosophy and Psychology,' Sam said, climbing through the window.

'What?' Katya asked, turning to face him. The room darkened suddenly, as Sam pulled up the planks and wedged them back in position. She remembered the last time she had gone into a room before a man she didn't know.

'The kittens – the little one's Philosophy and her big brother's Psychology.'

Sam walked around the room, lighting candles. As the light grew, Katya could make it out better. The floor boards were bare, and the walls had been stripped, or rather, someone had started stripping them, but stopped. In places the plaster was exposed, while other parts had various layers of wallpaper still stuck to them. The place looked and smelled damp. A sleeping bag was laid out on a small square of dark-blue carpet along one wall; a rucksack and a few books lay next to it. In the middle of the room there was a rectangle of rush matting with a small single-burner camping stove and a battered saucepan on it. In one corner, underneath a crazed china sink with a tap that dripped continually, there were two cracked saucers, one with a little milk in it, the other empty.

Sam fished about in his plastic carrier bag and came up with a tin of cat food which he opened with a penknife from his pocket.

'Here,' he said, ladling some out with a blade from the penknife. The two kittens jostled for position, but there was never any doubt that the little one would have to wait her turn, which suggested that she wasn't just little because she was the younger of the two.

'Why don't you give food to the litt . . . to Philosophy first?' Katya asked.

Sam shrugged.

'That's the way it is. That's Psychology for you.'

Katya made a face at the bad joke.

'I suppose the little one is philosophical about it?'

Sam gave her an apologetic grimace.

'I'm afraid so.'

'And what name would you give me if I were a stray kitten?'

'Mad.'

'So you could say, She's mad? You don't believe what I say, then?'

'You haven't said much. But I believe what you *have* said. Why wouldn't I? It doesn't mean you're not mad. Don't you think you're mad? I mean, would you describe yourself as sane?'

Katya thought about this. In all honesty, she didn't think she could call herself sane.

'Well, no, but that doesn't mean I'm wrong, or imagining things.'

'It's no good asking me about right and wrong, or about real and imaginary. I don't really see how those words came up in the conversation we were having. I just said you were mad. If you like I'll call you Katya, or would that mean I think something particular about you?'

'You're just playing with words. You want to confuse me.'

Sam found a tin of soup and started to open it.

'Words are confusing. I get more confused the more of them I know. So it'll be Katya?'

'No,' Katya said, still standing at the edge of the room. 'You can call me . . .' She stopped and thought. 'Nothing. I don't want to have a name at all.'

'That's a pity,' Sam said, looking disappointed. 'I was hoping you'd be Chemistry. Never mind, nameless, if that's what you want.'

'That's what I want. And you still mustn't touch me. Promise?'

'OK. Promise. Want some soup?'

While the soup heated up in the saucepan, Sam washed two spoons in the sink. When it was ready they sat on the floor and passed the saucepan back and forth, dipping their spoons into it and the bread which also emerged from the carrier bag.

'What do you do about money? How do you buy food?' Katya asked.

'I organise,' Sam told her and left it at that. 'Why don't you get some sleep? You looked really tired in the Square.' He indicated the sleeping bag. Katya looked at him and he shook his head. 'It's all right. I won't bother you. I'll sleep here on the matting. There's a loo in the room next door which more or less works; you'll need to take a candle with you.'

Sam woke up wondering why someone was flashing the lights on and off. His first thought was that it was the middle of the night, his second, that the police had come for him, surrounded the house, and were going to mow him down with automatic weapons if he didn't give himself up immediately. He caught himself as he was beginning to slip back into sleep and a dream he didn't want to have.

The flickering was a candle beside Katya, who he could see as a dark shape, sitting cross-legged on the sleeping bag, with her back against the wall. He stayed quiet for a moment and watched, allowing his eyes to adjust to the low wattage. When they had, he saw that there were tears streaming down Katya's cheeks, like a river in flood silently overflowing its banks. She wasn't crying, she made no sound; it was as if she didn't know about the tears. He might have been watching a silent movie, or through a soundproofed window, or he might have gone deaf.

'You all right?' Sam whispered tentatively, only just remembering not to call her by name.

She didn't glance at him; there was no more than a flutter of an eyelid at the sound of his voice breaking into the silence. A movement made him lower his eyes. He saw one of her arms relaxed in her lap, the hand palm-upwards, the other seeming to stroke the forearms over and over, from elbow to wrist. It took a moment before Sam understood.

Katya had not managed to sever an artery; but she had made a terrible mess of her arm. Sam's penknife had made bloody ribbons of her flesh; in places the underlying fat was visible, the blood seeping up like an underground spring. Katya let Sam lead her gently to the sink, and run cold water over the lacerations. She appeared not to notice. The tears continued to fall down her cheeks, and she whispered, 'I'm very bad. I'm very bad,' over and over again. She seemed to feel no pain, it was as if the arm that Sam held over the sink was not connected to her. She watched him washing it, and tearing up a T-shirt to make a bandage without giving any sign that it had anything to do with her at all. Sam sat her on the rug in the middle of the floor. The sleeping bag was blood-soaked; he put it in cold water in the sink and left it there. Katya sat in the middle of the room as if nothing were happening at all. As if she were an audience waiting with exemplary patience for something to happen, but if it didn't – well, no matter, never mind.

Sam finished clearing up. He was not frightened by what had happened, at least not by the blood and the mess. Looking after the travellers' kids had made him useful at first aid. But Katya herself worried him. At first he tried to talk to her, but she didn't answer. It was as if she were enchanted. After a while, when she was bandaged and sitting obediently on the rug, she began rocking gently back and forth, still silently weeping, saying nothing.

'Shall I take you home?' Sam asked her, squatting down in front of her.

Katya responded for the first time, not with words, but with a violent shaking of her head, and wide, horrified eyes. The shaking continued until Sam assured her that she could stay where she was, that he wouldn't take her either home, or to a hospital, which had been his second suggestion.

'What do you want, then?' he asked her.

Katya started rocking again, holding her bandaged arm against her as if it were a baby.

'Shall I look after you? Do you want to stay here and I'll look after you?'

Katya fixed him with her eyes, focused for the first time, and nodded with all her strength. She began to cry again, but this time sobs came along with the tears and rocking.

'Can I touch you?' Sam asked.

Katya pushed her bottom lip out slightly, and her chin trembled as if there was something she wanted terribly but could not ask for.

'Don't worry,' Sam told her, putting his arm round her shoulders very carefully. 'I won't catch anything. You got rid of them all, anyway, didn't you?'

Katya smiled very slightly, like a cunning child whose clever plan had been found out. Then she allowed Sam to put her head gently on his shoulder, and the two of them rocked in rhythmic silence until Katya was stilled by sleep.

Katya spent the best part of a week sitting on the floor, in the middle of the room, in the basement of the derelict house. Sam cared for her like the infant she had become. She peed and shat where she sat, and each time Sam mopped up the floor, washed her down and rinsed her clothes. He brushed her hair twice a day, tying it, once the tangles were out, neatly at the back, and washed her face and hands before spoon-feeding her from the jars of baby food he organised on his brief daily trips out. When she vomited the food up, he cleared up, wiped her mouth carefully and gave her orange juice to sip. In between times, when she slept fitfully, or rocked, apparently contentedly (though the tears continued unstoppably, it seemed), he fed Psychology and Philosophy, and hugged Biology who suffered watching his master give so much attention to the new interloper.

Katya never uttered a word, though from time to time she whimpered. Every day Sam checked her arm and put on a clean bandage, after washing it and applying disinfectant cream. The arm looked nasty, but there was no infection. It would heal, though Sam knew that without stitches there would be large scars left. It never crossed his mind to take her against her will to the hospital, or the police. She was his responsibility, she was with him. He did what there was to do for her with complete commitment, but there was no one outside the two of them in the room to whom he was responsible. Parents, doctors, police, were not his concern. He never thought about *their* concern. He didn't wonder, even several days later when he had had hardly any sleep and was almost dropping where he stood, how long this could go on, if it would ever stop. He devoted himself to caring for Katya, as he would have cared for a sick animal that turned up and looked to him for help. But after a few days it seemed to him that there was more than that.

Sam came to think that Katya was very special. She was someone he had been looking for. He understood that she was making a journey, freeing her mind from the burden of her body, allowing someone else to take care of it, so that it could sink deep underground and work through – something. It was *for* something, he was sure. He recognised that Katya was crazy, but it made no difference. Katya had got to a place that all the people he'd known since he left home had believed existed, but none could reach. None of them had had the courage, or strength, or saintliness, perhaps, to undertake such a dangerous journey. If she returned, Sam knew that she would be changed. Sam had thrown off comforts and everyday routine, but his mind never got free of ordinariness. He began to feel like a disciple. He may not be able to risk his mind, but he could be an enabler of someone who could take the risk. He took care of Katya's body while her mind was elsewhere, keeping it in good condition, because she would need it when and if she returned. Madness, for Sam, was not synonymous with truth – he was too earthbound to believe that, but he didn't discount the possibility that it might be. He wasn't afraid for Katya now, for the risk she took with her sanity in the search for good and evil, because he knew it was a risk worth taking. Sam wanted to know what she would come back with, so he was happy to mop up the mess her body made, and take the risk, along with her, that she would never come back at all.

Sam kept his little basement world together. Cats, dogs, humans; cleaning, feeding, watching over, waiting patiently, for something to happen, or nothing, if that was how it was to be. He was a practical angel who attended to the material needs of his universe: a world of physicality that needed to be sustained so that the immaterial could exist. He thought that, perhaps, God's job was not very different: a kind of daily char that kept decay at bay. Sam had found a place for himself in the world that he had made. He felt useful, and he thought that God, working on a grander scale, admittedly, must feel useful, too.

19

IT WAS ONLY ever a matter of time before Katya and Sam were found. It was surprising, really, that they weren't found sooner, because Sam's organising activities had become increasingly risky. The range of his needs as the carer of their little band was broad – cat and dog food, baby food, cleaning materials, medical supplies, clean clothing, including underwear for Katya – he couldn't steal all these things from one place, but the more shops he went to, the greater the chance of his being caught. A mixture of stealth and the protection of the gods had kept him safe and all of them free for longer than they could have reasonably hoped in a suspicious and nosy city.

The neighbours, peeking through the net curtains, tired of clicking their tongues and muttering angrily at each other, finally got the courage to call the police.

Sam opened his eyes as dim dawn half-lit the basement. It took him a moment before he realised what it meant, and by then the room was crowded and noisy. Biology bounded around the room, barking and wagging his tail furiously, jumping up joyfully in greeting at each of the policemen in turn as they climbed through the window. He was thrilled by this new turn of events, loving the excitement and energy he'd missed since Katya had arrived. He'd had a sullen, unhappy week, sulking at the attention she was receiving from Sam, but now sparks flew and Biology felt adventure in the air. The cats were not so pleased. They disliked the sudden noise and light. Little Philosophy cowered in Katya's lap, which for the past week had been so still, providing her with a satisfactory haven when Psychology threatened violence. She suspected that the new activity meant an end to the reliable, warm place of safety, and felt, once again, irredeemably small and unprotected. Psychology had fled into the lavatory, and waited for things to quieten down.

A large man caught Sam by the front of his T-shirt and pulled him up.

'Come on, you, you've got no business here. It's private property, you're trespassing. What's the matter with her?' The policeman nodded in the direction of Katya, who sat, still as a statue.

'I'm looking after her,' Sam said, as the man pushed him against the wall. Biology ran frantically around the room, barking continuously.

'Get that fucking dog out of here,' the policeman yelled at one of his colleagues, who caught Biology by the scruff of the neck and hauled him to the window.

A third man got Katya under the shoulders and stood her up. Philosophy's claws were stuck in Katya's skirt. For a moment she couldn't get free and hung vertically, trying frantically to pull her paw away. Finally she succeeded and dropped to the floor, scrambling for her balance, and raced for the lavatory, where Psychology arched his back and hissed dangerously, his previous fear overcome by satisfaction at having her cringing, wide-eyed, nowhere-to-hide look back once again.

In the police car Sam tried to explain about Katya, who sat quietly looking out of the window.

'We have to stay together, I have to take care of her.'

The policeman sitting between them threw him a contemptuous look.

'You couldn't take care of a cat. God knows what we won't be able to charge you with, sonny. She can't be more than fifteen, and mentally defective, too, by the look of it. Look at the state of her.' Katya was wearing only a large T-shirt, and knickers, that were still soiled from the previous night, since Sam hadn't had a chance to clean and change her. 'You're in shit, but you won't mind that, judging by the filth you were living in when we found you. Prison'll be too clean for you.'

Biology had escaped from the policeman who had dragged him out of the basement. There was no sign of him as Sam and Katya were put into the car. Philosophy and Psychology stayed where they were, life having returned to normal for them, or almost normal, since there was still a little food left in an open tin of cat food by the sink. Normal would return when that was empty and it would be back through the window, out into the street, trying to get the lids off dustbins. Later in the day, workmen arrived to bang nails into the boards over the basement window. The cat food wasn't quite finished, so Psychology was still enjoyably batting Philosophy away from it when the hammering started.

THREE

Go on, believe! It does no harm.

– Wittgenstein

20

THEY CALLED ESTHER later that morning, a few hours after Katya was picked up, having found her listed under missing persons. Esther had got on the phone to Rob but his answering machine told her he was at the hospital. When she got through, she told him that Katya had been found and that they could go and fetch her.

'I can't,' Rob said. 'Felix has had a relapse. I can't leave him.'

Esther was stunned into silence for a moment.

'I'm talking about your daughter,' she said finally, in a tone that suggested he hadn't understood what she had been referring to. 'Your family.'

'Felix is my family. I have to stay with him.'

Esther registered the pain in his voice even through the shock of what she heard him say, but in a moment years of anger fell into place and were redefined by fear. Where was *her* family? She had made one with Rob and the baby, and that had blanketed her knowledge that no one in the world had ever belonged to her, not really, not as of right.

A hideous growth of rage emerged: anger at her adopted parents for not having given birth to her, a cancer of unacknowledged fury at never having been sure of their love. They'd coped with the fact that she was, by definition, a stranger, by pretending it wasn't true. And she had continued the pretence with Rob and Katya. Even when Rob fell in love with Felix, she felt he was still *her* family; that the existence of Katya *made* him family, and that he had to be first and foremost theirs, love notwithstanding. When he was unreliable, it was a fault in him, a failure of his character that didn't alter the fact of his being family. Only now she realised that family was a movable concept. Loving someone changed the focus of commitment. She had never understood this before, because in her experience what she lacked was the real thing, and having invented the real thing she thought it was immutable. Rob cared for Katya, she knew. She thought that he probably still cared for her, too. But his commitment was to Felix. Love was more important than family, and death had a priority over life.

Esther was numb with the horror of finding this out, and at seeing how little she had understood about the world. She couldn't feel reasonable about it. She was betrayed, left alone, and no one was there to help, no matter what.

'What am I going to do?'

Hysteria cracked her voice.

Rob spoke quietly, offering reason and calm.

'I'll get to you as soon as I can. Take Katya to the hospital. I'll ring you this afternoon and find out what's happened, and we'll take it from there.'

'But what am I going to *do*?' Esther howled again.

'Just be grown up.' Rob tried to hold back his own anger by being brisk and sensible. 'If you can't manage, get Ben to help. He'll love it. I'll be with you as soon as I can.'

'Fuck you! Fuck you! Fuck you!' Esther screamed uselessly into the mouthpiece.

Rob said, 'I've got to go,' and put the phone down, leaving Esther to scream alone into the electronic silence.

And she was left with responsibility for Katya. Why? Why should she accept it? Her mother, whoever she had been, had rejected her. Why should she be expected to do any better? Because she was probably older than her own mother had been? Because she was educated to be reasonable and should know better? But why should knowledge and experience save her from the murky undergrowth of her deprivation? Why should she be deprived – have always been deprived – of her deprivation? The truth was that the woman who had given birth to her and the man who had helped to conceive her had thrown her away, like so much unwanted rubbish. *That* was the truth. Why had no one allowed her to feel this? Why had no one held her in their arms and rocked her while she howled at the enormous injustice of not being loved as of right? Of not being genuinely part of someone's life. And, if she had never belonged to anyone, not really, then how could she make a place for someone, a genuine place, as of right, in her own heart? Why should people expect her to be able to cope? She could not, she would not cope. How the hell could she, of all people, deal with a crazy daughter, and make wise decisions, take responsibility for them, and for everything? It was not fair that such a thing should be demanded of her, Esther (whoever she really was), who had been given nothing more than a substitute tricked up with words. She did not even know her own name.

A madness descended on her and she stormed around the flat, picking things up and banging them down loudly, opening doors in order to slam them, lifting the telephone receiver and hissing her refusal into it before throwing the whole machine hard against the wall. She stamped through the flat, through room after room, and then started all over again, muttering furiously, shaking her head fiercely, refusing the reasonable voice of her adopted parents. A child having a long-postponed tantrum.

Finally, she was exhausted and sank to the floor, becoming part of the mess she had made. The telephone was beside her, making a whining, continuous noise, like a complaining animal. She whimpered a duet with it, half sob, half moan, until she drifted off into something like sleep.

21

The top portion of the page contains faded, illegible text bleeding through from another page.

THE ELIZABETH WHO was who she was had no name. That strangeness of the morning had been cleared up. She was not Elizabeth at all, she was someone else.

The priest responded to her question, 'What was my name?' with a raising of his shoulders and the spreading of his hands, the long fingers separating in a gesture of helplessness. His sombre face showed no emotion, unless the final draining of blood from his already almost colourless face could be interpreted as a response to feeling.

Elizabeth – whoever she was – sat on the edge of the stool in silence. Her black eyes were wide with shock. It was as if a spell of immobility had been cast, she was so still. She did not blink, she did not breathe: no part of her moved in the smallest degree. Internally, however, there was turmoil. Her mind scrambled, as if down a sheer cliff face, to return to something she had left behind at the bottom and needed urgently. Her head spun with the vertigo of the drop beneath her, with the change in altitude, but there was no bottom. No matter how far down she got, there was never solid, level ground beneath her feet. The story she had been told was without resonance in her own memory.

And yet.

There were the dreams; the moment before waking when she fought for breath and died. There was the strangeness. She tried to find names and places to replace the nebulous feelings, but she could not reach them. The priest could not help her with this; his story was of crowds and small groups huddling together, without names. But, as she stared into his bleak eyes, one thing emerged from the fog of forgetfulness. The tall man; the long, sallow face; long-fingered hands appearing from beneath rough dark, cloth, holding something; and a voice, compelling yet fearful.

'I remember you,' she said quietly. 'I thought you were an angel, leading angels.'

Father Anselm lowered his eyes.

'And everyone died?' she asked him.

He nodded.

'Except you.'

'Why can't I remember them? Why didn't they – you – kill me, too?'

The priest shrugged again.

'Whim,' he suggested. 'The whim of a woman who had no children of her own. A man who saw the advantage of another pair of arms to help about the house, and a dowry in the future. Accident or God's will. What do you think?'

'I think that God could not have been watching over such terrible events.' She thought for a moment. 'But if He exists, He must have been watching; and if He was, then He must be evil. He must be the evil creator of an evil universe.'

'But He saved you.' Father Anselm looked at her curiously. It was a question. There was no wrath at her blasphemy.

'To be saved by something evil, in order to live among the evil – what can that mean?'

'And if your survival was no more than an accident?'

'What is an accident? I am me, I was saved when everyone else died. I do not feel like an accident. And you would tell me, if you were hearing my confession, that there was no such thing. Everything is God's will, how can it be otherwise?'

'But I am not hearing your confession. You are hearing mine. And I repeat the word – accident.'

'Then, there is no God?'

She was aware, as she finished speaking, of the silence around her. The stone walls did not hold and return their whispers, the Virgin was no more than a form carved out of a piece of wood, the pity in her eyes just a trick of the light that no longer worked.

'God cannot be evil,' the priest said quietly. 'If that is so, and it must be, then . . .'

He waited.

'Then,' she said in a voice that was barely audible, 'it's true, there *is* no God.'

Father Anselm looked at her. One corner of his mouth twitched slightly, like the beginning of one of his unaccountable smiles. He didn't speak.

'But there is evil? If such terrible things happen, then there must be evil.'

Father Anselm spoke.

'We inhabit a world where flesh destroys flesh. And the question: *What for?* cannot be asked, because there is no answer. There can be no answer when flesh asks the question. If there is a God, He cannot see us, He cannot know us. If there is goodness – and there must be, if there is evil – then we cannot see it, we cannot know it. While we inhabit the world and the flesh, we live in the shadows, in the dark, where light cannot penetrate. While we are substance, we exist without hope. There is no God. Not for us.'

'But you are a man of the Church?'

The smile formed on Father Anselm's lips.

'And I was the man who read the letter. The Church is of the world. The Church is flesh. It is there to prevent questions that have no answers, and to prevent people from seeing the answer that comes from no answer.'

'But you are a minister in the Church.'

'And so I know it well.'

'When I came here, you were praying.'

'You saw me stand in front of the altar. You saw my lips move. I speak to the god of the flesh in his own language.'

She remembered something.

'And you smiled when you crossed yourself.'

'I have spoken of this to no one but you. I spoke to you today because you had a question that proved you to be as different as I knew you to be. I have told you the truth about yourself, and the truth that you already knew about the world. I owe you that. I am responsible for your present existence, just as I would have been responsible for your death. That is why I'm here, why I came to this place. To wait and see what you would become.'

'I have become a person without a name.'

'Take one.'

She thought for a moment.

'No. It's better to be without.'

There was a long pause. She tried to absorb the story that Father Anselm had told her, but apart from the dreams that touched what the priest had told her was her reality, and the recognition of Father Anselm himself, she couldn't make the story her own.

'Shouldn't there be pain?' she asked eventually. 'I don't feel any pain.'

'How long does a kitten feel pain when it's torn from its mother? If there is no memory – of the event, of life before – where would pain belong?'

'I'm not a cat.'

'No, and so you've felt strange and different all your life since then. You've noticed the distance between you and others, and the look in your parents' eyes.'

'But I love Christian . . .'

'Perhaps he's the only one who is truly your family. He came after, and he accepts you without judgement.'

She remembered who Father Anselm had been.

'Do you know everything? Do you know all the answers to all the questions?'

The priest hung his head and remained silent. It could have been a gesture of shame, for what he had been, for what he had caused. But it seemed to her that she saw the ghost of the strange smile flicker across his mouth as he lowered his head. After a moment he raised his head, and there was no hint of a smile.

'I am your servant,' he said quietly.

She was confused.

'But I'm just a girl. You are a priest. I don't understand.'

'There is work to be done. You *will* understand. I told you, before you insisted on the truth, that you would be alone, isolated, outside of everything. More than you have ever been. More than you can imagine. You will need me. I will serve you.'

She blinked at him, recalling something.

'In the dream, the one I have just before I wake every morning, there *is* a name . . . Esther . . . the name is Esther.'

'Will you be Esther, then?'

'Yes. I'll take that name. I'll be Esther.'

They were all looking for, and complaining about, Elizabeth. Christian had been getting under everyone's feet: his father's while he was trying to chop wood – get out of the way, he'd end up chopping off his hand at this rate, where was his sister, why wasn't she keeping the child out of his hair? His mother's who furiously prepared the root vegetables for the day's soup – this was Elizabeth's job, where was the girl, hadn't she enough to do without doing her idle daughter's chores too?

Both adults had the same thoughts. Hadn't they kept and fed the child all these years? Hadn't they given her her very life? Where was their thanks? What good was she? Never there when she was needed, and unmarriageable, with her dark – her devilish dark – looks. Who would want her? How were they to be repaid for their moment of weakness? For that was what it was. Softheadedness. A mistake. Those people – they were what they were. No amount of baptism and good Christian upbringing could change that. And then, after saving her, the boy had come. After years and years of fruitless trying. When they had given up all hope, then, when it was too late, when the girl was already with them, the boy had been conceived. Both of them felt cheated. Like a joke had been played on them. Well, take the child of Antichrist into your house and what do you expect?

Elizabeth's father and mother had the same streaming thoughts running through their heads, separately, but neither thought these thoughts in words. Each word was approached, as it were, sidled up to, partially sighted, and then veered away from. No picture entered their minds of the moment of their generosity – that vision had vanished from their memory as surely as it had vanished from Elizabeth's. Their thoughts were no more than a sullen clogging of the brain. Never spoken, never shared. There was never anything, from that time, between them, nothing more than an occasional furtive glance, half caught by one and immediately cancelled by the other. Nothing thought, nothing said.

Esther arrived home, although now she was released from the word. It had never seemed quite right, anyway. She had told

Father Anselm that she wanted time to think; she would return – back – and see what she thought. He nodded. Everything was different, of course, from the moment she was within sight of where she had grown up. There was no longer any nagging worry about her feelings, or lack of them, for the people she had called parents. And Christian, as he came running towards her, still lived in a warm place in her heart. They were kin, whatever her origins. Life had made them related. She felt no affection for the house, either, and, thinking this, she realised that her new assessments of her feelings were questions to herself about what she would miss. She understood that she had decided to leave. It was only Christian who would pull at her heart.

Her father stopped chopping wood when he saw Elizabeth approach. He held the axe at the top of his swing, his arms raised above his head to strike. Esther saw nothing of him, except his hands clutching the wooden handle. Once they had been around her neck, ready to squeeze the life's breath out of her. Her father. And had those hands dealt death blows to the others – the ones she couldn't recollect but who had belonged to her? Her father. She focused now on his face, coarse and reddened from a life of hard work. Did she hate him, her killer and her provider? She thought she didn't, she was only perplexed that he could have lived all these years with her and the memory of then. Perhaps he had bad dreams. But she was certain he didn't. There had been only that sullenness, a resentment, that she had thought was his character, just who he was. And who was to say that that wasn't true? She saw clearly the limitations of this man, his smallness, his crabbed, miserable soul. But this was a good man, a good enough man, to the world.

'What are you gaping at? Where have you been?'

She ignored him. Christian came running towards her, and she opened an arm to him. They walked towards the house, while Christian chattered about a bird's nest he had found. At the door he said, 'Mother's cross,' and slid out of her embrace to wait until the coming storm had died down.

Her mother glared at her.

'Useless girl. Do we feed you so that you can run wild? God will punish you for your sins.'

Her mother's face was as mean as her father's. Esther had never felt inclined to run to her for comfort and warmth. Her thick body had never seemed a place of security. Esther could not remember having once nestled against her mother's flesh. And yet this woman was her rescuer. She focused on her hands, rough and flaking, dealing mortal blows to the root vegetables before throwing them into the pot of water. She remembered, suddenly, a hand taking hold of a wrist, and the stranglehold relaxing. Her saviour. This sour, bitter woman who was her mother and her saviour.

She did not speak a word. There was nothing she wanted from this house. She did not blame these people for a crime against her that she could barely remember, she felt no anger. They were not her people. There was only disgust at the smallness of their souls, and contempt for their God, who accepted their worship. A small God for small people who never looked up from the dirt at their feet; who never turned their sight inwards or wondered at anything. For such people, religion was no more than a way of preventing thought. If these were good people, then she wanted nothing of goodness. The world she saw about her had turned everything on its head. It was darkness and blackness. The light must be elsewhere.

She knew she could punish them. She could take Christian with her. He would go with her, given the choice, and they would lose what she had lost. But she loved Christian, and she had no idea what lay ahead. The priest said isolation, danger. The road to the light must be a dangerous one; why else was it avoided? She knew she must leave Christian behind, for she had to leave everything behind. And it had been made easy for her by the people who called themselves her parents, and the rest of the town who had been there. She had left everything behind long ago. Now there would be no difficulty. Christian must stay. Whatever she felt for him, he was not her people, either. He would have to find his own way.

Esther returned to Father Anselm knowing that her old life was over and wondering what that might mean. There was a quality of dream about her walk from her house to the church. If she asked herself why she should trust the priest who was responsible for her condition, she didn't find an exact answer, other than why not. No one had turned out to be what they seemed. Her parents were not only not her parents, but the murderers of her real family. She herself was something quite different from what she had thought. It was one thing to feel strange, quite another to discover that you were strange. What grounds were there for trusting or not trusting anyone?

As to the new life she walked towards, isolated, alone, at risk from the world, she couldn't imagine what the reality would be, but isolated was what she had always been, so why not make it real? What was to happen, would happen. She was no longer part of any community. The people she had grown up with were foreigners – or she was. The Church that structured, and made life meaningful was a sham and a lie, and there was no room in the world for those who saw this. And her origins? What did she know about Jews? Who were they? What did they believe? She had never heard anyone talk about Jews (though now she understood the town's silence on the subject), but she was imbued with the knowledge that they were dark and different. And, different and dark as she might be, she had never thought of herself as one of *them*, any kind of them, and Jews were hardly to be thought of at all. Jews were dangerous, vile, Christ killers – she knew that much, and now she knew she was one. The route back to life could not be as a Jew. In any case, there were none. Not that she knew of. Not hereabouts.

But it turned out that isolation was not to mean that Esther would be entirely alone. Father Anselm watched her solemnly as she entered the church, and led her into his room. They sat at the wooden table where he had taught her to read and where the burnt-out candle of the night before and a manuscript lay.

'You are sure?' he asked her.

'That I want to leave them? Yes.'

'About the Church, about God? That is the real break you have to decide about.'

'They have lied to me. Goodness is compliance. Wherever the Lord is, it is not with them. I want to find the truth, what is real.'

Esther looked sure and certain. She sat straight-backed, her face set with decision. The child, the girl who did the family chores, had vanished. Something new had entered her and shone from her eyes. A purpose, perhaps.

Having seen this, Father Anselm returned his gaze to beyond her left shoulder.

'There are others. You are not entirely alone. Some of them still live within the community – secretly, not active, but helping those who are. The others – there are not many – live beyond the boundaries of the town.'

'In the woods?'

'Yes. Those of us who remain on the inside help them with food and clothing. We do what we can. You must join them. I will lead you to them when it gets dark. Are you afraid?'

'Yes. But also excited. Who are they? What do they do?'

'They try to live a life that is truly holy, in accordance with the knowledge in their hearts. You will find that the road to the true Church and the true divinity is very different from what you have learned.'

'From what you have taught me . . .'

Esther looked at him curiously.

'It is necessary. I would give anything to live with them, but my position as a priest is much more useful. I hear confessions, I learn the secrets of people's hearts. I know the thinking of the Church. I am an agent of truth. There are sacrifices to be made. Trust me. I will serve you.'

'Why do you speak to me like that? Why should *you* serve *me*?'

'Because you are holy. Your question and your refusal to give it up are signs of that. In the early days of the Church, before it was overcome by the agents of the Devil, there were men and women who *knew*, who were touched by the truth. Chosen to lead others towards it. And so it is with you. It's a hard road, Esther. Your beginnings set you on that path, perhaps. My error in leading the flagellants was, perhaps, ordained too. How are we to know? I am guilty of a great crime, and yet, here you are, saved, and it is my privilege to serve you.'

'But I know so little. I'm frightened. I don't think I want to lead anyone anywhere. I don't want a servant. I want . . .'

'You must release yourself from everything you have known,

176

from everything you have been told. I believed once that one had to punish the flesh, to scourge it, in order to make it obey the spirit. There was a grain of truth in my belief. The flesh is the substance of the Devil, yet mistreating it is only to pay homage to its power. To deny the flesh we must deny its power. Do you understand?'

Esther shook her head.

Father Anselm smiled and placed his hand over hers on the table. She looked down at it, and a chill ran through her when she remembered the first time she saw it, holding a letter that promised salvation for some.

'You will, my child. You will.'

He led her through the darkness, holding his skirts high so that he could step carefully through the undergrowth. Their destination was a hut in a clearing, deep in the woods, that had served once as a temporary home for charcoal burners. She followed him as if she were a sheep, being led but without any sense of a destination. Inside she felt empty, as if leaving everything she knew for everything she didn't know had hollowed her. There was no fear, no excitement, only one step and then the next. She might have been going to her execution or her baptism; neither carried more weight with her. The dream she had entered as she walked away from her old home had settled fully on her. Esther was a sleepwalker without a past or a future: someone who had been divested of everything, so that now nothing held any danger.

22

ESTHER'S HEAD SPUN names like a tombola. Elizabeth, Esther, Katya. Elizabeth, Esther. Round and round and senseless. But, senseless as it might be, her heart was pounding, and, without coming fully awake, she longed to scream out a warning: Danger, take care. Doom and death seeped through her bloodstream. Betrayal and defeat of something . . . that deserved better. She heard the sound of her own voice calling to – Esther. Yes, *Esther*, though not Esther herself.

23

THE HUT IN the clearing was dark and empty. The priest lit the tallow candle he had brought with him. Its dim radiance seemed to increase the shadows rather than bring light. There was a small table and two chairs in the centre of the room, and a straw mattress in one corner.

'Where are they?' Esther asked in a low voice, as if she were afraid of disturbing something that lurked in the shadows.

'Someone will be here soon enough. There are hiding places all over the woods.'

'Will I have to wait here alone until someone comes? How will they know who I am? How will I know them?'

'Someone will come before the night is out. I sent a message while you went home. I'll wait here with you, I don't have to be back until the morning. You must trust me, Esther.'

The oddness of the situation, that she should be spending a night alone in the woods with a priest, struck Esther only as something else that she had caused to happen with her question. Everything was too extraordinary to find any one thing exceptional.

Father Anselm moved a wooden chair out from the table and indicated that Esther should sit.

'Who are they, the others who live in the woods?' she asked him.

The priest stood behind her and lifted her cloak from her shoulders.

'Do you remember Joseph?' he asked her softly.

'The son of the weaver? He disappeared a year ago with Annette. They ran away together.'

'Yes, but not in the way you imagined. They live here in the

179

woods. And Stefan, who everyone thought had drowned in the river.'

'You said a mass for him.'

'Yes.'

The priest was still standing behind her chair. Esther had turned to look up at him when he spoke the familiar names. His fingertips rested lightly on her shoulders, as if they were gently keeping her in place. She could not remember if they had been there since he took off her cloak, or whether he had placed them on her while he was speaking. She stared down at them. The thin, delicate fingers looked as if they were at rest on an instrument he was about to play.

Uncertainty crossed her face. No man, no priest, should be so close. She could feel the heat of his body along her spine.

'My child,' he said, his voice as dark and hushed as the shadows at the edges of the room. He tightened his grip on her shoulders.

'What . . . ? Please . . .' Alarm took over her features and she pulled away. The priest's fingers pressed more firmly against her flesh and held her in place.

'We must talk about the true religion,' he whispered in a tone that seemed to distort the meaning of his words, though Esther could not say exactly how. He kept one hand on her and reached around her with the other for the empty chair. He sat facing her, so that they were only inches apart. The heels of his hands now lay on the edge of his knees, so that the long fingers fell indolently in the space between the two of them.

'Everything you have been taught has been lies. You were right when you said that God was not concerned about our daily lives. God is concerned with nothing of the flesh. He does not watch us. He does not punish us. What is there to punish? The sins of the flesh are nothing more than the behaviour of the flesh. What pitiful kind of God would concern himself with a hand placed on top of another? You must learn to lose your fear of everything you have been taught is fearful, my child. You must reject the sins of the Church of the Sinful. They are there to hold you in thrall.'

Father Anselm's fingers straightened, and lifted to form a

bridge between their knees. Esther tensed, and pulled back slightly at their touch.

'No, my child. You must not fear the touch of others. To do so is to continue in error. It is a risk to your immortal soul. You must fight the lies you have been told, and throw off the obsession with the flesh. You must give yourself freely and show that you are released from the flesh. That it is nothing. Mere substance. Then we can free the spirit to soar to the heights of the seraphim and beyond.'

Esther was confused. This was a priest and an educated man. They were the only two in the town who could read. Who was she to make judgements? She understood what he said, and yet her flesh recoiled at his touch. She must free herself from the results of the lies she had been told. Was that the cause of her fearful heart? And yet there *was* fear and distaste. Did she feel these things really? Or were they no more than a sign of the meanness of her spirit?

Esther, who had been Elizabeth, was full of questions. They tumbled around inside her head like too many clubs in the hands of a novice juggler. But the answers did not come. Questions and no answers. Nothing but doubt and uncertainty.

And, as if the priest saw deep into her mind, he said, 'You will be beset with doubts, Esther, my child. Uncertainty is now your condition. That is the pain you must experience. The price. The cost of freedom. You must trust me. I am here to help you and guide you. That is my true calling.'

Still confused, Esther said, 'There are so many changes. I am afraid. I'm not very brave.'

'Trust me,' the priest told her again.

Esther cried out, 'No!' when Father Anselm reached towards the fastening at the neck of her blouse.

'Shh,' he said softly to her. 'You must be brave. You must be free and brave. His will be done.'

He pulled the drawstring and slid her blouse down over her shoulders. Esther stayed motionless, barely breathing, but a tremor behind her ribcage rocked her body so that she visibly quivered.

'Shh . . . shh . . .' Father Anselm soothed. 'Concentrate on the truth. Remember the questions in your mind.'

She told herself that fear was cowardice, disgust, small-mindedness, her horror and shame at her exposed breasts nothing more than the distortion of truth that her doubts had uncovered. She fought with herself against herself: Esther against Elizabeth, the doubter the adversary of the mindless drudge. She knew the questions she had asked were right, and, being right, she could find no logic to counter Father Anselm's teaching. Her feeling of horror was well explained by the priest, who was, moreover, her protector; the friend who would help to save her from the stake.

Esther bit down on her lip until she tasted blood at the touch of the priest's hand on her breasts, first one, then the other, the pallid fingertips exploring their texture, and savouring the long nipples. When he put his lips against them and drew them into his mouth, she thought she saw the smile again as she cried out in shock at what he was doing to her.

Everything about her pleased the priest. The quivering of her flesh under his hands and mouth; the tang of blood as he pushed his tongue past her gritted teeth; the small cries that were forced from her in spite of her attempts to be silent and allow what must happen to happen. Her willingness would have halved his pleasure, which was now complete, after all his years of watching her dark, alien beauty from beneath his heavy eyelids. He had savoured this moment in nights of candlelit reverie, his reward for living so many years in a God-forsaken hole, ministering to ignorant pigs of peasants, who could never in their wildest dreams imagine the quality of his breeding and his mind. Now he was repaid, and with the Jewess who fate had saved for his pleasure. How he smiled to himself. How much he had to smile about. They had reprimanded him, and sent him to this pisshole – but he was not to be crossed. When he heard the sound of the cracked bell for the second time – the time after he had led the flagellants into the town – when they sent him back to minister (as a penance to those he had damaged, they said) he had sworn by his sinking heart that he would triumph against them all: the dullard peasants, the feeble apology for a Church, the devil Jews. Many times over he had triumphed – quietly – over all of them. And now, again, here was another sweet victory to savour with his mouth and hands and heart. And there would be more to come.

He ejaculated almost as soon as he entered her, pushing her virginity aside with the power of the secret warrior that he was. Esther screamed in pain as she was torn, and the sound triggered the spasms that pushed him deeper and deeper inside her, and finally left him empty.

Father Anselm stood up and let the skirt of his habit fall into place. He stood over Esther, watching her body convulse with pain and shame, her hands trying to cover her face and the exposed place between her legs; trying to conceal the double, confusing shame of tears and nakedness.

'So now you are baptised in the true religion, my little heretic.'

.The priest's voice had an edge now, something new and sharp, to Esther's ears. But she was not sure of anything any more. Was she free or was this something else? Had the tone of Father Anselm's voice really changed from concern to glee? She didn't know. She felt that nothing she thought or knew could be right. In her abdomen, the pain radiated; in her mind, there was confusion. Both were terrible, and yet, being in pain and uncertain was, perhaps, not worse than some lurking thought that she pushed firmly down to a dark place where no light would shine on it. What could she do but trust the priest? If she didn't, what was there? She had left all protection behind, and she had done so because of her own belief that things were not as they appeared. That still seemed true. The questions remained, through the pain and the fear, so what else was there to do but listen to someone who knew better than she possibly could?

Father Anselm was right, she supposed. Her shame was shameful; her disgust was nothing more than her fear of transgressing what she knew to be lies.

She sat up, wincing at the stabbing pain between her legs.

'Put your clothes on,' the priest barked at her.

'I'm sorry,' Esther said, apologising for her foolish tears and her resistance, though still there was something like the taste of bile in her mouth.

'Put your clothes on,' Father Anselm repeated in the same tone.

She pulled on her blouse and tightened the drawstring. It was strange, but she felt all the more exposed.

'I'm leaving now,' the priest told her casually.

'But you said you would wait until someone came.'

'You have the candle. What have you got to fear from being alone?'

'But what if no one comes? What will I do?'

A great, dark fear began to fill her.

'If you are not brave enough to spend a few hours on your own, how do you think you will fare at the life of a heretic?' There was a sneer in his voice. 'Someone will come, I told you that. Sooner or later, they'll come. In the mean time, I have work to do. Do you think you're the only person who needs my attention? Wait here, and do not be a foolish child. Or perhaps you would rather return home?'

'Someone will come here, then?' Esther asked tremulously. Once again, part of her felt she had failed. It took little courage to be alone in the woods at night, compared with spending the rest of your life as an outcast. And she had been selfish. Father Anselm was a busy man, risking his life for others.

'I'm sorry,' she apologised again. 'But . . .' Another look of doubt came into her eyes, and fear along with it.

'What is it now?' The priest asked impatiently.

'Will they expect me to do . . . what you did?'

A harsh sound that was almost a laugh came from the priest's throat.

'So you are still concerned only with your flesh? What if they do? What difference does it make? You sin against the orthodox Church, and then you sin against the true one. Is sinning all you can do? Do you only have a talent for that, and no ability at all for sincere learning?

Esther stared at him, her mind whirling again with the difference between what he said and what she felt. The priest stared hard at her.

'Do you think what we did was wrong?'

Esther hesitated.

'You used to tell us it was.'

'I spoke to you then as a priest, as a man of the Church. I spoke of the morality that belongs to the Antichrist that we both, in reality, reject.'

'But you sounded so sure. That to let . . . to let a man touch you before he was your husband was . . .'

Father Anselm sat down heavily at the table and looked contemptuously at Esther on the mattress.

'You are a foolish girl. How can I be of help to the true believers if I do not stay visibly within the precepts of the Church? The Church says that the flesh is sinful; yet it elevates the body by making its desires of supreme importance. If you need to shit, you shit. Do you understand? Otherwise, evacuating the bowels would be all anyone was concerned about. They would think of nothing else but how and when and in what conditions their shits were performed. You must follow the demands of the body, that is the true attitude to the flesh. Do what you need to do and think no more about it. You feel good after you shit; you feel good after you fuck. The pleasure is in the release from need. It's done with, now we can think of more important things. So long as there is pleasure, so the true believers say, there is no sin. Take what pleasure you require, give what pleasure is required. Nothing could be more simple.'

Esther listened in silence, the tears drying on her cheeks. But there had been no pleasure for her. She did not know if Father Anselm had felt pleasure, he did not appear to, but she supposed he must have. But if she did not, then it was a sin after all. She wondered if she should say so, but decided to stay silent. Father Anselm had told her that the route she was taking was painful and difficult. She had not understood that inner turmoil was part of the price to be paid.

'My child, you must learn sincerity,' Father Anselm said, his voice once again that of a priest, and his eyes hooded. 'You must beg forgiveness.'

'Who from?' Esther asked, as Elizabeth was submerged once more. 'God can't forgive me because he is not here with us. Who can I pray to? Where am I to look for the truth?'

'You must listen to me. I am your teacher, and your servant. I offer you the way to the truth. If you reject it, you are lost. You must listen to what I tell you and obey me. You have not yet come far enough to be entrusted with the great secrets. You have much to learn. Now, be silent. Wait in the candlelight and trust me when I tell you that someone will come for you. You will not have to wait very long, I promise you.'

He got up and walked across the room and, bending

down, took Esther's face between his bony hands. His mouth
descended towards hers and pressed down on her lips. His
tongue entered her like a sharp reminder of what he had done
to her earlier. Esther felt him seem to suck the life from her
lungs, and take her saliva greedily as if it were food in time
of famine. She pulled away a little, but his hands clasped her
jaws firmly and kept her close to him.

'What will it be like to live as a heretic?' she asked when the
priest finally released her from his grip.

'It will be like it is for every true believer in the true Church.
You will feel the fire of truth burn within you. You and your
kind will be consumed in a blaze of truth.'

The priest stretched his mouth again into the semblance
of a smile and, without another word, left Esther alone in
the hut.

The candle was half gone. It would not last the night through,
but Esther waited on the straw mattress, hoping that her
new friends would come for her before the candle sputtered
and died.

The life she imagined ahead of her was one of reversal. What
she knew would be turned on its head. She, who was so very
much what she had not known herself to be (a victim of belief;
a child of what she had learned to think of as the Antichrist),
would have to lose all her belief in order to find out what she
wanted to know. For a moment, sitting in the half-light on the
straw mattress, she forgot what it was she wanted to know. The
question escaped her, though she knew there was a question.
Perhaps just knowing that was enough. But it came back to her
– *What for? That* question. Then, it made no sense. While she
was within the society that forbade the question, it was the only
one to ask. But now, outside the rule and law of God and man,
the question lost all sense. *What for?* belonged to the world that
God had made. It seemed possible, suddenly, in the corners
of Esther's mind, that it was all *for* nothing. Accident hovered
dangerously in her mind as a possible explanation. No God,
no intention. Her escape, her very existence, the existence of
the world itself – all nothing but accident. But this answer was
more impossible than the original question. She may have left
the world she knew, and rejected its teachings, but she was
and would always be of it, even if that meant nothing more

than that she was against it. *What for?* was the inconceivable question; *accident* was the inconceivable answer. They did not belong to the times. They were not for now.

She longed for the company of the others who lived in the woods, not only because the candle was burning dangerously low and she was alone, but also because she wanted the company of people who would help her to think the way she needed to. She wanted to be taught. The priest had taught her to read and so the marks that had meant nothing had been given order and meaning. This was what teaching was for, and she knew her disordered attempts at thought would rearrange themselves into sense once those who knew passed on their learning.

She wanted, also, to know that there were others. Not that she disbelieved the priest, but, even so, she feared with part of herself that she was utterly alone in the world, and that the woods were inhabited only by shadows.

A moment later she caught herself in prayer.

'In the name of the Father, Son and Holy Ghost . . .'

She stopped herself, but felt bereft. There was nothing any more to pray to. There was only silence and black night.

Esther lay back on the straw mattress and closed her eyes. It didn't seem to her that she slept, but there was someone else: a woman who wept and called out a warning. The voice trembled with concern and fear. *Be careful. There is awful danger but I don't know how to help you, or what to do. They will hurt you.*

The meaning seemed to come almost without words, but Esther recognised a hopelessness that matched her own sudden feeling of desolation. In her sleep, if that is what it was, she wept too, for the terror of the other voice, and for her own fear.

'Help me. Help me,' she called to the voice inside her head, and, after a moment, the other one answered in a new tone, almost a gasp of astonishment – of discovery.

I know you, the voice whispered. *We are family. You are what I never had but also lost. Stay with me. Stay close. Don't let them hurt you.*

Esther listened to the voice that was not her own, that came from a place far away, in sleep and not sleep, and heard that it was her own voice too. It seemed to echo back and forth between them: her voice, other voice, until it hovered in a space that belonged to both.

Take care, the voices said, each to the other. *We need us. We have found us*.

Esther's eyes opened in alarm. They responded to something that she could not yet sense with her waking self. The candle had burned itself out, but a cold light broke through the gaps in the shuttered window, giving the hut an eerie glow. It was barely morning. Esther listened, but could not catch what her ears were straining to hear. There seemed to be only the sound of life waking in the woods. Perhaps that was what had woken her. She remembered the voice in her dream and lay still for a moment, wondering about it, until she realised that she was not at home, that dawn had broken, but no one had come.

Then the sound of nature, and the stillness of her half-perceived fear was shattered.

The door flew open, crashing back against the wall of the hut, and men appeared, silhouetted in the frame of sudden light. Their sound seemed to come a moment after Esther saw them, and she watched their mouths opening and shutting. She couldn't move, but lay still, wondering that her friends should appear so suddenly, and with such violence. Perhaps, she thought, in a time that had slowed everything so that it all appeared to be happening under water, perhaps, she thought, they are testing me. She tried to smile a welcome, to show them that she knew them and was one of them. And then she realised that Joseph and Stefan were not among the faces in the doorway. Time reasserted its normal speed and brought sound to her ears. She heard the men shout to each other.

'There! Take her! We've got the heretic Jewess! Bind the hands of the she-devil! Tie her down.'

She saw confusion and fear, mixed with malevolence. One of the men was dressed in ecclesiastical clothes and smiled victory to himself; the other three, rough men, looked fearfully at her. They snatched her up from the mattress and tied rope around her wrists so tightly that the pain overcame the beating of her heart. Then they pushed her through the door, one man with his palm hard against her back, another dragging her by her upper arm, so that she stumbled, pushed and pulled in the direction of a cart that waited in the clearing.

A voice in her head screamed panic.

Take care! Take care! Oh, please, please, let her go. Esther . . . Esther . . . the voice called, weeping with the terrible loss of something newly found. And then there was another voice, a soothing incantation.

Shema, ysrael, Adonay Elohaynu Adonay echad . . .

The voice stayed with her, in the background, all through the next weeks. When she was alone in the dark, the prayer reverberated round her head loudly enough to drown out her terrors. When she sat in the dazzlingly bright room, where solemn-faced men fired questions at her, the voice half sang the prayer at her, softly, like a lullaby to soothe her panic. Beneath the *Shema*, she thought sometimes that she heard the sound of sobbing, like a background throb that beat in time with her heart and the tempo of the prayer. She welcomed both the sounds and hugged them to her, comforted that she was not alone. There were times, when the men with cruel mouths spoke of the fire, and the pain it would bring, when the sounds in her head – the prayer and the weeping – seemed to surround her, as if arms held her, protecting her from the horror of what was to come.

She did not have to be brave; she had only to exist in time. It was something she had done all her life. She did not imagine a future that was to be cruelly cut off; she saw only now, and, beyond that, a misty veil, not dark and fearful like the night alone in the woods, but merely what could not be known. There was pain when they beat her and tried to extract their truth from her screaming nerve-endings, but not for long. Just a searing moment, and then nothing more than numbness as the prayer increased in volume.

They had taken her to the city, where she had never dreamed of going. The only familiar face she saw in the next two weeks was that of Father Anselm, who arrived one day to give evidence against her. He came into the room and directed a glance, as ever, at her left shoulder, while the familiar smile played on his curled lips. He told them all they wanted to know.

She had come to him, he said, his head lowered with reverence and humility, with questions that only the Devil could have put into her mind. He warned her, no, begged her, to confess and throw off her error. He fought with the Devil in her to bring her back from the brink of mortal sin, back from the path of the Antichrist. But, finally, he had known it was hopeless. She was a Jewess, after all, daughter of swine. How could baptism with holy water change the tainted blood? All the blood of Christ had not saved the Jews, and could not turn a Devil into a saint. She was evidently a sorceress. Her adopted parents, who, in their innocent goodness, had saved her, had told him of milk turning sour, of nights when she was seen to rise from her bed and walk backwards about the room. They were simple folk, and in great fear of her. She tried to steal the mind of their son, a mere child, with tales of wandering souls, and the secret places of the earth where the Devil reigned. At night, the child screamed in fear at the stories she told him; by day, he was afraid to walk on God's good earth. All these things were told to him by her distraught benefactors. And Father Anselm himself had had a terrible proof of the succubus she was. She had come to him that night, after she told him about her questions (though he saw now that she had been trying to tempt him with them). When she failed to jar his faith she had returned in fleshy form, devil-naked, her breasts and private place bared and wanton. She offered her body, clawing at his own, tearing at his priestly habit, a harlot of the Devil, sent on a mission of defilement.

Then, Father Anselm knew, there was nothing he could do. She could not be saved, and it was his duty to God and man to send a message to the Inquisitor. When he had pushed her out of the church, he followed her and saw her, in the hut, behaving so foully that he could not bring himself to describe it to the pious members of the Inquisition. The daughter of the Devil was a creature without a soul, less than an animal, who had been unwittingly harboured in their midst.

The men nodded gravely at the priest's evidence. He had proved his piety before, bringing others of the town to their attention, so that heresy and witchcraft could be stamped out as soon as it raised its head within God's community. He was a good man, a wise but humble priest who ministered to those who were his inferiors in every way. He cherished the well-being of his Church and his flock. They thanked him solemnly.

Later, in a corridor, it was suggested by someone in purple that his efforts over the years had not gone unnoticed. He might hope for greater responsibility and a chance to serve his Church in a higher capacity.

Father Anselm smiled quietly to himself on the journey back to his own church. He was a man alone, above them all. He had them all at his mercy. He played with them like toys. The thought of his new victory against *them*, all of *them*, whirled around his head like a tempest, so fast, so violently that it was almost indistinguishable from pain. He was a superior man in a pitiful world. He stood out, above them all: a man alone.

24

THE SOUND OF howling woke Esther. It was not her own, though the sense of loss and the anguished weight inside her made her think, at first, that it was. She knew it was a real sound in the waking world when she felt her lips pressed hard enough against each other to prevent any howling of her own. She turned her head to her right and saw the telephone receiver lying on the floor next to her. She thought it funny that someone should have made the disconnected signal sound so exactly like the pain she felt inside. It was the cry of helplessness, of something wrong and nothing to be done about it. It wailed: Do something, I can't do anything myself except howl for your attention to my trouble. Like a baby; like herself.

She reached out and lifted the receiver without getting up from the floor, and pressed the button. It purred again, and she dialled Ben's number. Who else was there? She had to have someone. She had told Ben to fuck off. She had told herself she didn't like him, but now she had a terrible need, and *someone* had to fill it. She had drowned the defeat of asking Ben for help in the noise of the tempest she had made.

Ben, of course, was used to being told to fuck off, it was part of the territory of any psychotherapist. He hadn't taken it seriously then, and he didn't remind Esther about it now. He had guessed that she would crack, and that she would need him. He had been right; well, he usually was. He was happy to take control of things.

Esther was happy to have Ben take control. Someone had to; she seemed to have stopped working.

'Ben, I can't move,' she croaked into the phone. 'They've

found Katya . . . but I can't . . . I don't seem to be able to . . .'

She was greatly relieved to hear his competent tone interrupt the sentence she couldn't complete. She listened carefully, and answered his simple questions like a child giving evidence about a crime she didn't understand.

'I'm on the floor . . . I made a terrible mess in here.

'Rob can't come, and something awful's happened to Esther. They've taken her. She was all I had.

'I can't move.

'Yes, I'm sure. Nothing moves. I don't know what to do . . . Ben, something's got to be done . . . about . . . everything. About Katya . . . and Esther . . . and I can't get off the floor. Ben?'

Ben arrived a few moments later and took in Esther lying curled up on the floor in the centre of the storm damage. He put the receiver she had dropped back on to the phone, and guided Esther through the wreckage towards her bedroom. When she was in bed, Ben sat beside her, and spoke to her in a clear and careful tone.

'Esther, listen to me.'

He waited until she looked in his direction. Her lips were pursed, her brows furrowed with the attempt not to cry. She was making an effort to help Ben help her.

'I'm going to pick up Katya, then I'm going to take her to Anderson House – remember the place I told you about? She'll be well looked after there, and then I'll come back and we'll have a talk about you. Do you understand?'

She did understand, but, even if she hadn't, the gentle authority in Ben's voice would have been enough to make her hand herself and her daughter over to Ben's care. She nodded, and a tear slipped down one cheek.

'I'm sorry,' she whispered, perhaps for the escaped tear, perhaps for her inability to take charge, perhaps for having told him to fuck off. It didn't matter.

'It's all right,' Ben said, stroking her forehead. 'I'll be back soon, and we'll talk about what's going on with you. Don't worry. Just rest a little, and I'll sort things out.'

'But . . . Katya . . . ?' Esther asked feebly.

'It's all right, leave it to me. I'll take care of everything. Trust me.'

For a little while, Esther worried about the burden she was placing on Ben. He had his own family, and his work, a wife, children and patients who needed his attention. She felt bad about demanding that he drop everything else and sort out her life. But she didn't feel so bad that it overcame her relief that he was going to take care of things. Ben was prepared to put his other commitments aside because she needed him, now, urgently. She had misjudged him. She had almost rejected the one person who was really there for her, who cared enough to help.

Esther let the muscles in her neck relax and sank her head gratefully into the pillow. She allowed her mind to go blank. Ben would organise everything. He would reorder the mess, and straighten things out so that she would be able to think properly again.

It was already dark when Esther's absent mind was jerked back into herself by Ben's return. He had turned on the light beside the bed. His face loomed over her and he held her hand in his, squeezing it to gain her attention.

'Esther? It's me, Ben. Esther?'

She smiled up at him, remembering. Gratitude and apology rushed out of her, stumbling over each other to make themselves heard.

'I'm sorry, Ben. I just couldn't cope. I should have listened to you . . . before. I shouldn't have let them put her in the hospital. I'm sorry I behaved . . . the way I did. Thanks . . .'

Ben shook his head, waving the apology away and telling her not to think about it.

'Is it all right? Is Katya . . . OK? How is she?'

'There's nothing for you to worry about. Everything's fine. She's being taken care of. We'll talk about it in the morning.'

'But I should speak to her.'

Ben shook his head again.

'Not now. She's exhausted. Let her sleep. You both need to rest.'

He bent down and kissed Esther on the mouth, a light brush of tender concern that deepened imperceptibly, until it was something else. Ben pulled back the duvet, increasing the pressure on her mouth while he reached for her breast. Esther noticed that she was naked. Ben must have undressed her when he put her to bed. She didn't move either to touch him or avoid his touch. She held still, not wanting sex but unable to reject Ben, who had helped her, and who she had misjudged before. Her distaste for a physical connection with him seemed surly after what he had done for her. They had been lovers, she had wanted him as much as he had wanted her, and if she didn't want him now, she told herself, as she thought Ben would have told her, it was no more than a neurotic reaction, a rejection of her own feelings.

Ben confirmed her thoughts. He lifted his head and looked at her.

'What's the matter? Don't hold back. Don't stop yourself feeling.'

She didn't feel as if she were holding back. She was drained. The sense she had had when she collapsed, that everything was too much, had begun to return. Sex seemed a very minor activity. An irrelevance. She was not interested in it.

'I don't feel . . .' she tried.

'You do,' Ben interrupted, slipping his hand between her legs. 'You won't let yourself. You're punishing yourself, denying your needs.'

His fingers worked away at her vulva as he spoke, intent on proving her need, rejecting her denial.

She tried to pull herself back into physicality, towards desire, as Ben undressed and slipped into bed beside her. She tried to feel pleasure when his hands ran over her body, stroking and coaxing her. Her mind would not join in. It remained separate, so that she seemed to watch the pair of them on the bed, as if reflected from a mirror on the ceiling. She gave up and let her body get on with it alone. It knew what to do, and responded well enough to convince Ben that she was there and part of the proceedings. She shut her eyes and stopped looking at what was happening on the bed, letting her mind wander back into the blankness it had discovered in Ben's absence.

Esther managed to stop herself uttering a polite thank you when Ben had finished. She realised only just in time that it would be an inappropriate response. After what she thought the right amount of time she lifted her head and looked at him.

'Ben?'

'All right?' Ben murmured.

'Yes, I'm fine now. Tell me about Katya.'

'She's all right.'

Esther looked perplexed.

'What do you mean, "all right"?'

'She's being looked after. She's all right. You mustn't worry.'

'But I should see her. We have to decide what to do. Is she going to stay at that place – Anderson House?'

Ben grunted and turned his back to Esther. She listened to his regular breathing for a moment, and wondered why she didn't feel as protected as she had earlier. The phone rang, but Ben didn't stir at the sound of it. Esther reached across him and lifted the receiver.

'Mrs Adams? Is that Katya's mother?'

The voice was young and urgent.

'My name's Sam. Did he tell you about me? I'm a friend of Katya's. She's been with me for the last week. Please, Mrs Adams, you've got to get her out of there. She mustn't stay in the hospital.

Esther was mystified.

'What? I don't understand. Katya's at Anderson House. Who are you?'

'No, she isn't, she's in a psychiatric unit at St Pancras. I got in to see her. They wouldn't let me in, but I walked in and found her. They're drugging her silly. They've got her on something so strong she can't speak properly. She's terrified. Please, you've got to get her out of there. You don't have to worry about it, I'll take care of her. I'll look after her.'

Esther still could not make sense of what was being said. She shook her head firmly.

'She can't be in hospital. She's at the place Ben took her to. They don't use drugs. That's the whole point. They're looking after her, letting her rest. They don't believe in using drugs . . .'

'Is Ben Mr Redfern? The man who picked her up from the police station?'

Esther nodded, glancing down at Ben asleep beside her. Sam took her silence as confirmation.

'I tried to stay with her. He – Mr Redfern – bailed me out and gave me ten quid. He told me to go away. But I wouldn't. I wanted to know what was going to happen to Katya. So he let me go with them in the car to that place, that Anderson House. Then he told me to go away again. But Katya didn't want me to. She kept calling out to me not to go, so he let me stay, because she was getting so upset. I waited in a room downstairs, it must have been two or three hours – and then an ambulance arrived and they took Katya away. She was fighting them and screaming to be left alone, and I heard Mr Redfern tell the ambulance men to take her to St Pancras, that the duty psychiatrist was waiting to admit her.'

Sam retold his story as if recounting a nightmare, reconstructing it but barely believing the story he had to tell. He remembered his intention.

'Please, get her out of there, Mrs Adams. I'm sure she'll be all right with me. Please. You mustn't let them hurt her.'

Esther wasn't listening. She held the receiver with one hand, and shook Ben awake with the other. He opened his eyes reluctantly, unwilling to emerge from the comfort of his sleep.

'Where's Katya? Where is she?' Esther demanded, still shaking his shoulder as she spoke.

'I told you, she's all right,' Ben said sleepily, irritated at having to give reassurance when what he wanted was to rest. 'Don't worry.'

'Is she in a psychiatric hospital? Is it true? Did you have her taken away?' Esther's eyes were wide with disbelief and barely controlled panic. She wanted Ben to tell her this was nonsense, that the boy on the phone was . . . was what? She believed the boy. She knew he spoke the truth. Still, she wanted Ben to tell her he had got it wrong. That he had misunderstood.

Ben came to abruptly. He noticed the telephone cord that ran across his chest as he turned to face Esther. He saw her clutching the phone, and the sound of someone trying to get her attention. And he saw the way she looked at him. He sat up and rubbed his face with his hands to wake himself up, and to give him a moment to think.

'It was for her own good. She was out of control,' Ben began, putting on his professional voice of reason, to undercut Esther's demanding horrified tone. He put his hand firmly over hers, still clutching and shaking him by the shoulder as if she were trying to shake the truth out of him, and lifted it off him. She shook his hand away and looked at him for a long, silent moment. Then she took in Sam's voice, calling her name. She spoke into the mouthpiece.

'Sam, did you say your name was?'

She gave him her address and asked him to come round. Then she let go of the phone. It fell on the bed. Ben picked it up and put it back on the hook. He pushed back the cover and got up. While he put his clothes on, he explained what had happened with Katya.

Esther only heard certain words and phrases: *hysterical; self-destructive; dangerous to herself; religious mania.* She tried to listen carefully, but was distracted by the look on Ben's face. It was set and determined, like a child caught out in a lie and refusing to acknowledge it.

'I didn't realise she was so ill,' she heard him say and then Esther came to.

'But you kept telling me that I should take her out of the hospital.'

'I was mistaken. When I saw her – I spent two hours with her – she wouldn't listen. She was deluded and screaming about being evil and contaminated. She was hurling herself around the room, beating her head against the walls and door. She would have done herself serious damage if I hadn't stopped her.'

'How?' Esther demanded.

'How what?'

'How did you stop her?'

Ben finished dressing.

'I gave her an injection.'

'What of?'

'Largactyl,' Ben said, straightening his tie.

'But you don't believe in drugs.'

Esther's face was still disbelieving.

'No, but when a patient is out of control – can't be reached . . .'

'You drug them and then send them to the local loony bin.'

'Don't be silly. Psychiatry is a practical business. You're using emotive words. Katya is very ill.'

'I know. You kept telling me that she needed psychotherapy, that she mustn't be drugged, that we had to get to the root of the family trouble. You kept saying that, and getting into bed with me. And you got into bed with me again, today, after you sent Katya to the bin.'

'Don't be ridiculous. I told you, what we do together is separate. Esther, you are not yourself. You had an hysterical outburst this afternoon. I had to put you to bed . . .'

'And then get in it with me?'

'Stop it. I'm doing what's best for Katya. She can't be treated by talking until she's amenable. She's got to cool out first.'

'You mean she's got to come round to your way of thinking?'

'If you like. You want her to think like you do, don't you? You were the one who said she was mad.'

'But you were the doctor, you were supposed to know what you were talking about. Until it came to doing something. I just let you have charge. You must be right, I am mad.'

'I'll call later, when you've calmed down. We can talk about your daughter's treatment then.' He turned, then stopped and looked at Esther sitting up naked in the bed. 'Shall I leave you a couple of pills? I think you should take something, you're overwrought.'

He shrugged when Esther didn't respond and made to leave.

'Ben,' she called to him as he opened the door. He stopped and turned.

What?'

'Was anything legal done about Katya?'

'She's been admitted as an emergency patient under a section of the Mental Health Act.'

'How?'

Ben looked surprised at the question.

'A letter to the hospital saying she was in need of emergency treatment. The duty psychiatrist confirmed my diagnosis.'

'A letter from you? Signed by you?' Esther asked quietly.

'Of course I signed it.'

Esther looked away from Ben into the distance as if she were retrieving a memory.

'Try and sleep. It'll all make more sense to you when you've rested,' Ben suggested as he left. But Esther continued to stare ahead into blank space, seeming not to have heard him.

Recently she had noticed without noticing a girl in a T-shirt that had written on it, 'LEAVE ME ALONE'. She whispered the slogan like a mantra.

'Leave me alone. Leave me alone. There's nothing I can do. Leave me alone.'

She spoke it aloud – to her daughter, to her dreams, to all the demands that there had ever been that had culminated in her daughter and her dreams.

'Leave me alone.'

By the time Sam arrived, Esther had spun a cocoon around herself that was almost visible. He had the impression that only Esther's surface was functioning. She opened the door to him and stood aside to let him in. They both stood in the hallway in silence. Esther held one arm across her chest, gripping the other above the elbow. Several times, she looked as if she might be about to speak, but didn't. Sam was still wearing his torn white T-shirt and decayed jeans. Finally he spoke.

'She shouldn't be in that place.'

Esther looked up at him, apparently startled.

'She's ill. Ben – Mr Redfern – is a psychotherapist, and he thinks she should be there.'

'I'll take care of her. She won't be any trouble to you.' There was no hint of blame in Sam's voice. 'Shall I make you a cup of tea, or something?'

'Who are you?' Esther asked, moving towards the living-room. Sam followed.

'Sam. A friend of hers. I met her in Soho Square. I've been looking after her.'

'But you must have known she was ill. Why didn't you call?'

'She trusted me. She didn't want to be taken back to the hospital. She needed time.'

'Time for what?'

Sam shrugged.

'Time. You know.'

Esther shook her head.

'I don't know. What did she need time for? To starve herself more? To gouge bigger holes in herself? Don't you think you were being very irresponsible?'

Sam looked around the room. It was warm and friendly. He stared at some photographs of Katya as a child, then at some near by of Esther when she was younger. When he had finished he turned round and looked at Esther.

'I don't know, to tell you the truth. I knew there was a chance . . . a risk . . . but I thought she was asking some interesting questions and if she had time she might get some answers.'

'So you risked her well-being, her life, perhaps, just because you decided she had interesting thoughts?'

Sam looked unapologetic, but thoughtful, as if he were engaged in a serious debate.

'But isn't it the same either way, the risk? I mean, if you let her stay in hospital and they give her drugs and do stuff that she doesn't want, isn't that a risk? She won't be the same person. They want to stop her asking questions.'

'They want to stop her asking questions that she was taking too seriously. She was endangering her life.'

'I know, but it still seems a difficult decision to me. The risk you take because you don't like the way she's thinking, and the risk I take because I do. The only difference is that Katya wanted to take the same risk that I did.'

'But she's not thinking rationally. At some point you have to stop taking her views into account. Supposing she wanted to pour petrol on herself and set light to it?'

Sam thought for a moment.

'Can I make a cup of tea?' he asked.

Esther sat down in an armchair, exhausted by the conversation. Sam went off and bustled about in the kitchen. He came back ten minutes later with a tray and two mugs of tea.

'Here,' he said. 'I put milk in. Is that OK?'

Esther nodded.

'What if she'd died?' Esther asked.

'I don't know. It would have been terrible. It would have been my fault. But what if she died anyway, now, or before?'

Suddenly Esther's face streamed with tears.

'I'm tired of this,' she said, ignoring her wet face. 'I had this debate twenty years ago. Sitting around in rooms talking about individual liberty and the right to . . . the right to, God knows what. But we were just talking then. And we weren't talking about our children. This may be a new conversation for you, but I've done it already.'

Sam looked genuinely interested.

'What conclusion did you come to?'

'None. That's the point. Oh, I suppose we opted for the right to be as mad as a hatter, but we didn't know what we were talking about. We never took the pain into account. Katya's not *thinking*, she's off her head. She's dangerously mad, and someone's got to do something. She's hurting herself, she's suicidal. She thinks she's the Devil and she ought to die. Do I just let her go on thinking that, and being in hell, or do I let her have drugs that take the terrible thoughts away?'

'*Make* her have drugs . . .'

Esther rubbed the tears off her cheeks in an angry gesture.

'Oh, you silly boy.'

Sam winced amiably.

'I know what,' he said brightly. 'Why don't the three of us live here? I'll take care of things, and I'll make sure Katya eats and doesn't do anything silly. We can just see how things go. How's that?'

Esther stared at him. She had stopped crying, almost stopped breathing.

'I'm very good at looking after other people. Really. And you might find it easier if I'm here as well. I'll be useful around the house, and you wouldn't have to worry too much about Katya or anything. I'd take care of both of you.'

'Why?' Esther demanded, monosyllabic with astonishment.

'I'm not doing anything else. I like Katya, and I like you. Well, I would, I suppose, since you're her mother.'

'That's not very good logic. Perhaps you're stupid,' Esther wondered aloud, more to herself than to Sam, who seemed so impervious to sense that she began to think of him as absent.

Sam thought about this for a moment.

'I don't think I am stupid, though I might be a little naive, compared with many people.'

'And you think that a little naivety is what we all need right now?'

'That's quite a good way of putting it,' Sam acknowledged. 'It can't do any harm to try.'

'It can do a great deal of harm.'

'Yes, but so can what's happening now. The harm balances out, doesn't it?'

'Not if being in hospital is right for Katya.'

'And you.' This was said gently, with a quiet understanding. Esther accepted his insight without becoming defensive.

'Yes,' she said.

There was silence for a moment.

'Are you sleeping with her?' Esther asked.

Sam shook his head.

'Do you love her?'

Sam nodded.

'You love a fourteen-year-old girl you've only known as mentally deranged. Do you really think that's love? What happens when – if – she gets better, and she becomes just like everyone else?'

'I don't think that you become someone else when you go crazy. But I wasn't really thinking ahead. I want to take care of her now. Do you love her?'

'She's my daughter.'

'Do you love her, though? Did you love her when she wasn't crazy and have you stopped loving her now she is?'

Esther gave up her attempt at being Sam's elder and better.

'I don't know. I don't know what it's supposed to feel like – loving someone. I don't think I ever have, or if I have, it doesn't feel like it's supposed to feel. It doesn't feel like anything at all, except worrying sometimes, and a kind of – fondness. An admiration . . . I don't know.'

She shrugged and shook her head helplessly at Sam.

'Did you love your parents?' Sam asked, interested.

'They weren't mine. I was adopted. I don't think I liked them very much. I was angry, I suppose, that they weren't mine. No, I didn't love them.'

'My parents were mine, but I didn't love them. I don't think they loved me, either. But I loved other things and people. When I was a kid, my dog, and a girl who lived near by who

I played with; and then when I grew up.' Esther blinked at this. 'And lived with the travellers, a woman, and lots of the children. And now I love Katya.'

'You make it sound easy.'

'It probably is, unless someone tells you it's difficult. You don't have to love everything, just because you're supposed to. Katya's not like she is because you don't know whether what you feel for her is love. That's your problem, but it's only about a way you use a word. Katya's like she is because she's Katya.'

'That's not what Freud, Jung, Melanie Klein, Bowlby, and Ben would say.'

'I don't know any of them except Ben. But isn't there anyone who disagrees with them? Doesn't anyone say that people are what they are, as well as what their parents have made them?'

'Not aloud.'

'Who says it's not allowed?'

Esther laughed and let it go.

'Sam, people can be damaged. Your parents are the only model you have for making relationships. If you don't have a good model . . .'

'But no one has a good model. And some people are OK and some aren't. And anyway, what good is it worrying about damage way back when, when there's a problem here and now?'

'Because you need to understand *why* a thing is before you can remedy it.'

Sam scratched his head.

'Then why did Ben put Katya in hospital?'

'Because she was too ill for him to get through to.'

'So all that stuff is no use if you're the wrong kind of ill?'

'Yes.' Esther was getting impatient. 'Psychotherapy is no good if you've got flu.'

'What's Katya got, then?'

'Something organic, I suppose.'

'Then it doesn't really matter if your parents loved you or not, does it?'

'All right. Forget Freud. But the child's sick and unhappy. I don't know how to help her. She's psychotic.'

'She's asking questions. She wants to know what she is, what we all are. There's nothing wrong with that, is there?'

'But it's driven her mad. She thinks she's the Devil, or God, or something.'

'But supposing she is?'

'Is what?'

'The Devil, or God, or something.'

'If you believe that, I've got nothing to say to you. It makes no sense.'

'Well, if it were true, it wouldn't make sense, would it? I mean, the point about God and that stuff is that it doesn't make human sense. Supposing she decides that there's something in it – God and all that. You don't have to agree with her, but you may be wrong, and why shouldn't she believe whatever she likes?'

'But we don't live in a world where belief in God is useful. Everything is explained without it, or near enough. That's why she's mad. It's not a thought that belongs to here and now. Thinking the impossible is . . .'

'Bad for your health?' Sam suggested.

'Esther's going to die of it,' Esther said, without thinking, and then realised what she was saying. She stopped and stared, wide-eyed, at Sam, but she wasn't seeing him.

'Esther. You mean you? We're talking about Katya, aren't we?' Sam asked, confused.

Esther was thinking hard. Sam thought she had a funny look on her face when she answered him.

'Yes, of course we are. I was thinking about someone else. All right, Sam, we'll try it your way. But you'll have to take care of her. Do you think we can get her out of the hospital?'

Sam was surprised at Esther's sudden agreement.

'Yes, but I suppose you'll have to give them undertakings about keeping her on the drugs and so on.'

'Well, you'd better move your things in.'

Sam had all his possessions with him in two plastic carrier bags. Esther showed him up to the spare room next to Katya's bedroom and left him to settle in.

They brought Katya home that evening, after several telephone conversations, and a meeting with her doctors. All kinds of promises were made, and Esther's bag rattled with tablets the pharmacy had made up for Katya for the coming week until her outpatient's appointment.

Esther, Katya and Sam stood in an awkward silence in the hall, after the front door had shut behind them. Esther waited for Sam to break it; he had, after all, taken that responsibility on himself. It was as if she waited for him to introduce Katya to her, whom she could not recognise or see, as in some royal protocol, until formal introductions had been made. The same seemed true for Katya, who walked in, smiled politely when it was required, and gave appropriate answers to questions that were put to her directly. ('Now, you will take the tablets your mother gives you, all of them, won't you, Katya?' 'Yes, I will.' 'And you won't go running off again, will you?' 'No, I won't.')

Sam tried to take up his role.

'All right, I'm going to make a cup of tea, and then we can all have a proper talk. Katya, will you come and help me?'

Esther waited in the sitting-room and wondered what she was doing. Having dreams was one thing. Having an understanding of the pattern of things was one thing. Good to think about. But the reality of taking responsibility for a sick daughter was something else. A commitment. An action. And suddenly, in the silence of the sitting-room, she couldn't see the connection between what she had understood about the way individuals were connected to past and future, and having Katya at home. There had been a logical connection, she knew, but, for the life of her, she couldn't remember what it was.

Katya stood in the kitchen watching Sam make tea, still unnaturally remote because of the drugs she was on. It was better to be at home, she thought, and Sam made her feel safer than at hospital, but she didn't know what was going to happen. And she didn't know what her life was for, with everything changed so abruptly: the schoolgirl pointed at an assumed future was vanished, a crazy person to whom future was meaningless in her place. She hoped that someone, Sam probably, or God possibly, would explain things to her, but she was very unsure that there was anything that could be explained.

Sam had very little idea of what was going on, or what would happen, but he supposed he'd find out. He wasn't worried, only curious.

'How are you feeling?' Esther asked Katya tentatively, over the teacups.

Both women looked at Sam, as if he were the only one in the room capable of answering the question. He blinked at them. Katya, very upright and stiff, dropped her eyes to her clasped hands in her lap. Esther shot a look of panic at Sam, who responded with a happy-go-lucky well-here-we-all-are sort of shrug.

'Can I go to my bedroom?' Katya asked, keeping her eyes down.

The tea party broke up, and, after Sam had escorted Katya upstairs, the flat became a place where three separate people, each in their own territory, tried not to impose on each other, or tried to avoid each other, depending on how you looked at it.

Esther was certain that she had made a mistake bringing Katya back from the hospital. She sat in her workroom in the dark, simmering with anger at Sam for persuading her to do it.

Around midnight, there was a light knock at the door, and Sam's head appeared.

'You all right?' he asked.

'What's she doing?'

'Praying,' Sam said with a slight nod, coming into the room.

'Jesus!'

Esther stared aggressively at Sam, defying him to make the joke that was on the tip of his tongue. He swallowed it and Esther continued.

'She isn't going to get better here. I shouldn't – you shouldn't . . .'

'Praying isn't actually mad. Lots of people do it who aren't mad. It's no madder, as such, than sitting on your own in the dark for hours.'

'There's a difference,' Esther snapped.

Sam squatted by the arm of Esther's chair.

'Look, Katya may not ever be normal in the way you think normal ought to be. Maybe she'll spend the rest of her life praying and listening to voices in her head. But there are worse things.'

Esther couldn't think of any, her face said. Sam continued unabashed.

'I'll make sure she eats, and if she gets frightened, and she wants them, she can go back on the tablets.'

'But she'll have to be looked after all her life. You're not going to do that, are you?'

'No, but maybe she won't. Perhaps she'll only need to be looked after sometimes, when things get bad. Suppose she doesn't get completely better; it means she won't get her A levels, go to university, have a career, have a family. Maybe she's got an illness that makes all that impossible. It's bad luck, but she isn't dead.'

For a second, before the thought became intolerable, Esther knew that this was precisely the problem. Katya, the normal little girl, had been in her care, her responsibility. But it was a limited one. Each step in her development had been a new move towards independence. When she first learned to walk, when she went to school, when she started to try her hand at cooking, when she spent hours up in her room talking about private things with her friends. It all meant that she was going to grow up and go away, a loosening of ties, a move towards adult friendship with her mother and away from emotional dependency. Esther had not, could not ever envisage having someone for ever dependent on her. Now she felt cheated and panicked by a new view of her future, and, in truth, she wished her daughter dead rather than tied to her for ever by necessity.

She had invented a family, but in reality it was play acting. If she had been distraught earlier about discovering Rob's lack of commitment, it was something of a sham. If she had allowed herself to consider him really commited, for ever, death do them part, her panic would have been very much worse. And it was implicit always that Katya, too, would go. Those were Esther's terms which, until now, had never looked as if they might be challenged. She had, from three feet above the world, made her model of family, the thing she thought she lacked, but now, the model was earthbound. It was making demands that she had never envisaged. She felt that in some way she had been tricked. By whom, by what? It didn't matter. It wasn't fair.

But it was also a plain fact. She had made a thing – a person – who would not necessarily go away.

'But maybe,' Sam went on, not noticing the terror his previous words had produced in Esther, 'maybe she'll find a way to ask the questions without giving herself pain. Her prayers might be answered, after all. You don't know they won't.'

'So what? Is she going to become a nun?' Esther hissed viciously.

'I don't know. Anything's possible. She might become anything, or nothing. The idea of God and the Devil has been around for a long time, so there must be something important about it. Perhaps good and evil still matter, and Katya's right to think they are more important than other things.'

'You're not suggesting that Katya's going to find the answer to the problem of good and evil, are you, Sam? Even you couldn't be so naive.'

'I don't know for sure that she won't. But I suppose probably she won't. That doesn't mean she should be stopped from asking.'

'But there's no conclusion to come to. Questions about good and evil are for children, or philosophers who can't buy a pound of spring cabbage for themselves, or – the mad.'

'Perhaps Katya's all three. You can't stop her thinking, all you can do is hope she'll grow out of it. But some people don't, and if you happen to be someone who's stuck with having to ask difficult questions it's going to make a difference to the way your life is.'

'The Inquisition stopped people from asking questions,' Esther said with more urgency than Sam could understand. He thought for a moment.

'You mean killing them? But it didn't work, did it? Because here's Katya, centuries later, and she's still asking questions. So the questions go on even if the people don't.'

'And that's the risk you're prepared to take on Katya's behalf?'

'Well, actually, Esther, it's the risk that you've got to be prepared to take.'

'And you think I should?'

Sam gave his amiable grin again.

'I don't see what alternative you've got.'

Esther stared at Sam for a long time before answering. When she did, it was in a quite different tone of voice.

'No,' she said. 'I suppose you're right. I think I'm going to do a bit of work before I go to bed. See you in the morning, Sam.'

Sam nodded briskly and got up.

'OK,' he smiled. 'Sleep well.'

The variously crazed plates were displayed around the room, against the skirting-board at floor-level. Esther's first thought as she gazed at them was that she would like to get back to her flower designs. She got an image in her head of a papaver, in full, round, hairy bud, almost burstingly ready to bloom but without flowers yet, none the less. The colour and texture would be satisfying to paint, and look ripe and interesting in the middle of a fruit plate, with perhaps part of a leaf here and there spreading to the edge.

She knew that wasn't what she was going to do tonight.

Esther picked up one of the original plates from the floor, one with the three bright colours marked out in black outline, as yet coexisting, not like the later ones, where colour battled colour for prominence and position. She cupped the edges of the plate, walked over to the window by the kiln, and brought it up to eye-level as if she were examining it for flaws. Then she opened her hands and let the plate fall on to the hard tiles that surrounded the area of the kiln. She watched it shatter, her hands still open in front of her, as if she were expecting to have to catch a ball. The plate broke into a dozen or so pieces, scattered over quite a wide area. Esther stood back and folded her arms, looking thoughtfully at the remains.

An hour later a new design was ready to be painted on to a fresh plate. Esther sat on the floor with her sketch pad resting on her knees, and examined the plate, checking back with the broken pieces on the floor, which she had rearranged into the original circular shape, leaving a fraction of an inch between the shards. It wasn't a perfect fit; some of the pieces had a bit missing along the edge, but the basic shape was there. The circular pattern on her sketch pad used the same colours and black outline as all the plates, but this one had followed the breakage lines on the dropped plate. This time the black outlines were in fact the edges of the broken pieces and did not, therefore, delineate the boundary of each colour. The outlines contained an arbitrary mix of colours: some were blue and yellow, some red and blue, some red and yellow, and some contained all three colours. The boundaries now marked only space, and colours met directly.

Esther knew that the new design was disturbing. It was not comfortable and made no sense without the earlier designs in the series. But she also knew that this new plate must stand alone, without reference to the others. It would not be part of the dinner service. She would make only single plates from this design in spite of its origins. Whoever bought them would have to take them for what they were, or what they imagined they were. A cock-eyed pattern; a slippage between colour and design. It didn't matter what people thought, or what erroneous origin they gave it.

She spent the next two hours painting the first plate. It was a slow task because the meeting of colour and colour had to be precise, the black outlines of the old design had made it easy. She used her finest brush, no more than a few strands of sable, and held her arm steady by cupping her wrist firmly in her other hand. With each change of colour she had to wait for the adjacent colour to dry enough not to bleed when she applied the new one. It was getting towards dawn by the time she had finished. These plates would be expensive, if she priced them according to the time she took to make them. Then it struck her with absolute certainty that no one would buy them anyway. She could hear the ringing, confident voices of the women who owned the shops she sold her designs to.

'Well, it's just not – commercial. It's such a – mess. You know? I don't mean to be rude, but your fruit and flowers designs are so much more, well, they sell. This just wouldn't look well on the table.'

Esther knew she would smile amiably.

'I'm planning a series of papaver plates, from bud to flower. You know, poppies?'

And the shop owner would smile too, with relief.

'Wonderful. How many can I have?'

Esther stared at the finished, but not quite dry, plate. She didn't mind. This pattern was hers, anyway. She wondered what to call it. *Then Again*, she thought, but knew that she would not, in fact, give this particular pattern any name at all.

She went to bed and lay in waiting for sleep, hoping she was not too late.

25

Shema, ysrael Adonay Elohaynu Adonay echad . . .

The words of the prayer boomed in Esther's ears, like a great sea crashing against a cliff. They engulfed her senses and left nothing for fear to cling to.

Baruch shem kevod malchuto le'olam va-ad . . .

She knew them now, she had remembered what had been forgotten; the images of death by violence, broken bodies rendered limp and lifeless, and the silence that came with it, a silence created by the words of the prayer her father spoke, and continued to speak even when his own voice had been silenced.

Veahavta et ad eloheycha becol levavecha ooverchol meodecha . . .

They came again, now, when fear and intolerable pain threatened, to comfort and protect her. They would stay with her, like the sensation of the small group that held each other, all touching, all holding, all being touched and held.

Vehayoo hadvarim ha-ayleh asher anochy metsavcha hayom al-levavecha . . .

There was heat, but as yet no flame touched her. When it did, the *Shema* would embrace her, close her eyes to the sight of her body being consumed, dull her hearing, her smell, her nerve-endings against the crackle of flames and crisping of burning flesh, and the agony of a slow and terrible death.

Veshinantam levanehcha vedibarta bam beshivtcha bevaytecha
oovelechtecha vaderech ooveshachbecha oovekoomecha ookeshartam
le'ot al-valecha vehayoo letotofot bayn ayneycha . . .

The sound of the words soothed like a balm that placed an
invisible layer between Esther's mortal flesh and the flame that
was to punish her for her impossible questions.

Oochetavtam al-mezoozot taytecha oovish areycha . . .

The sound soothed the pain and the fear of what was to come,
but the words were in a language she did not know. They
were the sound of comfort in her childhood, the sing-song
meaningless incantation that a small child heard and repeated
like a spell. But along with the return of her memory of the
time before everything she knew was lost, came translation:
the recollection of sitting on her father's knee and hearing him
tell her in her own language what meaning the sounds carried.
It came back now, the vernacular, in a rush, beginning as a duet
with the Hebrew, but overtaking it, like a singer who could not
keep time.

Hear O Israel, the Lord is God, the Lord is One. Blessed is His name
for ever and ever. You shall praise the Lord your God with all your
heart, and with all your soul, and with all your might. And these
words which I command you this day shall be upon your heart.

Esther opened her eyes.

The price of memory had to be paid. The words, now that
they were attached to meaning, could not stand undisputed.
They were the words that denied the question. Her question.
She could not praise the Lord with all her heart and soul and
might. The words were not upon her heart; the questions were
upon her heart. The questions were prior to the teaching of
the Church; the only teaching she had known as she grew up,
but the questions were also, it turned out now, prior to her
origins. The questions came first, even before her real forgotten
beginnings. She discovered that she was not what she was – a
heretic, an aberration to be exterminated – because of all the
years of *not* being what she was. She was what she was –

213

herself, her thoughts – for all the time that she existed: then, now, and . . . for ever more.

She had no choice but to own her questions, and by doing so lose the comfort of painlessness that was offered. She had rejected the cross that was held towards her when they bound her to the stake, and now the sound of the prayer, the incantation that numbed the pain, faded, chased away by the inevitability of her thoughts.

Her senses came to life, sharp and vivid, ready to take in everything that was happening to her, all the pain, in all its forms. Her eyes were open and she had no choice but to see.

The rest of the prayer came to her, along with the memory of her father, her real father, smiling as he spoke them, with the pleasure of doing what the words enjoined him to do.

And you shall teach them diligently unto your children, and shall talk of them when you sit in your house, and walk by the way, and when you lie down and when you rise up. And you shall bind them with a sign upon your hand and they shall be frontlets before your eyes. And you shall write them upon the doorposts of your house, and upon your gate.

The prayer was beautiful, in the sound of the original Hebrew and in its translation. Esther took pleasure in it while she understood that her questions, her thoughts, did not allow her to take comfort from it. She would not have children to teach diligently, and if she had she could not teach them what her father taught her. She could not pass on unquestioning faith, but she recognised a great truth in the second part of the prayer. That *something* should be passed on: what is known, what is understood; what is not understood and cannot be, but can be asked; the reaching out, the sense of future, of offering something essential to the future. It would not necessarily be comfort; perhaps the nature of future itself would demand that comfort change to something more difficult. If the questions went on being asked, a universe of possible answers was available. The future would answer them as best it could, or deny them, according to the nature of the times. Perhaps it would even be possible to return to faith eventually, a new faith that rose out of questions; a possible faith that arose from the possibility of questioning.

It *was* possible for Esther to conceive teaching something to the children, and talking and living with it every moment of every day, for now and for ever more.

Esther did not struggle for consciousness. She woke, fully herself, Esther the mother of Katya, but also Esther containing the story of the other Esther. Her dream belonged to her now, awake as well as asleep. The distance beween sleep and waking was bridged with awareness. Esther's story was done; she had it all now. All there was. She had lived through it, to the end.

She lay in the morning light, remembering, recollecting Esther's life and the moment when there had been contact, when her alarm had cut through the barriers of sleep and she had called out her fears and her connnection with a troubled child of another century. There was, apart from grief, a great contentment that the connection had been made. A place that had stayed hollow and hungry had been filled, and, unexpectedly, not with the real family, the absent mother and father that she imagined belonged in that place, but with something else, something larger and more solid that fitted the empty place precisely.

Esther, who became Elizabeth, and then was Esther again, was long dead. She was not to be mourned over, but remembered. She had tracked her missing origins and discovered that what was essential was there all along. Who she was was of no more than historical interest; its discovery gave her a more complete story. But *what* she was, and what she had to be was her real discovery, and her gift to Esther six centuries away.

Esther pondered on the agony that the times imposed on a child who asked the wrong questions and could not stop asking. The actual pain was unimaginable.

Agony was the condition of and exit from life for the uncountable dead of the past, and still was for the majority of the countable, living masses of the present. More agonies, more death than anyone could imagine. Esther tried to envisage the number of the stars in the universe; the edge of infinity; the single droplets of water on the surface of the planet. But she knew she was tricking herself into painlessness; numbing herself with numbers for which her brain was not equipped. She was merely making herself dizzy.

Try thinking about one person's pain. Try a single agony. Acknowledge it. Add it to the unfinished sum that would, in the end, *at* the end, become a total of what had been understood. Only one individual's total, which was all there could ever be. It was beyond Esther's comprehension how the individual totals might be totalled, and what significance such a result would have. Moreover, it was not her business. She had to take what could be taken, and to understand what could be understood. It was the least and most that she could do.

She inhaled deeply, and with the outbreath let the other Esther go. What remained was her question, and it seemed to Esther, as she got up and prepared for the day ahead, that *What for?* was as good a question to ask as any she could think of.